# PRAISE FOR DAREN DEAN'S WORK

### Far Beyond the Pale, A novel

"In FAR BEYOND THE PALE Daren Dean grandly and seamlessly joins terror and tenderness, gravity and sublime lightness, and he does so through the narrative voice of a boy so endearingly and vulnerably real that he turns into lost kin you keep worrying about long after the book has been put down. Dean writes like the laureate of fallen angels. He is an important new voice in our literary culture."
—**Robert Olen Butler**, *The Empire of Night, The Star of Istanbul, A Good Scent from a Strange Mountain, Hell, Tabloid Dreams,* and others.

"Dean shoots from the hip and his characters follow his example. Alive with language, FAR BEYOND THE PALE makes you feel like you're sitting in the back of the car with the windows down, listening to the cast wonder about what comes next, and you slap on your seat belt to make sure you are safe for the raucous ride."
—**Michael Farris Smith**, *Nick, The Fighter, Blackwood, Desperation Road, Rivers, Salvage This World*

"Daren Dean writes in the school of Larry Brown, Harry Crews, and William Gay. His fiction is funny, deep, ironic, and just twisted enough to hold a reader tight. In his novel, a kid grows up, the mean grow meaner, and we come to care about what happens in this Missouri town that could be just over the next rise from Faulkner's famous Jefferson, Mississippi."
—**Clyde Edgerton**, *Raney, The Bible Salesman, The Night Train*

"Visceral, authentic southern language flows throughout the starkly honest prose, performing a brutal, violent dance that is all at once hard to watch, yet impossible to turn away from, qualities that are inherently essential in all successful, dark works of literary fiction."
—**HuffPost**

### I'll Still Be Here Long After You're Gone: Stories

"Thank goodness Daren Dean has filled in the giant hole Larry Brown left behind. The stories in I'll Still Be Here Long After You're Gone provide us

with unforgettable blue-collar protagonists fighting for—or against—respect, love, and justice. I pulled for these characters, scene after scene, in their roadside bars, cheap motels, country churches, trailer camps, even outside the burning love-nest of an ex-spouse. Dean's stories are gritty, honest, and beautiful. I want more, more, more."
—**George Singleton**, *Staff Picks, The Half-Mammals of Dixie, Novel, Why Dogs Chase Cars*

"*I'll Still Be Here Long After You're Gone* is, in a single word, harrowing-- in the truest sense. Dean's stories dig deep, churning up the psyche of his reader, bringing to the surface a darker side of humanity that may make us flinch, but never look away. Teaming with desperate characters forced into brutal choices, ratty motels, smokey bars, fire, storms, the wrath of God and the sweetness of the Holy Ghost—this short story collection feels like it was made for me, a lover of authentic, rural noir. Country as hell, I'd have to say that he gives Daniel Woodrell a run for his money and then some."
—**Steph Post**, *Hopeculum, Lightwood, Walk in the Fire, A Tree Born Crooked*

**The Black Harvest: A Novel of the American Civil War**

"It may seem a bit odd to call a novel set in the nineteenth century timely, but the partisan warfare at the heart of Daren Dean's The Black Harvest has never really gone away. It's happening all around the world right now and right now, in the fall of 2020, we have even seen a few preliminary skirmishes here in the United States. Dean's closely researched account of guerilla fighting in Civil War era Kansas and Missouri shows just how very, very bad it can get. With the antic verve of Cormac McCarthy's Blood Meridian and the Old Testament rigor of Andrew Lytle's The Long Night, this novel represents historical fiction at its very best."
—**Madison Smartt Bell**, *All Soul's Rising, Ten Indians, Devil's Dream*, and many others

"*The Black Harvest* injects you into the heart of America's blood and still-bleeding past. Daren Dean has written a masterful historical novel. There has never been a better time to read it."
—**Aaron Gwyn**, *All God's Children, Wynne's War*, and *Dog on the Cross*

"Dean's writing also offers a striking brew of poetry and punch, combining

unflinching realism with delicately woven imagery . . . A remarkable tale of war and its ghastly ramifications."
—**Kirkus Reviews**

"The language of American Christianity contours Dean's storytelling, a tongue he learned from a charismatic pastor in his own family. Like the Biblical Jacob, Ashby wrestles God — or some shadow of the divine — throughout the book. Carnal impulses and heavenly whispers compete for his attention; this conflict between flesh and spirit animates The Black Harvest."
—**The Columbia Tribune**

**This Vale of Tears, A Novel**

" . . . spectacular, distinct writing in This Vale of Tears brings us into the vivid and memorable worlds of the Scofield and Phelps families. This is a beautiful and affecting novel, and Daren Dean is a unique and powerful storyteller of the American South."
–**Karen Bender**, National Book Award Finalist and author of *Refund, Like Normal People, The New Order*

"He introduces us to an ensemble of unforgettable characters who hunger for love and vengeance and whose lives are haunted by the places their hearts and guts land them in. From the opening scene, Dean grabs us by the lapels and won't let go. In language that shines with lyricism, grit, and wit, he makes us know the Scofields and Phelpses and feel their hard and troubled lives."
–**Randolph Thomas**, *Dispensations* and *The Deepest Rooms*

"The words in *This Vale of Tears* have a way of burying themselves beneath your fingernails. Even now, months after I've read it, I still find its sentences ringing in my ears like a dirty southern breeze. Daren Dean is a compelling new voice in American fiction."
—**Chris Tusa**, *Dirty Little Angels* and *City of Falling Stars*

"Dean writes with great restraint and intelligence, effectively depicting the downward spiral of the two families and engagingly showing how their grim destinies are intertwined. They all live amid the ruins of their collective

descent, and Fairmont, Missouri, is vividly portrayed as a forlorn site of former promise. Furthermore, the author has a notable talent for creating atmosphere; a kind of sad predestination hangs above the Phelpses and Scofields like a darkened storm cloud, just waiting to finally burst."
—**Kirkus Reviews**

### Roads, A Novel

"From the opening page, Dean propels the reader into his story and never taps the brakes as his characters move toward an inevitable reckoning. Dannie Gail Posey is the novel's young heroine, and we cheer her on as she navigates a violent world that *seeks to entrap her even as she dreams of escaping it. Roads confir*ms Daren Dean as an important new voice in rural noir."
—**Ron Rash**, *In The Valley, Serena, The Risen, The World Made Straight, One Foot in Eden*

"His latest is a novel called ROADS that we should all be reading. His command of prose is so strong that I feel some of his sentences are just like that old one-two punch; they send me reeling and then stay with me for days."
—**Jon Boilard,** *Junior,* Junk City, Settright Road, The Castaway Lounge, A River Closely Watched
Dean deftly creates an atmosphere of claustrophobia and desperation that practically seeps out of the pages. Dannie's attempts to make sense of both her past and present echo protagonists' struggles in some classic Southern novels, with this grim, twisty tale providing its own cast of memorable characters. And perhaps most impressively of all, every bit of the story's tension manages to implode in a jaw-dropping final act. A gripping tale of brutal murder, betrayal, and redemption that will challenge readers' assumptions.
—**Kirkus Reviews**

### The New Salvation And Other Stories

"His work lines up alongside authors such as Larry Brown, Daniel Woodrell and S.A. Cosby. And while his prose bears a different style, Dean borrows a key element from Cormac McCarthy: their books are shot through with a common confession, that this world — and all the creatures in it — run wild. Whether that wildness proves brutal or beautiful depends on a person's ability to understand and harness its energy."
—**The Columbia Tribune**

**ALSO BY DAREN DEAN**

Far Beyond the Pale, A Novel
I'll Still Be Here Long After You're Gone: Stories
The Black Harvest: A Novel of the American Civil War
This Vale of Tears, A Novel
Roads, A Novel
The New Salvation And Other Stories

# SHELTER ME

Daren Dean

LIVINGSTON PRESS
University of West Alabama

Library of Congress Control Number 2025943306
Printed on acid-free paper
Printed in the United States of America by
Publishers Graphics

Typesetting and page layout: Joe Taylor
Proofreading: Kelly West, Brooke Barger, Savannah Beams
Cover Design: Kelly West

# SHELTER ME

*To Cassie, Claira, and Finn,*
*for teaching me that home is wherever they are*

*Now on the day, you call for me*
*Someday when time - no more shall be!*
*I'll say, oh death, where is your sting?*
*Oh shelter me, Lord, underneath your wings*
*I say shelter me, Lord, underneath your wing*
*Shelter me, Lord, underneath your wing*
**—Shelter Me by Tab Benoit**

Livingston Parish
Satsuma Grove, Louisiana
*Dog Days of August*


## ANGELINA

The couple next door was going at it again. A screaming match followed by a hollow thud. She had come to think of their house as the
bad luck house since there had been at least a half-dozen tenants in
the past couple of years. Lazy Jeff and Heaven always seemed to have
sharp-tongued arguments ever since they moved into the neighborhood six months earlier, and more than once she had heard gunshots,
so the noise she'd heard was at least a little ominous. Heaven had
once bashed out the driver side of his Toyota pickup window with a
baseball bat.

She sat up in bed and felt the pull of her oxygen mask and
tubing that she had come to think of as Death's halter and reins.
It seemed to her as if she were being ridden down into the dust of
mortality by that demon, Cancer. She wasn't the only one on Eden
Church Road on oxygen, but then she was considerably younger
than Ms. Lynette just down the street, and she couldn't help feeling
a certain righteous anger. Breast cancer had hit Angelina hard and
in the prime of her life. She had been in remission for four years,
but then it had come back with a vengeance. The sound of the
neighbor's bitter argument brought up old nightmares and regretful
memories. She wanted to hold onto the good but the bad had a way
of creeping in at the edge and fogging up those visions.

Angelina Mulvein was raised up with horses as a girl in rural

Fairmont, Missouri. She absolutely hated to be called "Angie" so she made certain when she moved to Louisiana to introduce herself to everyone she met as Angelina with a steel-fire look in her eyes just in case that other nickname even crossed their minds. She had showed horses for 4H as a teenager for as many classes as her grandpa could put her in: English and Western, flags, and reining classes. In her dreams, she still rode her white Arabian-pony; a bay saddlebred with a midsection like a barrel; a chestnut quarter horse; there was also the muscle memory of the feel of the horses between her legs and the squeaking of saddle leather. There was the thudding of their hooves on the hardpacked earth and she could still feel their galloping in her own chest like a second wild heartbeat. The muscles in her calves were hard as softballs from riding. The smell of the grass and horseweed; the fertile odor of the black earth. The taste of ashy dust on her tongue after a truck slid around the corner on the new gravel. The cloud of white dust floated heavily in the summer air. Her horse pawing the air when thoughtless passersby honked their truck horns to be friendly. Her hand holding the reins or grasping the coarse, hemp-like mane. The memory of riding a gray appaloosa her grandpa had dubbed Cochise bucking and plunging beneath her and the sound of his hooves turning up mounds of grass in the pasture—the snorting breath exhaled visibly on a crisp morning, cantering across a green field covered in wild daisies. Queen Anne's lace and wheat growing slant in the ditches. She held the reins loosely and allowed the horse to lead the way down to a wide stream her grandpa referred to simply as "The River" as though there could be no other. He called the blacktop road at the end of his long cedar tree lined gravel driveway "The Black Road" for the smelly black mix used to resurface it.

But when she awoke, she was no longer on the little Missouri farmstead but a foreigner in Satsuma Grove Louisiana or "the real south" as Mr. Jule, her neighbor, had put it when she first moved there with Tripp. She could still remember when they reached the state line, after driving forever through a dense corridor of trees on both sides of I-55 by way of the rolling hills of Mississippi. Finally, she saw the highway sign, *Bienvenue en Louisiane* with the little fleur-de-lis emblazoned on everything like a brand.

At the time, it had seemed like she had arrived in a different country. The roads needed resurfacing badly and the interstate high-ways most of all. In Satsuma Grove, the main roads were lined by businesses mainly housed in repurposed brick buildings that looked to her like they were about ready to fall down in their ancient strip malls and were in need of razing. Everything looked like it was rotting and mildewed. Why had Tripp brought her to this hellhole of pocked roadways and crumbling strip malls? Louisiana was the flattest place she had ever lived, with its dead alligators on the road shoulders and stands of cane with water sitting up around homes that looked like they were built in the middle of a pond, even when they weren't. She didn't yet know about beignets, drinking coffee Americano, po' boy sandwiches, pralines, bead-throwing parades, no-fault car insurance, or especially how unethical the town and parish governments could be. It seemed like every month you heard about a mayor or other elected official embezzling money from their constituents. The laws locally, and at the state level, were set up to favor the banks and the rich. The banks didn't even have a notary public like the ones back in Missouri! She couldn't believe it when she was trying to find someone to witness her signature for a legal document. *Bless your heart*, they said in response to a woman's distress. They expected you to pay a lawyer hundreds of dollars for what local banks did for free up north because they called witnessing your signature, *legal advice*. Despite all the inequity, natives would gush, "I wouldn't want to live anywhere else." It was as if the rot were invisible to them or maybe just in spite of it all. They had grown up betwixt-and-between disaster and an ebullient festival culture that rocked Louisiana to a Cajun, blues, country, and zydeco beat. It took her awhile, but she had made some adjustments concerning how things were here. Now she was over forty, she was no longer a young naive girl, even if she felt she some-times looked younger than she actually was, though not in the early mornings when her face was puffy and had pillow creases. She prided herself on the fact that her legs still looked good. At least, she had looked good until the doctors had started pumping her with drugs and cutting away body parts. The free wig from the cancer support center she wore to hide her hair loss didn't help either.

She took her chemo pills at the old-fashioned porcelain sink and then went to the window and peered through the blinds at the little rental house that would probably be better for the entire subdivision if it were demolished. The rent was too cheap and as a result attracted a certain undesirable element to the neighborhood.

The neighbor's house and the house she lived in had been hauled in on trucks thirty years ago according to Mr. Jule but they were turn-of-the- century houses with crawl spaces the neighbors hadn't liked because their homes were all newer ranch style brick jobs on concrete slabs. They said the old homes with green shake siding looked like picaninny shacks and would bring down their property values, but they couldn't do much but complain since it was the Arceneauxs who owned the houses. In a move to placate the neighbors, Old Man Arceneaux, now long since passed, had put asbestos siding on the houses and painted them white after hauling them in.

When it came to exactly who they rented to, the Arceneauxs weren't particularly discriminating. If the renters were white and claimed to be Christian and could prove employment and produce the first month's rent, that was about all they needed for Miss Jackie Arceneaux these days. Her leases were one-page documents that didn't mean much except that she could throw out her tenant by the end of the month if she had cause and she had had plenty of reason to do this over the years. She ran things now that the old man was gone, and at 69, she was still one tough old bird. A perpetually exasperated woman with a Jiffy Pop hairdo. Angelina had watched the Sheriff's department serve three evictions over the past three years. Miss Jackie would be out there with her arms crossed, dressing down her tenants as they ignobly carried their worldly possessions out on the front lawn in the throes of their post-rental activities. The Sheriff would stand next to her overseeing the operation and *yes ma'aming* everything she said the entire time, inscrutable behind his aviators. Angelina usually tried to ignore the other renters until they did something so terrible as to warrant a call to Miss Jackie or 911 since they were usually gone in a matter of weeks or months.

The Arceneauxs were well known in Satsuma Grove and throughout Livingston Parish as upstanding citizens. Some Arceneauxs were police officers, others were business owners, and more sat on the Chamber of Commerce. They did what they wanted to do and always had. If her renters didn't toe the line, it was left to Miss Jackie's discretion. Everyone respected and feared her, and working men, and even older folks, deferentially referred to her as Miss Jackie because everyone around there had worked for the Arceneauxs at one time or another. They had been among the ruling class in Satsuma Grove for as long as anyone could remember. Angelina was an expatriate Yankee, so she had always simply called her Jackie. For her part, Jackie gave her a break because she paid her rent on time and she didn't believe in holding the accident of her birth against her. People often teased Angelina about being a Yankee, but they said it betwixt and between those southern districts of amusement and accusation. Angelina had originally moved to Louisiana with her husband Tripp because he had been promised a job to make big bucks as a welder on an offshore oil rig called Thunder Horse working 14 hours on and 14 off. The money was good but the hours had taken a toll on their relationship.

Ironically, the woman next door was named Heaven. No one knew where Lazy Jeff LeBlanc had found her but most of the older folks on the street had known him by reputation since he was a boy. Angelina only knew he worked for the Coast Guard. They had a long conversation about it while he watched as she planted azaleas in front of her own porch, though Heaven bitched him out afterwards just for talking to her. Angelina heard her screaming at him: *Is that how you like your women? Bald? Should I shave my head bald for you? Is that how you get your rocks off?* Angelina didn't let it bother her at first and just scoffed about it. Later that night she cried while she was taking an Epsom salts bath. Her sad toenails had fallen off due to the chemo treatments.

Their houses were a little too close for comfort and she could hear every word since Heaven didn't bother to modulate her voice at all. If anything, Heaven tended toward the vitriolic, the more subdued and laconic Lazy Jeff grew in his responses. It was as if she thought she were some sort of actress whose front porch were a stage and she was projecting for the audience sitting in the back rows.

Lazy Jeff regularly disappeared for great swaths of time. This left Heaven bored and lonely. Heaven was probably in her early thirties, give or take. She liked to have big drinking parties and ran around with younger men, mostly redneck tweakers, behind her husband's back. Young men who wore camo pants tucked into untied work boots with sleeveless tee shirts to show off their biceps and tats. Jessica, Angelina's daughter, referred to them as no-good "yee yees."

They whistled at her and shouted, "Oh yeah, baby!" when Jessica stepped off the school bus last year even though she was wearing her distinctly androgynous school uniform, which amounted to a dark blue polo and khaki skort. Jessica pronounced the men gross, pathetic tweakers. This deeply concerned Angelina about her daughter's easy familiarity with drug terminology. How much did she really know?

Angelina had seen enough to know that Heaven was selling meth out of the house when Lazy Jeff was gone. She had called Jackie with her suspicions, but she hadn't done anything about it yet. Who would want drug dealers renting from them? Most of the other houses were elderly people or "decent" families. The lone exception was the lady in the corner house who rented her RV out like it was in a trailer court under a tall green carport. Her neighbors on Eden Church Road said it was against the city ordinance and couldn't wait for her to get caught, but after an anonymous phone call it was discovered her son-in-law was a local police officer, so she continued to get away with it. An electrician everyone called Davey Baby, a man in his early 60s from New Orleans, lived in the trailer with his Australian cattle dog. His customers loved him for his habit of calling everyone *baby*. This habit, a common one down in New Orleans, seemed to endear him to whoever he was talking to. Anyone on the street who called after him might hear him say, "I'll be over there in a sec, baby!"

A cop car started parking up the street during the week in the afternoons about the time the neighborhood children were walking home from school but suspiciously they didn't drive by when the late model vehicles with teens and twenty-somethings were coming and going on Friday and Saturday nights. When the green porchlight came on, it seemed to be a sign that Heaven's house was open for business. Angelina didn't know what they were selling. She guessed they were selling meth, pot, and oxy. She wouldn't have cared but it was clear the situation right next door was going to end badly for everyone.

An Acadian ambulance was sitting in Heaven's driveway. Someone had explained to her that you had to sign up for the ambulance service like getting a membership to a Snap Fitness, or so she was told. If you were in an accident, didn't you just call 911? If you were unconscious in an accident, did they pat you down for your membership card before loading you up?

In Louisiana she had witnessed something unusual in how things were done legally and illegally on nearly a daily basis. Angelina pushed down on the blinds and watched as Heaven met the driver almost as if he were her long lost lover. She took the meaty EMT driver by the hand and led him to the screened-in porch, declaring her dismay in such operatic fashion that Angelina had to suppress an outright shriek of laughter. She left her room and went into Noah's old bedroom to peer through the blinds to see into Heaven's living room window since Lazy Jeff hadn't found time to hang a curtain. When the ambulance driver and Heaven went into the living room, Angelina watched from her new vantage point in time to see Heaven kneeling in over Lazy Jeff who was lying motionless on the hardwood floor in the middle of the living room.

The EMT set down his giant satchel that looked like he was selling door-to-door samples. He took Heaven by her shoulders with his oversized paws and physically moved her to the couch where she sat slouched down in a pair of ripped jeans and a green top with spaghetti straps which fell strategically down to her elbows to reveal the top mounds of her officious little breasts. She covered her face with her hands, ostensibly a gesture of grief. The butterfly tattoo on her forearm seemed to spasm like a moth fluttering into your peripheral vision. The EMT's bulk took up the window and Angelina knew he was working on Lazy Jeff's body until he stood, wiped his forehead with the palm of his hand in a gesture of consternation. Heaven stared at the EMT, her eyes smeared black with mascara and her lips formed into a dramatic pout. He sat back down on his haunches, retracting equipment from his medical satchel, and began to perform CPR. She watched with her hands clasped together as if remonstrating with God. The paramedic shook his head again and mumbled something unintelligible.

"Don't *aks* me no more questions! I done *tode* you all I know!" She was pouring on that accent for the paramedics who seemed to respond to it with little grins aimed at one another. She sobbed and threw her tiny frame at the big man who awkwardly patted her shoulder with his sausage fingers engulfing her rounded shoulders. The sound of her wailing shook the house as she caterwauled over her husband's body.

"I'm sorry, ma'am," he said.

"Why!" Heaven screeched. "Why me . . . my Jeff! Oh, I will always love you! Only you!" The way she slobbered over him was disgusting since it was so obviously disingenuous. The EMT murmured more syllables of consolation in his bearish voice until it was a low and indistinguishable rumble again.

"Shoot!" Angelina snorted to herself. She had seen all she needed. Talk about your one woman gothic horror shows! She couldn't help thinking of that Bette Davis film she had caught on AMC where Davis played a femme fatale. It was obvious to Angelina that Heaven was that kind of woman, and she was on something besides. Her eyes were bugging out of her head. She was scratching her arms like she had fleas. The EMT was aware of it as well, but he had probably seen it all before. Meth was big here, maybe she smoked crack, and no doubt the EMTs had seen plenty of tweakers croak in front of their eyes. Angelina wondered if he had overdosed or if maybe the vicious little creature had poisoned him.

Heaven seemed oblivious to the reaction of the paramedics, so caught up in the moment of her performance. She knelt over Lazy Jeff and rested her head on his chest as if she wished she were the one who had died. At the same time the big paramedic went out to confer with his obviously bored partner, who was talking to someone on his cell phone in the driveway.

Angelina walked quickly back to the kitchen for lukewarm coffee. She couldn't drink anything cold due to the neuropathy, a side-effect of her chemo treatments, and a few minutes later the EMTs were outside readying the stretcher for Jeff's body when she returned to the window. Now that her audience was gone, Heaven leapt up off her husband's body, stood over the corpse and delivered a vicious kick to the side of his head. "Why don't you *aks* me if I'm crazy now!" Heaven laughed with her head pointing up to the ceiling just like a super villain. The young woman turned suddenly and stared directly at Angelina before she rearranged the blanket they used for a curtain so she could no longer see through the window. The dead expression of pure evil on Heaven's face made Angelina's blood run cold and goosebumps pop out on her forearms. She closed the blinds and walked smartly to her front door and locked and bolted it shut.

When the ambulance drove away the lights and siren were off. Two days earlier he had been all smiles and even waved at her and other neighbors while he rode around the neighborhood on his battered John Deere mower. She had actually felt pity for the cuckolded bastard. Jeff LeBlanc had been a nice enough man, a little slow, but had tangled with the wrong woman.

Heaven was standing in the front yard watching the ambulance drive away with her arms wrapped around herself. Varnado and Daryl, who partied with her all the time when her husband was gone, stood shirtless next to her like gang members awaiting new orders just as the clouds like great and angry gray brains unleashed a pounding, tropical rain.

An unnamed storm spun overhead for several days as rainfall accumulated two to three inches per hour in many areas, equaling roughly three times the amount of water left behind by Hurricane Katrina. The fleur de lis of the Saints' flag hanging on the side of Heaven's porch flapped wildly like an exotic bird as the unnameable tropical storm blew through Satsuma Grove on its way north lashing Livingston Parish with its ragged tendrils like watery ribbons around a maypole. A jagged branch of purple lightning lit up the black, rain-laden clouds and raced from the heavens to the earth on the far distant horizon. A few seconds later, thunder echoed across the vault of sky.

## PRESLEY

A wicked storm moved in off the Gulf over Louisiana and churned clockwise like a hurricane but instead of moving off to the east it seemed to get hung up on the jet stream and spun, a malicious pinwheel on fire with jags of lightning. Before we even knew it, its cloudy, rain-filled arms had dumped enough rain until the Comite and Amite rivers, lonely creeks and bayous, became swollen and ran over their banks and bled out like ruptured veins across Livingston parish. The storm beat our house like the fists of a giant against the roof.

I could tell you about other swollen rivers and other parishes too, but this is my story and I'm going to tell you what I know. If someone tries to tell you it didn't happen this way, just know . . . they are a liar.

This was only the beginning of sorrows like the Good Book says. Anyway, that's what my old neighbor, Miss Lynette Richard said. Her husband, Mr. Dixon, said the two of them were ten years older than dirt. Her hair is white like a brand new cotton ball out of the package. She says her hair is "premature" but she's decided to embrace it. Jami Lynn said she might be embracing it, but it makes her look like an old lady. Miss Lynette reads her beat-up rose-colored Bible every day. Her name is embossed on the front cover in gold in the lower right. She was a nurse for thirty years in Baton Rouge and New Orleans. The last job she had was at Oschner hospital and she had a thousand stories about working there.

You could always count on Miss Lynette, drinking her

Community Coffee on the porch at a little table out there. She'd give you some fancy pralines if you came up and talked nice to her. She liked to complain to her husband Dixon, the truck driver, about life in general like griping and moaning was an actual sport, but always in a *charmy* sort of way. She once called Jamie Lynn tawdry but then immediately apologized to me for it and burst into tears. She hugged me and I felt weird about it but I couldn't hold it against her. Jamie Lynn was guilty of tawdriness. That's how our house looked on the inside but it still felt hurtful to hear Miss Lynette say it since the charge stuck to me too.

When I'd get into my angry-depressed moods, Miss Lynette would say, "Lower some heaven, before raising some hell." She tells me she loves me, pets my hair like I'm her granddaughter, gives me money for my birthday, makes Mama and me little jars of home-made pepper jelly, and sometimes she looks at me like she can see my future and big tears fall down her wrinkled cheeks. It must be bad. I don't know what that's all about. She can be a little weepy some-times if you ask me but she means well. Sometimes I'd call Mama "lady" or by her given name, which is Jamie Lynn if you must know, to avoid accidentally calling her Mama in front of a man. I know it's weird, but she doesn't want any guy to think she's old enough to have a girl as big as me.

I'm not going to lie, it makes me feel calm and loved to let Miss Lynette hug me every so often, but I don't hug back. Jamie Lynn is not a big hugger unless you're a man with big roaming hands. Something inside me is too scared for that kind of affection. Scared I'll start caring too much and then something bad will hap-pen. Disasters always happen when you love somebody or something too much. Take my word for it. It's bad luck.

Some people might think it funny that I'm the one quoting the Bible when I've got a reputation for being a little wild and having a smart mouth. At South Side Elementary, they tried to yell at me whenever they asked me a question for running the halls, *What do you say, Presley? Yes, what . . . ?*

See, down here in the deep south you're supposed to say *Yes Ma'am* and *No Sir* and all that jazz, but just because someone's old or a teacher with a stick up their butt don't make them the boss of me so I'd cross my arms, toss my hair back, and laugh! *Yes, okay,* I laughed in their faces! Those cruddy office workers and our fat principal with her hair piled high to boot! See, when people ask where I'm from I always have to say "all over" since that's the truth. I had been living with Daddy in Denver when I was little and they're not so crazy about all that "Yes Ma'am" stuff so I had to learn to be more old-timey and proper. Daddy was from the Midwest originally, but I was born in Raleigh, North Carolina. He always said, *You are a born Southerner!* But there's regular southern and then there's Louisiana southern. See, it gets real complicated down here with all the Cajuns down south, the north Louisianans all *gone-with-the-wind-like* where the old plantations are, the Baton Rouge Football rednecks, and the "gumbo pot" like they say in New Orleans. It's like at least three foreign countries in one.

They say I'm a bad kid. At least I admit it now, but I had my reasons and I'll get to all that so just don't you worry. My daddy spent a pretty penny at Sylvan last year to make me better at math–it didn't take. I'm a whole year older now. I still suck at math. It doesn't count that I'm a genius at art! Art doesn't count in school! It's not on the end-of-year LEAPS test. Daddy said it's because they're barbarians.

My daddy loved me very much but he and Jamie Lynn couldn't get along so he ended up moving to get away from her. I heard him tell someone over the phone once, *I love Jamie Lynn Fontenot. That's why I married her, but I can't live with her no more.* Not long after that he moved to Denver. Dad left my little brother, Austin, living with our grandmère in Baton Rouge now. I see him every couple of weeks and he says things like *merci* and *monsieur*. She's originally from down Morgan City way.

Just in case you don't know it, Baton Rouge means "Red Stick" since someone said Indians used to mark their land with red sticks dripping with animal blood. Gross right? Mama couldn't take care of both of us but I'm the lucky one who got stuck with her here in Satsuma Grove, known as a nice place to raise kids, for white people. Black people live here but it's almost as racist as over in Denham Springs. They had a big reputation for the KKK though I wonder what the difference between those who are just regular suprema-cists who claim to love their black friends but call them "no good N-words" behind their back when they go down the street. Besides, most kids I know around here, black or white, live with their mama (no dad) or their grandparents anyways. What I'm saying is, they ain't raised right. They need Jesus! But even Jesus with all his superpowers and angels at his side wouldn't want to deal with the mess we got going on around here.

Daddy became a physical therapist and worked at a hospital, but he said Mama was too crazy. She took "meds" for her nerves. I heard him tell someone she was a pill-popping alcoholic and he just *couldn't* with her—not anymore. He caught her in bed with Mr. Dan, the science teacher at my school, and that's when Daddy moved out for good. It was so embarrassing! Everyone at school and our entire neighborhood knew! Teachers and kids were all talking behind my back. I could have died!

It was about that same time the teachers at school told Jamie Lynn I needed to be tested for ADHD and might need medication because I was dumb at school but they couldn't come right out and say it, so they hinted around until the lady took me to see someone. I went to a therapist, who I'm pretty sure worked for the school and no matter what I said they were basically like, *Yep, pretty sure you have ADHD*. All just because I don't sit there like a robot or love learning about the history of Louisana and Huey Long "The Kingfish" gover-nator or math! All those linears, integers, and whole numbers buzzed in my head like honey bees trying to find the right flower to pollinate. I guess I must have something 'cause I can't concentrate on that junk. Daddy says I started walking and talking at only 10 months old. He couldn't believe there was anything wrong with me except plain old-fashioned sassiness. He liked to say, "You are a born contrarian!" and then he'd laugh.

One time I got mad about doing stuff around the house and I told her she drove Daddy away and that made her cry because it was the truth. Jamie Lynn can be a real you-know-what sometimes when she goes off her meds. She goes a little fugazi and not even any of her boyfriends can stand to be around her for more than five seconds when she gets that way. She'll tell you how the cow ate the cabbage if you're not careful like Mr. Jule likes to say.

Mr. Jule lives cattywampus to us across the street. He's been like a grandpa to me since we moved here when I was in fourth grade. He used to give me $2 bills every year for my birthday. Last year he even deep-fried a turkey for us on Thanksgiving Tukey Day.

It was a little burnt, but it was nice of him to think of us.

Just above the brick fireplace was a painting of The Last Supper, and much to my surprise, Jesus and his disciples were all black! Mr. Jule was the only black person on our street. He like to call me Dahlin' and pet my hair and give me a hug and call me his little girl when I was younger. I felt safe in his arms when he would catch me up when all the kids were out and playing on our street. He always smelled like Newports and Bacardi. He'd tell me stories about being in the Army and being stationed in *Ha-why-ah*! I wasn't sure what he said at first but one day I realized he meant Hawaii. He loved kids. He parked his Hoveround in his driveway before and after school and shook his finger at all the speeders.

One night he invited us over with some other people from our street and we ate grilled chicken, fried potatoes, onions with loads of ketchup, and topped it all off with Dauber cake for dessert. With everybody watching, he asked me to sit right next to him and he sang an old country song about *Waltzing* in the state of Texas because he was born there and missed it back home. I had to ask everyone what waltzing even was, which made the adults laugh for some reason. I never heard of it before. He sang it in his old-timey voice. It sounded like the scratched records he played over in his man-shed.

Before he finished singing the last line, he reached into his shirt pocket and pulled out a little mouth harp and played a solo on it. There was something so special and genuine about him and his singing. We were all crying when he finished. His eyes were red. He set his harmonica on the table to his right and dabbed at his eyes with a white handkerchief. He reached over with his hand, the color of dark chocolate pralines, took my hand in his so gently and kissed the top of it like I was his special princess. I don't know why he picked me to like so much, but it made me feel special. Everyone clapped like we were on stage.

Miss Esperanza, we usually just call her Miss Hope for short, has a strong accent but she doesn't look Mexican. She is very white looking, so it's confusing to me. Jamie Lynn used to say she thought Miss Hope was Cuban. Her hair was stained wine red with henna or sometimes white as a cotton ball. I only knew about using henna for tattoos. So to settle it one time Jamie Lynn asked Mr. Jule where she was from. He just gave her the deadpan look of a gunfighter,

Daren Dean

"Ma'am? Oh, her people are from south Texas." Jamie Lynn didn't know what to say to that and I just laughed so hard tears rolled down my cheeks. He never would say if her family was Mexican, Cuban, or what. I guess they were Texans. One time he said, "Where she's from they called her güera. Means she's a light skin Mexican. Her family is Tejano."

Their kids were all grown and one of them spoke with accents and two of them lived in the area. Even though Mr. Jule was black, he called other black people the N-word all the time. I even heard him call himself one once. Funny enough, Miss Hope got onto new immigrants for not speaking good English but then she would laugh at herself for saying it because she knew some people complained they couldn't understand her either. She liked to say, "whatever, whatever" when she couldn't think of the English word or when she needed a filler word for the rhythmic way she spoke. She said she used to be a cashier at the Southern Produce Company and she worked with a jetona woman who acted like she was her boss.

"What's jetona?"

"You don't know jetona?" She asked with a little twinkle in her eye. She looked around as if someone might hear her and whispered, "You would call it resting bitch-face."

"Oh!" I laughed. "Miss Hope!"

She laughed along with me but quietly and bent over at the waist. She put her hands on my shoulders, "Shh. Shh. Don't tell anyone and I'll give you a bottle of my homemade pepper jelly."

No one knew anything was going to happen until it did. Mama was laying in bed with a hangover moaning and groaning real dramatic-like, that wasn't nothing new. It had rained a little but it was no biggie, or no one was really talking about the rain like it was a big deal but it did start dumping rain in sheets and the clouds swirled over central Louisiana churning like a slow-motion hurricane. It was nothing to see water flooding up around someone's house in our parish like they were living on their own little island. Some folks even had boats tied up near their house for when it rained a lot just so they didn't have to wait for the Cajun Navy to come save them or simply to go to work if it didn't rain everywhere. Some people's houses were in places bad to flood. Later they would call this big storm that sat over Louisiana churning away dumping rain the *No-name Storm*. Now ain't that something! How's anyone supposed to remember a storm without a name? They give hurricanes names so people a hundred years from now will be able to say, *Remember when Katrina, or Rita, or Ike hit?* How're you supposed to remember a no-name storm? Well, now I'm telling you all this so you won't forget!

"Get me my ciggies!" Jamie Lynn moaned like a pathetic invalid from her bed. I love her, but my God! What a drama queen! "Turn that music down too! My head is killing me!" She was coughing and hacking and making disgusting snot noises in the back of her throat.

"Where are they? I don't see them." That was a lie, I was looking right at them.

"On the coffee table in the living room," she whined. "Get me my lighter too, shug. It should be with the pack."

"I can barely hear the music as it is! It's not that loud! The volume is only on the fourth bar."

"Jamie Lynn loves you!" Mama said. She talked about herself in third person the way I heard boxers do when Daddy used to watch it on his "Hurricane Television" out in the garage but he watched it all the time when he was tired of Mom's stuff only he said S-H-I-T!

I sassed her quietly and shook my head and backside at the same time since she couldn't see me through her bedroom door. I slapped my skinny rump at her too even though she couldn't see what I was doing. *Get my lighter too, slave! Turn my music down, slave!* I put the back of my hand to my forehead and pretended to faint onto the red couch for Mickey, my little Yorkie. He yipped and sneezed at me to be let up on the couch. When a dog sneezes at you it means they love you. I pretend-sneezed back at him. The lighter was a new Walking Dead Bic so I slid it into my pocket. Also, I'd already snuck a pack of her Maverick Gold 100s from the carton on top of the fridge. I was planning on smoking some of them with my friend, Olivia, but she probably wouldn't because she was so religious.

"You just wait!" Jamie Lynn said. "One day I'll die and you can just put me in an ole' pine box. I know you want all that prompt and circus dance! New Orleans, Swing Low Sweet Chariot!"

*Prompt and circus dance? Is she kidding me?* I hollered back. "What?" I held my breath waiting for her to answer. I can hear her

Daren Dean

better from the living room if I don't breathe.

"That's what you want, Miss Fancy britches! Remember, you *aksed* me for it just last week!"

"Oh!" I knew she meant pomp and circumstance. I don't know where she got this stuff. She was always making up words and expressions, but her loverboys never called her on her bullshit.

Olivia went to the Amite Christian Church right next to the Amite River up in Watson with her family every time they opened the doors and she even liked going to youth prayer meetings all the time. I'd went to a Christmas service with her and a few other things. It looked like a Church from way back forever ago. It was brick and had a steeple, but it had red and black walls on the inside with nice wood floors, white pews, and a huge stage with professional cameras and lights for praise services. It seemed too modern for a church on the inside.

Olivia would probably be pretty impressed when she saw me smoking. She'd tell me in her serious mom voice, "You're going to get cancer or you need Jesus in your life, Presley." It made me laugh just imagining how shocked she would act when I met her at the park. She said she liked me because I'm cool and she is a nerd; I like her because she's nice. Her skin is so pale, it's what I call fish belly blue. She's a genuinely good person. Like sent-straight-from-heaven-good! I like shocking her. It gives me a kick in the head.

I hoped we might even see Chase Danforth, a high school boy I had a not-so-secret crush on. I liked watching him playing soccer with his teammates in his cute little blue and white soccer outfit. His hair made him look kind of Emo since it was dark and extra long on top, but he was really more what I call a basic white boy—he was cute anyway. Jamie Lynn said I was boy-crazy like her—that's not exactly what people say about her.

"Presley, can't you find them?"

"Found them! I don't see your lighter though!"

"I've got one in here! Hurry, Mama needs a cigarette!"

"Well," I said under my breath, "if you hadn't gotten so drunk you could get your A-S-S up and get it yourself."

"What hon?" Mama said.

"Nu-thing! Nu-thing!" I called back to her like I was opera singing.

"What?"

"I feel pretty," I said just to confuse her. I can be real random sometimes.

I jumped off the couch and ran the pack in to her real quick with Mickey on my heels.

"Here you go, dearest Mummy!" I clutched the door like a life raft and poked my head and upper body around the door and tossed the pack at her. It bumped off her chest and fell into her lap. She was holding her head like it was a giant balloon filled with helium and trying to fly off into heaven against her will.

"Go fix me a cup of coffee, sugar pea!" she said.

"Sure thing, Nutter Butter," I said. Instead, I grabbed my skates and my pencil and little sketch pad and ran out the door before the Nazi-mama could issue anymore orders. After I put on my skates, something I hadn't done for awhile, I started skating out in the street with Mickey trying to keep up. I was a little afraid he might get under my wheels and I would run over him but this hadn't happened yet. I'm a big worrier.

"I feel like funkin' it up, feel like funkin' it up! I feel like funkin' it up, feel like funkin' it up!" I was singing and skating down the street and kind of bouncing up and down on my knees. I was singing that classic Rebirth song that every parade and second line does in New Orleans and they usually play it during festivals and parades in every town that has its own Mardi Gras. I shook my hands in the air as I skated. "Feel like funkin' it up!" It's funny to see how tourists react when they hear it for the first time.

I skated up and down the street heading past Remy Vincent's house. He had his own landscaping business, Red Stick Landscaping, though his own yard wasn't much of an advertisement for his work as Mr. Jule said. Mr. Remy's wife was Ms. Leah who ran the Dollar General. Remy hadn't even taken down the Mardi Gras beads someone had thrown up in the branches of the lemon trees lining the front yard like a privacy hedge. Their eldest son, Brandon, was outside practicing twirling his baton for the marching band to Gangnam Style blasting from a speaker carefully propped in the living room window against the screen. He had a younger brother and sister, Cindy the Slut and Skylar the Punk. *P. S. Don't think I'm being cruel since this is what everyone says about them.* Cindy was out of school but she still lived at home and she was out-to-here preggers. Brandon thought he was some kind of cheerleader-debutante. He was the nicest boy in the world and I sometimes thought he was more of a girl on the inside than me. On the outside, he was 6'5" and if he wasn't so nice he'd probably be terrifying. He had red hair, brown eyes, a big moose nose, and hands like bear paws made to fish for salmon. He threw the baton up to the moon. I stopped to see if he would catch it. He did a little 360, stuck out one claw and caught it when it eventually fell back to planet earth. Usually, he dropped it. I applauded like a fiend. He bowed like a giant circus bear.

"Hi Presley!" he said. "I like your blouse, girl!"

I looked down for some reason. I knew very well I was wearing a yellow Tipitina's T-shirt but I glanced down at it like I was surprised. "I stole it from Jamie Lynn. Shhh."

"That's so cool!"

"You're getting pretty good with that baton! You get any better and you'll be dangerous!" I spun in circles on the street in front of him with the tips of my skates pointed outwards. When I stopped on a dime, I started flossing in front of him. He laughed and he did it with me. He could do it perfectly. "You've got the moves!"

"You're so sassy." He shook his head and went back to his routine. He even did a cartwheel, for my benefit I'm sure, which is pretty awesome to see someone that big do one. You can't believe it until you see it. He could have been a lineman for the LSU Tigers. He was that big. I'm telling you. I always feel embarrassed to talk to him now but I tried not to let it show. He used to babysit me three years ago. He was a Senior now.

"Wow!" I said. "Just wow! Next time you throw it up and catch it, stick your hip out to the side like all, hey-girl—like this!" I skated a half moon in the street and stuck my butt out to the side like a cheerleader. "Ready? Okay!"

"I'll try that! But right now, I'm trying to concentrate on catching it before it conks me in the skull." He smiled real wide and then he remembered to grimace and hide his yellow and crooked teeth behind his upper lip. I'd seen him do it so many times before. He marched in place. He picked up his knees so high that it would have been way over my head. I think he was showing off those mad marching skills for me. He did flags the year before. You should have seen him then. The big bear waving the heck out of that thing. He was so proud of his school spirit.

I snorted, "Let your freak flag fly!"

He gave me a look like he was saying, *Really?* He knew I was teasing.

I gave him another ovation as I spun in circles around Mickey until my little drawing pad came flying out of the back pocket of my jeans. I had to stoop and pick it up. It was then I noticed the strangest thing in the parking lot of the elementary school at the end of our street.

"What in the world!"

"What is it?" Brandon asked as his his baton thudded to the earth. "Dang it!"

I ignored him and took off down to the end of the street as gracefully-dangerous as a roller derby queen. I put my hand on the stop sign there to help me toe-stop. Water was lapping at the end of the street and I picked up Mickey protectively. I'd never seen anything like this before on our street. On the other end of the street, I could see a pair of white egrets strutting around in the ditch. I guess that's why Mr. Jule referred to them as *ditchbirds*.

*Oh?* I thought. *I egret to inform you they aren't ditchbirds.*

Mr. Jule was always bragging when it flooded anywhere in the area that on Eden Church Road we were at 46 feet above sea level and it didn't even flood on this street during the 1983 flood, and not even during Hurricane Katrina! There was a big flood in 1983, back in the olden days, because all the old people on our street mentioned it whenever there was flooding around town. Just boring old people talk, like when they complain about the price of gas or their old backs. The real shocker was the two men in their fishing boat tooling around in the elementary school parking lot, now several feet under water. The water covering the road reflected the blue sky and the white and dark clouds overhead like a pretty painting.

"What are ya'll fishing for?" Mr. Jule called out to them.

"Whatever's biting on the end of my line, Yank!" One of the men answered with a Cajun accent.

Mr. Jule got all choked up then because he was trying to laugh and cough at the same time, "I know that's right!" He coughed into his handkerchief when he regained some control after his fit.

"Yank! Ah Lawd, I'm Texas Creole!"

"Oh my Gawd!" I said. I sat Mickey down at my feet, whipped out my drawing pad and sketched the men in the boat laughing and making random Cajun comments. They were speaking English for the most part, but it always sounded like they were saying things backwards. There was a sudden sun shower so I put my pad away to keep it from getting wet.

"The Devil beating his wife with a walking stick," the man in the back of the boat said. They both laughed at that one. Mr. Jule had driven his Hoveround to his backyard slow since he wasn't too worried about it. He had on his cowboy hat he always wore outdoors to keep rain or sun off his face.

"There my couyon, sha!" The younger man waved at me and then looked back at his partner with a wink. I couldn't believe it. I looked up into the heavens as if he could see the source of the shower. He said something in his backward sounding way with a big grin and then something that sounded like *Morceau du chou.* I wish I knew Cajun better but I knew it enough to know it probably wasn't good.

"Don't call me couyon, boo!" I shouted back at them sarcastically, standing up and gathering my stuff. "I know what you are! You a couple of ignorant coon-asses!"

They just laughed at me and started talking fast Cajun to each other. The crazier looking one shouted, *"On va se revoir plus tard!"* They made a circle with their powerful outboard motor and thundered off the opposite way down the street. Their boat cut into the water like a knife as a white spray arced into the blue sky. They disappeared going up toward the high school in their boat under the live oaks and Spanish moss.

The water was lapping at the stop sign and this was just down the street from our house. I'd never noticed the natural dip in the road there and now it was a few feet under water. The house across the street from where I stood balancing on my skates had serious problems because its front yard was almost completely under water and it faced the school parking lot so that sort of made sense. It didn't look like anyone was home now anyway or maybe they left when they noticed the flooding. Why hadn't anyone said nothing about flooding?

I looked up in the sky where the sun-bleached daylight was blazing down almost directly overhead. It was weird to see all this flooding when the sky was so clear. Milkweed seed floated through the air. It was like dryer sheets bouncing around in a dryer. Mean storm clouds, a terrifying purplish-black, were stacked like mountains and gathering with their black underbellies carrying a load of rain just waiting to dump more on us. Voices murmured and grumbled from on high like rebel angels against the blue of the sky and lazy cotton ball clouds that usually slept there.

"It's flooding!" I said. "See that! Tell your mama and daddy, Brandon!"

"What?" He put his hand up to his forehead like a salute to look in my direction. He squinted like a madman and I realized he couldn't see too good. He used to wear glasses, but I guess he'd stopped because I guess he didn't like the way he looked in them. He took a few steps my way before he suddenly changed direction almost like an old-fashioned cartoon character. For a second it looked like his feet were going in the opposite direction of his body. He disappeared inside his house. I saw two kids walking on the other side of the street wading barefoot in the water about a block away where it oddly also hadn't flooded yet. I looked behind the school and off to my right where a company had been working on building a new little subdivision and some of the new houses were already flooded.

"This ain't right," I said to Mickey. He licked my cheek. His little body shivered with fear. He sensed what was happening too. Animals were much smarter about these things than humans. I saw King, one of the neighborhood cats, on the Laryisson's roof. He was up there looking at me like I was crazy to be standing so near the water. He seemed unconcerned the way cats do as he licked his paw.

I skated up to the Laryisson's yard and walked across the grass awkwardly on my skates. There was a Virgin Mary grotto statue near the porch steps. There were dozens of different Mary statues throughout the neighborhood. It was as if the Holy Mother had replicated herself to protect the entire town. Everywhere you looked you couldn't help but see a statue or image of her. We weren't Catholic but I liked their statues!

It was a little trickier walking up the stairs so I sat Mickey down, but I used the rail that looked like a pipe a plumber might use.

Daren Dean

When I knocked on the door Mr. Dixon answered, I was relieved. He was a heavy-haul truck driver, but kind of strange. He liked to quote the Almanac (I learned what it was from him), Shakespeare, and somehow related anything that happened to a Greek myth. He told me the Myth of Sisyphus, though I said the Myth of Syphillis when I told Jamie Lynn about it. *That ain't no myth!* She said and flicked her cigarette into an ash tray like a punctuation point. Dixon hauled big stuff like cranes, generators, welding units and stuff like that. I had a hard time featuring it all, except for cranes. Everyone knows what those look like. His powder blue Kenworth was parked in the driveway without a trailer, so I knew he was home.

"How you doing, Presley?" Mr. Dixon answered the door with a lit cigarette in the corner of his mouth. His hair was a little cray-cray under his Saints cap. He had those Ray Ban type glasses that turned dark out in the sun that some old men like to wear. He had fluffy sideburns, a braided salt and pepper beard, and he rested his left hand on his beer gut. He squinted his eyes against the smoke when he said, "Lynette is asleep right now." He could tell I was disappointed that she wasn't awake and bustling in her kitchen making muffuletta sandwiches almost as good as the ones at Central Grocery in New Orleans.

His crow's feet crinkled when he laughed or smiled. His face was ruddy and his skin was dried out in odd places. He saw me noticing and said the doctor called them dead spots like counting rings on an old tree. Miss Lynette had shown me pictures of him from when he was young and handsome with jet black hair. In his short sleeves, his forearms now were red and bruised looking with burgundy liver spots. I wanted to ask him what was wrong with his arms but decided it wouldn't be polite—I was dying to know.

Mr. Dixon was a "big and tall" (like the J. C. Penney clothing department in The Mall of Louisiana) man with thinning but still wavy hair, gray at the temples, and something about his personality made him seem bigger than he actually was. He was smart and always reading true crime, mysteries, the Farmer's Almanac, and books about the Wild West. Normally, he was easy to talk to, but I didn't know what to say exactly so I just pointed down the street to the floodwater like a crazy person. He walked toward me where I stood on the porch so that I had to back up and then he looked out across his yard and down the street to the water lapping at the edge of our street almost like a beach. The first thing he did was look in the driveway to check on "Blue Betty" his pretty, powder blue Kenworth.

"You go tell your mama what's going on." Mr. Dixon plucked his cigarette out of his mouth and held it between his thumb and forefinger down by his side. "I knew there was a reason I caught the *frissons* this morning. I think probably everyone in the neighborhood ought to know if they don't now. Guess I'll have to get my generator going and the Bass boat ready. I 'spect its Cajun Navy time. Can't believe I hadn't heard nothing on the TV about it."

"Yes sir," I surprised myself by saying. I clattered down the steps, skated down the driveway and onto the street.

I was working my arms and skating hard to the house. I couldn't believe this was happening. It was exciting but then I felt bad about being excited since it was so serious. I started imagining the water flooding down the street and covering up our house, every house on the street even. The water was creeping down our street by the minute. My heart beat hard in my chest until I imagine us all swimming under deep water, treading water like in the ocean, and then whales and squids watching us from below trying not to laugh at us foolish land mammals. Mickey had already beaten me to the front steps of the house.

In my mind, I can already see the water covering everything up. It even rises over the trees up and down the street in my vision. It grows deeper like a Bible flood and drowns everything in Satsuma Grove. Tears blinded my eyes as I pulled up into the yard and face plant in the grass. I'm tough enough but I started crying and beating the ground with my fist. I had been so emotional. I wish my dad was here. Maybe he could save us. I feel rain drops now. It never really just sprinkles, not much anyway. In Louisiana if you feel it sprinkle, it's getting ready to rain down frogs.

I dragged myself up and bound across the yard and took little mincing steps on the toes of my skates. I untied and then kicked them off onto the porch and burst through the door with news that even old Noah from the Bible wouldn't want to hear. Just before I went inside I saw Joker, the black and white kitty that wouldn't let anyone on the street touch him. I felt bad that he might end up drowning. I gave him treats thinking I could tame him down but he would never take anything from my hand.

"Jamie Lynn!"

"Quit yelling!" She moaned dramatically from her bedroom. "O my head. What is it?"

"Mr. Dixon told me to tell you it's fixing to flood and we better get out of here."

"It's going to flood? Ain't heard nothing about it."

"Yes, we better get some things together and go to Baton Rouge or up north somewhere!"

"I ain't heard nothing about it on the boob tube."

"It's flooding just right down our street. The Cajun Navy already buzzing around in their boats in the school parking lot."

"Really?"

"Jamie Lynn! That's what I'm trying to tell you!"

"Well, bless your little heart! You don't have to get all huffy about it. Let me call Mr. Dan or Eddie or somebody. See if I can't find us some place nice to stay."

"We ain't got time for those idiots!"

"What?" She was hacking and coughing in the bathroom now.

"Nothing, Butter Nutter!"

## ANGELINA

Lazy Jeff had once come home early and caught Heaven partying with the young guys about a month before Heaven killed him. Angelina had witnessed the blowout since she no longer worked due to her chemo treatments. She was all but invisible as the bald-headed invalid in the neighborhood. Oh poor, Angie! She despised their pity. The physical side effects from the chemo treatments caused her hair to come out in clumps. She had even tried filling up a grocery bag with ice and putting in on her head under a colorful head scarf to hold it in place instead of purchasing a cold cap made for that purpose. She had heard a scalp cooling cap would help stop her hair from falling out, but it didn't.

Often, she would wake up in the middle of the night with swollen ankles and a charley horse in her calf muscle as hard as a softball. It also made it impossible to drink anything cold due to her neuropathy. Drinking anything cold was like someone shoved a branding iron in her mouth. Her cancer had progressed to Stage Four. It had been in her lungs and heart but the chemo had dried it up for now after they drained her lungs a couple of times.

When she looked in the mirror now—she wondered if she was still a woman. She had become so weak that at times Jessica had been left to supervise herself until she had simply vanished when she had been let out of the hospital after surgery. The landlord had looked in on Jessica once or twice and all was well, or so it seemed, but then Jessica had disappeared with her favorite things and Angelina had panicked. Her mind went to worst case scenarios like human-trafficking and child pornography since Jessica was a pretty young girl. It had turned out that her mother-in-law in Biloxi had simply taken her to live in her beach house near the dead, black beach devastated by the oil spill caused by the infamous Deepwater Horizon spill. She couldn't help wondering if Tripp hadn't been personally responsible for the ensuing environmental disaster. Jessica's bed, dresser, and little writing desk were still left in her all but empty room. She found herself staring at a framed picture of her daughter smiling over a Barbie princess cake when she was nine years old with Noah photobombing the picture in the background. It seemed like not so long ago, he sat on her lap with her nose buried into his brownish-blond hair inhaling that sweet little boy smell. It was the perfume of youth and the promise of a kind of immortality.

She didn't know what Tripp was doing now for sure but he had always dreamed of becoming a folk and blues musician. He had never been the practical one over the long haul. He'd get a job and be excited about it for a few weeks or months and then up and quit. He expected her to pick up the pieces back then. She used to manage the Hair Shoppe in Baton Rouge's Garden District. She had a half-dozen stylists to supervise. She had been damn good at her job. Her background was in restaurant and retail. Tripp would get a good job and convince her not to work. He wanted to take care of her or so he said. It was like being in a relationship with a charming teenager.

Following one of their more terrible arguments, he'd even told her he was ready to "change lives," and he had. He'd just packed up his clothes and a few things and left her and the kids as if they were recent acquaintances he'd met somewhere on one of the blue highways of life. Now he was shacking up with a singer, a light-skinned black girl, and he had decided he was in a much better position to raise at least one of their kids, so he had Noah living like a street urchin in the French Quarter in New Orleans. At the time, Angelina was so weak from chemo treatments she hadn't put up much of a fight over custody. Frankly, she was relieved Noah would be raised by family even if she had had her differences with his dad. She could have used Noah's help at home but every so often her friend Nikki from her cancer group used to look in on her though she was busy running 5Ks around the state. She was always talking about how they would both beat cancer.

Angelina had never been particularly religious in her heart. Lately she had started to attend Amite First Baptist and figured religious people were the best people to put her hope in. She had been raised an indifferent Catholic and even though she thought all of the Baptist rules against wearing skirts and having short hair were a bit old-fashioned, she liked that they believed God could and would do miraculous healings for them that believed. Although she had never given God too much thought before cancer, she meditated on that compassionate, red-beating heart from the imagery of her youth on handheld fans and votive candles. Now she attended every prayer service and even the Thursday night Bible study but the problem was she didn't really fit into any of the groups like the young singles, or the married couples, or even the retirees in the Prayer Warrior group since she was over twenty years younger than those retirees.

She turned the oxygen back on and pushed the mask to her face. She opened the blinds just a touch with her finger and thumb in time to see the ambulance drive away. Heaven held her arms in the air and did a pirouette in the weedy driveway where Lazy Jeff's ongoing project, a rusted gold *Bijou*, sat on the ground on four flat tires. Her conscience or fear of being observed must have hit her at that moment because she looked wildly around her, up and down the street, before hurrying inside. Just then a Satsuma Grove Deputy Sheriff's car idled slowly by Heaven's house.

Angelina allowed the blinds to snap back into place. A chill went through her body at the thought of how Heaven had killed her husband without conscience. When she thought about it she couldn't help wondering how long she had been poisoning him. She remembered he was always complaining about being dead tired and a long list of ailments that didn't make sense at the time. He had sounded like a hypochondriac of the worst stripe. Now she knew better. She kept replaying that hateful kick Heaven had given her husband's body in her mind on a loop. A murderer next door who had been in her own kitchen more than once asking to "borrow" just about everything that wasn't nailed down. She'd even had to tell her she couldn't borrow anything anymore because she needed it and if she lended it out then where would she be? Heaven had given her the most evil look a woman could give another woman. Her mind raced with possibilities. She reminded herself to never eat or drink anything Heaven offered. Not that she was much of a cook but just the same she would be on guard.

Angelina had left Jess with Miss Esperanza across the street the day she drove herself to the Ochsner Hospital ER alone for first chemo treatment. Miss Esperanza said to wait for Mr. Jule to drive her to the ER but he was in no shape to be messing with her. He could barely walk and he had to have regular kidney dialysis himself. His arms were perpetually covered in purplish-black scratches and bruises as if he had been running through the weeds. She didn't want to be anymore bother to anyone. She didn't want Jule feeling sorry for her. If there was a way to keep her problems a secret from everyone she would but she had to confess some of her fears to her neighbor. She was a mother figure to Angelina since she was in her late seventies. She would understand some of it. Tears burned her face just thinking what would happen to Jessica if she died suddenly. The only thing Jess was concerned with at the moment was Justin Bieber, Lady Gaga, Sam & Cat on Disney, and hoping to one day dye her hair neon pink like an acrobatic girl on TV she used to watch.

After blood tests, PET Scan, and a CT Scan, they determined her coughing fits were due to a cancerous fluid in her lungs and around her heart. They had drained her lungs twice now after two doctors had argued about whether or not there was any point. The Chinese cardiologist said he couldn't operate unless the Indian doctor drained her lungs. The louder they argued over her bed the stronger their accents became. While the Indian doctor maintained there was no point in draining her lungs since they would simply fill up again. He pointed at her emphatically and said that all they could do at this stage was to make her comfortable. He enunciated each syllable of the word in a patronizing way as if to make the cardiologist understand his own ignorance. Angelina could only lay helplessly on her hospital bed as the doctors quarreled as if she were an inconsequential possession. It was Christmas Eve, and nobody wanted to be there. She was all alone. She missed her children most of all and wanted to call them but her cell phone was in her purse, wherever the nurses had put it.

Besides death, her main preoccupation was what might happen to Jessica and Noah and who would feed Kitty Boy Floyd, her fat tabby tomcat. She hated the name but it had been Tripp's idea. Listening to the doctor's argue over her made her feel as insignificant as a corpse. Who would remember her? Who would care if she died on this day of all days! A day her family had always celebrated by going to Mass. She could still feel the heat of her grandfather's whiskey on his breath as he sang, "O Little Town of Bethlehem."

In the end, the heart doctor won the argument. The other doctor drained two liters from her lungs, a procedure that was a bit like tapping a beer keg or getting sap from a Maple tree. The doctors were finally integrated in their opinion when they gave her 3-6 months to live. That was being generous, they assured her. Was there someone she could call to help get her affairs in order? They could call hospice to come present her options. How had she allowed herself to get in such shape, they demanded to know. She didn't have an answer. Life had snuck up on her. That was two years ago now.

The news they delivered made her cry but later when she heard the hospice nurse had given Tripp a brochure and laminated menu and discussed her death with him she became very angry at everyone. How dare they try to ship her off to a hospice to die. At the moment, she steeled herself and decided she was most certainly not going to die either. She wasn't about to let anyone kill her off. The helpless look on Tripp's face when she screamed at him for his insensitivity made her even more pissed. She refused to die even if she knew Tripp not-so-secretly hoped it would happen.

She had clamped her mouth shut when the heart doctor asked her if she understood the implications. In her own heart, she told him to go to hell over and over again. She wasn't about to die. She refused to go to a hospice to die. She might die flipping them all the bird but it wouldn't be from a hospital bed. He noticed the fire shooting out of her eyes and quickly exited her room. A lone oncologist was the only one who had given her any hope. It was his opinion that she could live perhaps as long as another five years if she followed his protocols, which were to include chemo infusions every three weeks for the rest of her life. When that quit working, as it was bound to do, they would put her on a new chemo. There were a couple of options he was confident would work. Besides, he said, they were coming up with more effective treatments every day. She later found out the oncologist had houses in the Hamptons, Barcelona, and drove a Mercedes.

That was when she bought a Ruger LC9. Her daddy had taught her how to shoot as a girl but she had never seen the need before now though she used to go shooting with him. She might need to wave it around or, God forbid, actually use it on Heaven or one of her wife-beater clad minions.

Each time she had seen Lazy Jeff back from shore leave or whatever. Angelina didn't know if she should laugh or cry for her neighbor. He didn't know what Heaven was doing behind his back. She didn't think he was aware that his wife was sleeping with younger men. She was also fairly positive he didn't know she was selling drugs or helping someone sell drugs might be more like it. She'd seen the pattern: The Mountain-Dew-green porch-light flicked on. Not long after, two young men would show up in Heaven's driveway but never the same two, in late model pickups, blacked out Altimas and BMWs, or white Jeep Wranglers. Heaven would get in her rusty Malibu, which left the men dealing in her house alone. Ten minutes later, a white Chrysler 300 with gold grill and matching rims, pink top, and dark windows pulled into the driveway next to the house. The car basically screamed I AM A DRUG DEALER though the plates read GDFR. She never got a good look at the driver behind his tinted windows and on those drug days Heaven wouldn't come back home for hours. Maybe this way she could deny any knowledge of the deal.

A couple of weeks earlier the green light was on. She was sitting on her front porch drinking lemon tea and listening to a Podcast about juicing to fight cancer when two young guys pulled up in an old Chevy pickup. She was out there because she was waiting on her new water filter for a Brita pitcher to arrive. Ron the mailman was late and she glanced up the street every so often to see if she noticed the slouch–hat–wearing letter carrier bobbing through the neighborhood. Angelina rose to meet the young men as the driver got out the passenger side of the truck. She could smell the pot reek from the porch. They barely registered her under their heavy-lidded eyes.

"How you boys doing today?" Angelina smoothed down her house dress nervously. "You need some help?" She put a little gruff in her voice to get their attention.

"No," the blondish boy sneered. He was ambling toward her with a red plastic cup in his hand like he was going to a kegger.

He looked her up and down as if he was sucking on a piece of tart candy. She was an old lady to him—a bald old lady at that. "Not the kind of help you could give." The young man looked over his shoulder at his buddy coming around the other side of the Chevy with a smirk on his face. This one was taller but had that dumb country boy look about him like his 4H hog did something funny. His light hair cut into a mullet. What worried her was that he was bigger and more muscular than the driver but the driver looked cruel like he had killed kittens for fun as a kid. They were both eye-fucking her now to make matters worse.

"You all selling something then?" She asked in her best mom tone of voice.

"Nah!" The blond boy shook his head in the negative and snickered. An orange and red- flamed tattoo leapt out of the collar of his t-shirt and licked up his neck. His bottom lip protruded with what was most likely a wad of chewing tobacco. His eyes cut mischievously to his friend, who had a rollie tucked up behind his ear and was missing one of his front teeth.

"Is that all you can say?" Angelina demanded.

"No," he threw his drinking cup in the weedy rose bushes and looked at her defiantly.

"Well?" Angelina asked.

"You can pick up that trash in your bush," he nodded to the cup. Then, he smiled because he'd said bush and the innuendo tickled him. She thought about drop-kicking him into next week.

The punk tried not to tip forward as he stepped up and set one of his clodhoppers on her bottom step. He was very intoxicated and his eyes had that relaxed, rheumy look from drinking too much. She turned on her heel, opened the screen door, and pulled out an old wooden baseball bat she'd bought at a garage sale for home protection and held it casually down below her waist.

"I think you boys better move your asses on down the road if you know what's good for you," she said. "You can take your nasty mouths with you too!"

"Haha! This one's got spunk, don't she Daryl?" the blond boy said.

"I'll say she does," Daryl leered at her, "bet she could suck a golf ball through a garden hose."

"I'll make you think spunk!" She held up her Louisville slugger in a batter's stance.

"Speaking of spunk!" Daryl leaned over and whispered something in Varnado's ear. They both laughed like hell then.

"Like I said, is there something I can help you little boys with? Because there must be some business you think you have here since you're parked in my driveway."

"Me and Varnado are looking for Lazy Jeff," Daryl said, taking a sip out of beer from his own red cup. They weren't much on subtlety. If a cop pulled them over they'd go down quick for DUI, Angelina thought. "That is, I mean, Jeff."

"Well, he lives next door. He ain't home. He ain't been home for awhile now but you might be looking for Heaven. I'm sure she'll be real glad to see you boys." It was her turn to sneer.

"Aw yeah, Heaven," Varnado said in a now dreamy voice. They began to stumble across the yard.

"Forgetting something, ain't you?"

"No," Varnado snorted.

"You're forgetting your piece of shit truck," Angelina said. "You better move it in case I need to go to Carter's later or I'll have to have that thing towed."

The dark-haired young man named Daryl gave his partner a backhanded slap on his chest to indicate he was a moron.

"Oh yeah," Varnado tagged Daryl back with his left hand. "Better move my junky truck or this LADY here is likely to whip both our asses."

"You better fucken believe it." Angelina growled.

As he walked away Daryl mumbled, " . . . holocaust-lookin' slut . . ."

When she was younger she might have flipped them both off or even come down the stairs after their asses with her bat but instead she gave him the disapproving mom look and put her hands on her lips like her Great Aunt Opal used to do.

Daryl walked on over to Heaven's house, while Varnado made a show of getting into his truck and moving with with lots of fits and starts and burnt rubber before pulling into the driveway next door. Angelina was already muttering to herself about calling the cops. The young men beat on the door until Heaven came *flouncing* out all slutty acting with these guys who were obviously too young for her. Flouncing was one of those words her mother would have used to describe slutty behavior. She gave the dark-haired boy a pat on his behind as she allowed them to squeeze by her. Heaven gave her a wink over her shoulder before allowing the screen door to slam shut. Angelina couldn't wait for the day Lazy Jeff came home and caught her with these young guys or selling her drugs. He was lazy, but he had put one good beating on her before he bit the dust.

A few minutes later Heaven came out of the house with her purse and car keys only to jump into her car and roar off. Angelina sat back down so that the cat could get back in her lap. This show was about to get good. A black man with dreadlocks, dressed in crisp new dress clothes like he was going to church walked a pitbull down the street on a short leash. He stopped at the end of Heaven's driveway while his dog sniffed the telephone pole but then the dread-ed-dog-walker must have taken note of the strange pickup and kept walking. The cat sat as immobile as the Sphinx in her lap but flexed his claws into her legs as it watched the dog. The dog didn't appear to notice the cat and was attempting to drag the man back up the street from the direction they had come from. It lunged at a squirrel chattering a few feet up on the exposed roots of a live oak.

The brand new white Jaguar with fancy golden rims pulled into Heaven's driveway. A black man wearing expensive tortoise shell sunglasses, impeccably dressed in a gray suit and green bowtie, got out of the car and strode quickly inside with what looked like a fancy leather suitcase.

"Bow-tie Man," Angelina hissed to her cat. "There's Bow-tie Man again."

About fifteen minutes later, the two young men came out smiling like they'd just taken a trip to the moon and back on a magic carpet. The one called Daryl was carrying a brown paper sack like he was handling communion waifers on his first day as an altar boy. They jumped into their truck, backed out into the yard to get around the pimpmobile, and roared off down the street burning rubber and leaving celebratory *ah haws*, countrified laughter, and twangy country music in their wake.

Angelina said to her cat, "We just watched another drug deal go down." She said it to herself again because it wasn't something

Daren Dean

she would say everyday and it made her sound badass. "Should I call the police?" The cat gathered its back paws under its rump and blinked languidly.

Bowtie Man came out of the house, let the screen whop shut, and disappeared behind the blacked out windows—into the pimpmobile he went. A booming baseline rattled the Jaguar. She could hear the car's body pop, creak, and protest this bombardment of sound. Just as it rounded the corner, Heaven pulled into her driveway like she had just come home from picking up groceries at Albertson's. It was perfectly obvious what had just transpired. The wind-driven trees around the quiet house were barren and dead and looked like they had hatched a plan between them to faint on top of the joint one day. In the meantime, Heaven was in there whoring it up at her own little crank party. Something about the whole situation didn't smell right to Angelina. These drugged up young men going in and out next door worried her. What if they barged into her house? What then? Or was it also the pressure of her condition magnifying the problems in her mind? She kept reminding herself to take her happy pills, but she still forgot. When she did remember to take them, instead of feeling happy, she just felt even more tired than ever. Being happy and not caring weren't the same thing, a distinction her doctor didn't seem to recognize.

Her pastor said she ought to pray for people instead of casting judgment upon them. Maybe Jesus might help her and not in that funny, *she needs Jesus* way. She considered inviting Heaven to church but she knew this one would just laugh in her face as long as the young men and the good times kept coming through the front door. Heaven was young and still had her looks so the Good Book would hold no allure. The good angel on her shoulder told her to bake up some cookies and take them over and just "visit" with her as her mother used to say. But then Angelina laughed at herself just thinking how that would turn out. Instead, she grabbed her cell phone and called the local police department and reported drug deals going on in the house next door. The cop who answered the phone made her feel like she was crazy for calling so she would hang up. After a long pause, it sounded like male voices laughing in the background. She could almost hear the wink in her receiver.

The next day a police car sat a few houses down the street.

Angelina shook her head in disgust. She pulled on her robe over her pajamas dragging one of her oxygen tanks behind her. She didn't always need the oxygen but sometimes in the mornings she struggled with breathing a little. She thumped the tank down the steps behind her. The younger neighbors sometimes asked her if she got off huffing oxygen, which was laughable. She never felt much difference. She rolled up to the driver's side and knocked on the windows with her knuckles to get the attention of the officer who clearly enamored of his cell phone.

"They tell you to come watch that house?" Angelina demanded.

The cop looked up startled. "Ma'am?" He was so tall and large that it was difficult to see how he could have stuffed himself into his tiny cruiser. He needed it to be super-sized, she thought. Not only was he large, as in lardass fat, but she guessed he was close to seven feet tall. "Are you all right?"

"Yeah," Angelina said. "I'm just bald. Cancer. Chemo. Everything. Comes with the territory. Don't worry about it. I used to be beautiful like you probably used to be handsome, short, and thin."

"Ohhh." The big man looked terrified like maybe he was looking at a witch flying around the parish on her broom. "You don't have to be so . . ."

"They send you over here to watch the house. Bust up the drug ring?" Angelina asked. "If you're undercover your car practically has a bumper stick that screams, *powered by donuts.* You think Heaven and her bunch ain't going to spot you?"

"Excuse me, ma'am. I'm on traffic duty." The giant pointed his yardstick finger toward the elementary school down the street. "This way I make sure people slow down when school lets out. We want to keep our kids safe. The children are our future."

"Okay," Angelina snorted. She watched his face closely for any sign of irony but instead his large pumpkin head gazed up at her without ruse. "Well, I'm the one that called to say this one here's selling drugs out of her house. Her actual name is Heaven, if you can believe it. Lazy Jeff, her husband, owns it . . . or he did until Heaven killed him. He worked for the Coast Guard. He wasn't hardly ever here. I doubt he knew what this witch was up to, but you need to come back in a normal car if you're going to set up surveillance here,

Officer Shorty."

The cop squinted at her, "Name's Simoneaux by the way. Leroy Simoneaux. Everybody around here calls me Officer Leroy." He chuckled and then looked her up and down with as much interest as a man shows in a stranger's flat tire on the side of the road. Even this hulking man had no interest in her as a woman. She felt like an inanimate object that no one wanted. A knick-knack that belonged on a shelf in the little antique district over in Denham Springs.

"I'm Angelina, Officer Leroy," she clasped the neck of her robe.

Tears blurred her vision. She couldn't help lingering on the thought that she was unattractive and unwanted by even this giant. She had had beautiful brunette hair with blond highlights that fell past her shoulders like a damn shampoo commercial. Men used to scream like beasts in mortal pain when she walked by in fishnet stalkings, three-inch heels, and black gothic dress. Women were filled with envy and hated her or wanted to be her best friend. Now her breasts had been cut off, she was bald, and she was all alone. Her husband had left her with her daughter who didn't even live with her anymore. She wasn't even a woman now and there was no one to tell her any different. No man even looked her way in Walmart except to sneer or maybe pull his child away from her. Even when she went to Cortana or "the hood mall" it was like she was invisible.

The male and female nurses at the hospital took her blood, hooked her up to IVs in the infusion room like eunuchs or devoted nuns. "Enjoy the time you have left," they said dispassionately. "Make the most of every day. Make time with your kids." Her eyes filled with tears when they said that since she had no kids at home to make time with.

The chemo drugs kept her alive, the cancer at bay, but at the same time they destroyed her internal organs until she feared she would be found like a dried-up husk of a June bug on her back porch. Even her oncologist, Dr. Groth, refused to do physical exams whether it was because he was an absent-minded professor type or just awkward with women to begin with was another matter. He had never physically touched her except for the time she had burst into tears and he had put an awkward hand on her shoulder. The man had no compassion, which she could have forgiven if he hadn't been so incompetent. There had been a female oncologist, Dr. Laura Hart, whom she had liked but after a brief three months had left for a new practice in Houston. One of the nurses remarked, "She going to feel right at home there. Half my friends moved to Houston after Katrina, boo!"

Angelina had a few casual friends she did yoga with in her music class with Cancer Services where she massacred the mandolin. She even tried Tai Chi with a smiling, Chinese man who said to the class, "You pay sixty-five dollar to see Chinese man up close—what you think?"    Her own mother was now in a nursing home and didn't even know who she was anymore. She felt invisible except to the neighborhood children who thought she was crazy. She still felt achingly beautiful on the inside. It was the one thing she felt God had blessed her with. Now he had even taken that away. It wasn't fair. What had all of this life been for anyway just to end up as a lab rat to die from the poison they put in her veins?

She would occasionally feel sorry for herself only for the emotion to be followed by a surge of anger like the citrus spray of acid satsuma that reminded her that she was still alive. *Goddamnit!* It was at moments like this she would spontaneously hold up her middle finger in defiance at the grocery store in the health food aisle, in line at the pharmacy, or walking among the tourists in the antique district. Usually people pretended not to notice a tall, emaciated woman with striking angular features, dark maroon circles around her eyes, and a colorful scarf around her head.

She stood there gaping at the cop, expecting him to say what he was going to do about Heaven and her drug-dealing ways, but instead the cop was checking his cell phone and she leaned toward the window to see him 'like' a picture of a young woman in a yellow bikini on Facebook.

The school bell began to ring. The officer sat up visibly straighter as though the bell were a call to arms. Angelina stood there in her house dress as the kids streamed out of the elementary school screaming, walking, pedaling bicycles, and thrashing skateboards. Mothers in the neighborhood walked lazily home as their children tittered about the school day while lugging their oversized backpacks. Many of the children were lining up in their respective bus lines along the circle drive. Others were beginning to fill the sidewalks

Daren Dean

screaming with joy upon being paroled. Parent's cars were lined up grimly, bumper to bumper along the street. The crossing guard directed traffic with the intensity of a professional wrestler giving an on-camera interview.

"There's Crazy Woman!" A boy said to the little girl, probably his younger sister, walking at his shoulder.

"Crazy Woman! Crazy Woman!" The little girl cried in a sing-song voice. Her little cheeks burning red with robust health. She was so small she barely looked old enough to be in Kindergarten.

"That's MISS CRAZY WOMAN to you!"

The boy jutted his chin at her like a full-grown man about to fight after the little girl burst into tears.

"You're mean!" the husky boy said. He put his arm across the little girl's shoulders and heavy backpack as they walked down the street. He bent at the waist and whispered comforting words in her ear. How Angelina envied the little girl who had someone in this world who would console and protect her with such tender ministrations.

"Ma'am . . . " Officer Leroy pleaded but that was all he said. Despite his gargantuan size, he looked like a man well-acquainted with female vitriol. But Angelina couldn't help herself. Ever since the doctors gave her only a few months to live, she had had bouts with depression, followed by a righteous indignation that sometimes lasted days, and then helplessness would begin to build within her. She had decided back then to live just to spite the doctors, Tripp, and her own children, who had tried to write her off. God or Fate or just plain bad luck had decided to pass a death sentence on her for some reason. Past lives, past sins? That's what her pastor indicated. Bad Karma? That was what her Buddhist group believed. She refused to believe she had done something so terrible to warrant all of this. *Why, I've never even held political office!* She liked to use this line on people when they became too far-ranging and existential in their efforts at producing what they believed to be words of comfort but her delivery was a little too raw for anyone to laugh.

Parents were rubbernecking at her in her ragged pink and white house robe as they drove by. SUVs rumbled down the street at forty-five miles an hour or faster until they noticed the cop car and the crazy woman talking to him. The speed limit was twenty before and after school. The parents had all seen her since she liked to sit outside with Mr. Jule next door and wag their fingers at speeders as the children walked home. It had become a second vocation with Mr. Jule.

"Now Ma'am!" Officer Leroy ran out of patience. It was like a mad scientist in a white lab coat had flipped a switch. Electricity appeared to run through the cop's veins. She thought, *This is Frankenstein's cop.* "I'm going to instruct you to go back into your domicile. You are beginning to obstruct official police business." He then blinked slowly with both eyes. The word idiot immediately sprang to Angelina's mind.

"Official police what?" Angelina snorted. "You mean making sure people drive the speed limit in a school zone?" He just stared back at her blankly. If a fly had flown by, she wasn't entirely sure a giant green tongue wouldn't have come out of his mouth to swat at it. She wasn't sure if it was a natural reaction to the fear of what Heaven had done to her husband, fear of her own death, or the steriods kicking in that had made her feel such rage.

Angelina walked backed up her driveway with her arms locked in front of her shaking her head at Leroy the cop. When she turned to walk back to her porch she waved at Mr. Jule to let him know everything was A-okay. *Nobody worry about Crazy Lady!* Heaven came out of her house like an insane raccoon with her mascara ringing her eyes so they bugged out even wider than normal. She mistook Angelina's wave, assuming it was meant for her, and was now waving to beat the band on her way to her little Cooper to roar off to wherever the drug dealer and his krewe-of-meth holed-up at. Angelina sat in the chair at the black wrought iron table and drank half a glass of red wine in one gulp.

Benji and Jonathan, just two houses up and across the street came out of their brick house calling from the steps of their covered porch, "Oompa Loompa! Oompa Loompa!" It was the name Benji had given their cat and he would tell everyone all about his method for picking the name from his favorite film. He was a born storyteller, so even though the story wasn't all that interesting he could still keep you riveted with his voice, gestures, and facial expressions. Benji often burst into song in the middle of a sentence and had an angelic tenor.

"Lips of ambrosia" was how Jonathan had put it when it was

clear he was talking about something other than Benji's singing.

Benji was a children's librarian at the public library in Baton Rouge. Jonathan owned a little restaurant in the strip mall adjacent to the Bass Pro shop in Satsuma, which is how they came to live there together in the first place. Jonathan said his restaurant specialized in American cuisine. Though Angelina had never eaten there, she was sure she would love it.

Then it began to rain. The no-name storm spun over the area for several days like a pinwheel. It refused to move off, dumping between 20 and 30 inches of rain over East Baton Rouge, Livingston Parish, Ascension Parish, Tangipahoa Parish, and others. The water began to overwhelm all the little rivers and waterways in the area until they each began to spill out across the flat land of central Louisiana without warning. The floodwater didn't care about circumstances or who was rich or poor as it flowed north to south with dirty fingers searching for the Gulf.

## ESPERANZA

I can't help thinking about all the things that can't be replaced. The furniture and things don't matter to me but losing family pictures makes me sad. Mama and Daddy named me Esperanza, but now I'm old and my church friends and retired co-workers from Walmart call me Hope. It fit on the name tag more-better than my long name. It's the same thing. Mama says my name means Hope. They name me after my Great Aunt who died in a fire before I was born down in the little valley of San Benito where my Segundo family still lives today— the ones I know who are still alive.

*Oh Gawd!* Me and Jule get nervous when it starts raining too bad or whatever. Not many people know this, but his real front name is Garland. Everyone just call him by his other name.

We moved here in Satsuma Grove in the year of the 1983 flood. The front yards were lined with satsuma and lemon trees back then, but the bugs got most of *'em*. We already been married for many years. Now that was a bad flood because I was trapped here at the house with the kids. We moved here from Baton Rouge, but the neighborhood got bad. People breaking into your house and stealing. We had to move to feel safe. Before that we were in Texas. Mama was still alive then. I was so homesick. Jule tell me call Mama everyday if I wanted. Long distance was expensive. It was a big deal. It made it easier for me to adjust is what he said. It was so nice of him to let me. The kids was all *littler* back then. *Oh Gawd!* Mr. Jule was working in Baton Rouge as a foreman for LeBlanc Construction. The flood water was all around us. Oh, we was so scared! Jule said a young highway patrolman didn't want to let him drive on the flooded streets when he got to Satsuma Grove on his way home, but he was still young enough to make other men listen to him good. Men respected him. Some were afraid of him.

"Now Padnah!" He said when he told the story to us, "My family is over in that neighborhood trapped by them flood waters, and they're expecting me to come home with groceries for dinner or they're going to go hungry. You wouldn't want that, no?" The officer let him come on home to us then. He said the cop stopped him just because he saw a black man in a pickup truck and thought the worst.

The kids were little. We was all alone. Did I say that? He had a jack-up truck with big tires that let him drive in water even in the flood streets. Looking back on it now, it seems so silly. I was so emotional. He couldn't have done anything but be trapped with us. It made me feel better and him too. The kids scream and clap their hands as soon as Daddy come home! We was so happy! My English wasn't as good as it is today. I even worried about how I would call for help if someone couldn't understand me or didn't want to try. I told my sister, Bebe, about it. She's the one live in Texas. Tell her how she got to learn more-better English when we was young, and now she speaks it better than me! Whatever. I worried for the kids. Not for me. I guess we could have died or whatever, but nothing really bad would happen to the family until a few years later, and maybe I will tell that sometime.

River Road flood first and it was bad, you know? I guess that's why someone name it River Road! Oh, that's so funny. It is lined with those old live oaks and their silvery Spanish moss and those knee-roots they call 'em look like big black snakes poking out of the ground. Even though Jule couldn't get home at first we had our old neighbor Mr. Rene who was an bachelor and he worried about us. He had a big garage out back of his house, but it burned down after he died and a school teacher bought it. Ah, whatever-whatever! Jule began to fill those . . . whatevers. What you call 'em? Sandbags! He put ,em around our house with the help of other neighbors on our street behind the house until they were six bags high! Those same neighbors help with Rene's house too. We all help each other.

It took us long time to fill and stack the bags with sand. The kids could hardly hold the shovels. We stack them around the back of the house where the yard sat low. Margie was only 9. Now she's a school teacher. She call herself *Big Booty Judy*. Oh, she's so silly! Jesse was quiet and just turned 11 back then. Claude was 13 and he was my little man. They worked so hard they fell out plumb tired in the backroom on the guest bed where my sewing was usually piled up. They were so cute. I cried and cried. I don't remember why. I just cried a lot back then sometimes. Oh, I did. Even TV commercials made me cry.

When Jule wasn't working back then he would drink a whatever of Jim Beam, uh huh a fifth, and he get so nasty with everyone. That's probably why his kidneys are shot now. He was very mean, cruel sometimes. Full of anger but he couldn't say why, except he holler about being an N-Word. All the time with the N-Word. I told him quit feeling sorry for himself. Think about your kids. I ask him if he didn't love me and the kids one time. So long ago.

"Pshaw!" He said. "Pshaw! Why else you think I do all I do?" But he would never say the words except when we were together in bed under the blankets. Maybe something broke inside him when he was a boy. His granddaddy treated him like a slave working on his farm up in McComb, Mississippi when he was a teenager. They sent him from Texas to Mississippi. Had to leave everyone he knew. He never saw his mama again, but once. He still close with his brothers and sisters. Most of them dead now. I knew he loved me deep-down. It made me cry, he wouldn't say the words. It was hard for him to say he love me too. He afraid if he says it, he lose me. He says it to the kids, he lose them too. We lost one boy already, maybe he said it to him. He says he loves my pepper jelly and that is got to be close enough.

The storms are a-swirling again. A lot has changed since way back then. Jule has to use a whatever, Hoveround, most of the time. I says he riding a vacuum cleaner. He change but the devil got after him or God gave him bad health to teach him to be better, more nicer. Now everyone on Eden Church Road love him. We all love him. Now our kids grown, he practically adopted the Elvis girl across the way. That's what I call her . . . Presley. It's too hard to say. He hug her and give her two dollar bills and cards. She thinks a lot of him too. Her mama a bad woman though. She spread her legs at the drop

Daren Dean

of a hat. Shush now! Don't get me started! She don't even go to no church. We take Elvis girl to mass on Easter and Christmas. Men in and out of her mama's front door like, Lord, you wouldn't want to believe it!

It was pretty red. Like a brand new car, that Hoveround. He buy it cheap at the pawn shop because they said it couldn't be fixed but he knew it was something with the battery just like his old one. He can't stand too long. He laughed so hard because he fix it right quick. *They lost they ass on that deal,* he said.

The doctor told him, "Mr. Jule you abuse yourself so bad over the years, which is why you are in the shape you're in now." He hesitated for dramatic effect and clicked *tsk tsk* with his tongue like the doctor did.

"Abused?" His eyes got big when he tell it. "Yessir! Can't go change the past now even if I wanted to. Me, I'm the Black John Wayne, padnah!" He says it not blinking eyes. A white man on one of his work crews call him that once. Jule didn't make it up, but he was proud to hear himself says it.

A year later to the day, that old doctor up and died on him. Mr. Jule just smiled. He was so happy he had outlived Dr. Coffman. The doctor was younger than him. He died from lung cancer. He claimed he never smoked a day in his life. Jule said that was where he went wrong.

Daddy was out in the shed listening to his Slim Whitman, Buck Owens, Charlie Pride, and Johnny Cash records when I heard the weatherman on the TV set in the side kitchen say we better come go now.

"Oh my gawd!" I ran out quick as I could to the shed and stuck my head in the doorway without walking up the steps. "We'd better go, Daddy! The weatherman just says on the *whatever* we gonna get trapped here if we don't leave now!" I'd already started packing up the old Explorer. Even if he didn't have sense to know what's good for him.

"Huh?" Says he. I was on his left side so he couldn't hear me out of his left ear too good. Funny thing, if you whisper something you don't want him to hear, he hears you good enough. You shout it at him from the other room he say *wut* to you all day long. He *huh* or *wut* you until you're sick with it. He wear you slick. His ears don't know Spanish as good as I speak English. He says he can't understand me. I says, why? He says, I don't know what he means. Why?

"I'm making this here food," he says in the side kitchen in front of the carport. "Everyone want to eat chitlins when it's time to eat but no one want to help clean them."

We was driving up Highway 16 yesterday toward Watson when we saw the sign in front of the little green seafood shack by the road said "FAT FEMALES FOR SALE!" I laugh so hard. I seen it before, but it hit me the other way this time.

"Who don't want a mess of fat females? They gonna sell out them real quick, sugar!" Jule says, then elbows me.

I slap his arm, "Oh shoot! You can't handle one fat female!"

"Aw now," he said. "You ain't fat at all. Some men want a nice ripe fat one." He held his hands out in front of him and puffed out his cheeks.

That mean they got new female blue crabs for sale. We bought some crabs, some shrimp, and bright red, spicy mudbugs. Ooh, we was going to eat good! But now I wish we hadn't bought it 'cause Daddy was so focused on cooking it up he would rather get caught in the flood than let it go bad.

"Whatever! Your food don't mean nothing if we die in a flood!"

"I'd rather expire with the taste of crabs and mudbugs on my lips," he said. "That's what I call heaven."

## NOAH

When Tripp dropped me off at Angelina's with a hoverboard, a suitcase, two backpacks, and a Yamaha keyboard; I was pretty mad but there wasn't much I could do. I didn't want to move back in with her. It was boring in Satsuma Grove. The people were narrowminded and dim. They used to say the town had great schools, code for "no black kids" in this school. They mostly went to the school across town. That same day I was looking out on the porch when the white mosquito truck with a yellow flashing strobe light on top drove by spraying a fog of white chemicals into the air. The little kids playing out in the street ran through the white rainbow mist like they were being sprayed by a garden hose. I remembered doing the same thing when I was little. Lucky I didn't end up with an antenna growing out of my head and webbed feet.

When I was little, I called Tripp "Daddy" but after he picked me up last year and we moved to New Orleans he said to call him "Tripp" like I was all grown. I've been doing it ever since. I wouldn't even say Mama's name before that. I talked to her on the phone once and called her Angelina just to see how she'd react. I wanted to see if it hurt her. She didn't say anything for a few seconds and then acted like she hadn't noticed. I hadn't seen her in months. I did it to make him happy and to piss her off. Why did she have to go and get sick? I know it's not her fault but I was so little when she got it I really didn't know what to do with that information. I heard her and Tripp talking about it. They said she had only a few months left to live. When the hospice lady came to talk to us in the hospital room I felt a storm-surge rushing up and I puked right there on the floor. I love her and she loves me. Stuff gets complicated. I just played video games so I wouldn't have to think about losing her. She was so determined to live, she beat the odds they gave her.

I remember when I was ready to go with Tripp because Angelina's "friend" Floyd would come over and mess with me. He'd make me slap-fight him in the front yard until my cheeks turned bright red from his repeated slaps. Floyd was tall with long hair and I couldn't get by his long arms and sharp elbows. He thought his job was toughening me up but I guess I showed him when I burnt down the old carriage house where he liked to listen to his vinyl collection on an old record player, drink fat bottles of Coors, Juuling his brains out, and working on an old 1966 Ford pickup that anyone could tell was never going to run. He thought it was bad wiring that caused the fire. I just agreed. Screw him, anyway.

I hadn't known Floyd very long back then when he said he wanted to talk man-to-man with me. I was only thirteen at the time. I had a growth spurt and was just a little taller than Angelina. He stared accusingly into my eyes, "You wouldn't ever do anything to your mama? Would you?"

I was so surprised by the question I wasn't sure what to say. It wasn't something that ever entered my mind. I was speechless. I guess he took that some other way. Like, maybe he thought I had already done something. I don't know what. "I just don't ever want to hear about you doing something to your mama. Okay?" He stuck out his hand for me to shake.

My eyes filled with tears and this made me mad at him for accusing me of something so terrible. "No. Never, I . . . " When I put my hand in his, he clamped down on my hand with a threatening vise-grip. It felt like he was breaking my fingers and he got right in my face and stared into my eyes with a nasty look on his face.

"You get me? Understand me, boy?"

Angry tears ran down my face. I was surprised to be accused of something I hadn't done, had never come to my mind, and that the thought of it horrified me. I yanked my hand from his grip, "Screw you!" I went directly to my room and slam the door shut as hard as I could. I thought he might follow me but he never said another word about it.

Later, I wondered if she was afraid of me. Me, her only son. The boy who loved her more than any other man would ever love her. It hurt me to think it. I never brought it up with her. Words wouldn't help, I told myself. She must have said something about being afraid of me now that I was taller than her. I was still her son no matter how tall I grew.

Floyd never found out I was the one who burnt down the shed. He accused me of it eventually, but he never knew for sure. I waited for him to go on a fishing trip one weekend with his brother down in Grand Isle before I made her go up in smoke.

*Negligence,* I heard a fireman say after they put it out. *Plain negligence. Man smoked cheap cigars and Juuled in there. Been trying to get ahold of him, no luck so far.* It was a rental so there was no insurance to collect except for the old lady we rented from. She might have collected. I don't know. We were lucky she didn't kick us out because of it. I should have thought about that before.

I might just burn down his whole shitty house in Baton Rouge next time. Why did he rate a special place at our house? Let him go back to his actual wife. Angelina hadn't been going out with him for very long. Once Angelina told him about her breast cancer, it was all over then. Nothing had changed. She already had it then, you understand, but she wanted him to know she had to do chemo treatments. She was bad sick.

Angelina was running around on him. That was her big secret. He probably found out about that too, but not from me. Well, after that, he never came out to Satsuma Grove again. I was glad. I'd known he was a truly awful person as soon as I met him. Most of the time a kid or a dog can tell about a person, where grownups just can't. Adults have a kind of blindness that only kids can see. Adults don't hide their true selves from kids the way they do from each other.

I'd been living in New Orleans with Tripp and his girlfriend, Ayanna, over the past year. They were both trying to make it play-ing music on the streets and any place they could book. Ayanna had the voice of an angelic soul singer that made the tourists empty their pockets on Decatur. Tripp accompanied her with just about any instrument or object from bucket drumming to harmonica to washboard, mouth harp, mandolin to guitar or keyboard. He was seriously gifted with musical instruments. He could play a little bit of everything. Like he said, the problem was Bob Dylan and Dr. John could both out-sing him. This is why he needed Ayanna and me.

That doesn't mean they didn't have regular jobs. When Tripp couldn't find a gig he either "Set-up shop" somewhere on Frenchman's or Decatur where he might play trumpet or guitar or harmonica with a black fedora upside down on the sidewalk or his instrument case open for tips. Or, he was a sometimes bartender at The Maple Leaf or Molly's in the French Quarter but he also got fed up with the tourists, only that was where all the money came from. We all really wanted to play at Tipitina's. That was the goal.

*It's a symbiotic relationship*, he said to me once. *We're all in this thang together.*

Even before Angelina had cancer it seemed like they couldn't get along but it just got worse after. Angelina and Tripp fought with each other over everything. It could be just "please pass the sugar" or usually money problems, bills. Tripp was always the music type and sometimes he had money, but more often he didn't. When he did get some money as a welder he was known to go on benders, that's what Angelina called them when she was Mom and he would be gone for days. Claimed he drank so much he blacked out. Mom sometimes cursed him for it, but other times she was more sympathetic about it. He said his own mama and daddy abused and neglected him. Anyhow, it seemed like Mom got so bitter about her condition that she hated Dad, Jess, and me too because I looked like him.

"You're just like your father!" Angelina said. "You got a bad temper just like him."

I wish she didn't try to put all that on me when I was just a kid. I wasn't really like him at all, except I had a talent for music. If I had a hot temper, I was actually more like her. She didn't want to see that though. I was always more like her. If I had waited for her to cool down and say something about it later she would just say, *Did I say that, hon? Must be my chemo brain.* I really just wanted to feel like everything was good and would always be good between us. I couldn't say it. The words wouldn't come out right. It got so bad even Jess didn't want to stay with her anymore.

"You never had anything good to say about him my whole life," I said. "Why did you ever marry him? I mean, if he was so terrible. Why marry him?"

"The truth?"

"Yeah."

"Well," she rasped, clutching her fist between her breasts. Her dark brown eyes seemed to turn inward and get lighter as she played a memory in her mind. Her chapped lips turned upward into a private smile. "He felt sorry for me. He was really goodlooking and he had a cool car. Your daddy was so handsome. He drove a cool Orange Crush-colored Charger with a black stripe back then! He was a rich boy. Not really, but compared to me." She laughed and that turned into a wet cough until she started having a full-blown coughing fit and had to get a drink of water and go lay down in bed. She always got this little smile on her lips when she talked about Tripp when they first met. He was a rich boy and she was a poor country girl. She never said anything about being in love with him exactly. It was disappointing to think that they never really loved each other in the first place.

I guess that's when I started kind of checking her out. I would play video games while she was puking her guts out in the bathroom. I heard her in there hollering for help, I ignored her. Not because I don't love her but I just couldn't deal with it. When her hair started coming out, it scared me. She looked like a zombie. I started focusing all of my attention on my old Skylanders game back then. In real life, everything was out of control but in the game I did the fighting and it was straightforward and you could see the impact you were having. Winning was possible. If I could have shrunk down like Antman maybe I could have got into her bloodstream and fought the cancer somehow. Instead, cancer was invisible.

Angelina was wasting away before my eyes. She either ran to the bathroom to vomit or she had a Tupperware bowl by the bed that she had me or Jessica dump in the toilet when she couldn't get out of bed. Her normally olive complexion had lost its gold highlights. Her cheeks had become hollowed. Her brown eyes had turned dull. She was perpetually tired and in pain. It stabbed my heart. I didn't know what to do with the feels. I knew I was a terrible son.

Her insurance paid for me to have free counseling in the Sherwood Forrest area in a strip mall as the son of a cancer victim. The counselor was a young woman with large nose whose heavily made up face and curly hair and pantsuits gave the impression she was about to head out to her night job maybe as a hostess at Parrain's. The psychiatrist, an old man in his sixties who had only spoken to me once, told Mom that I had ADHD and wanted me to take Adderall. He passed the clipboard over his desk to her with ten signs of ADHD with every box checked. It looked like the form had been printed straight from the internet. Every kid who got sent there had ADHD, according to them anyway. One girl was just bad at Math and her room was messy so that meant she had ADHD. I told him I didn't have ADHD, I had PTSD! He actually took that seriously since it was the only time he ever spoke directly to me. His furry eyebrows arched upwards in a surprised and interested way.

What I didn't know back then, what I didn't want to know, was the hard truth of what Angelina was going through. They had, as she said, "chopped off my tits! Then they gave me these new ones. At least, I never have to worry about them sagging." She jiggled her chest a little and then her eyes filled with tears. I wish I hadn't done it now, but I thought it wouldn't be fair to your daddy. See, I was worried he wouldn't want me if I didn't do it." She felt pretty terrible about it. Jeezum! Who wouldn't?

I would hear her and Dad in their bedroom talking and crying together about it at first. It made me afraid of her but also afraid that I could lose them both in an instant. She could be so strong just like her old self one minute and then the next thing you know a commercial would make her cry. Tripp said she had always been like that, tender-hearted, and I just didn't remember.

She would leave me with one of the neighbor ladies when she drove herself to Baton Rouge General for her chemo treatments after Dad left us. He said he was going to see about a welding job over in Hammond but he never came back. He called us a couple of times from New Orleans and he and Mom would argue over the phone while I played my video games. Jessica, my sister, was in her room painting. I called her Jessica Pollock because of the way she scribbled and flung mad paint while listening to her Screamo music in her Hello Kitty Hot Topic t-shirt. That was her way of coping, I guess.

Sometimes Mom left us at home alone, when she went to the doctor, with a Redbox movie, A Little Caesar's pizza and two

Daren Dean

liter bottles of Dr. Pepper. The hospital doctors gave her three-to-six months to live. No one would talk about it in front of us. I didn't want to hear it anyway. It was terrifying. I distanced myself from her in my heart so that when she died it wouldn't destroy me. I tried not to think about real life. I could not find the words to explain this was how I honestly felt at the time. Dad had already distanced himself physically, then literally by walking out of our house and our every day lives. Money was tight. Mom couldn't work anymore. We were almost kicked out of our shitty rental house. Grandpa started sending us some money every month to help out. A lady from church helped Mom get on disability. Mom was embarrassed by it. It hurt her pride. She had always been a hard worker, a workaholic. She had always been a Type A personality and proud of it! The last job she had was managing a Glitz clothing store that mainly catered to college kids, in the Mall of Louisiana.

Dad said, "Don't drug our son!"

"He needs help," Mom said. "He's failing half his classes! You don't understand. You're never around. I can't raise him all alone."

"Who's fault is that?" Dad said.

"You're blaming me?" Mom said. "You left me because you couldn't handle reality. And now you're blaming me? I have breast cancer! You asshole! Why don't you run back to New Orleans. Go back to your little—"

"Don't say it," Tripp said in a quiet voice just barely above a growl.

"Child! Your child is what I was going to say. I can't possibly understand the attraction or what the two of you would even have in common! You're almost old enough—"

Tripp raised his hand and looked down at the floor. This gesture seemed to stop her mid-sentence. But he didn't say anything else. What could he? Not much. I hated seeing them fight. I think I knew it was over forever before they did. I heard about how grown-ups stay married for their kids, but I say they're not doing kids any favors.

A week later, Tripp, Ayanna, and me drove to Satsuma Grove in a green and black-striped Chevelle. He called it a muscle car. He was borrowing it from a big-wig he knew in the Garden District. People liked him. They sometimes gave him things because he was a cool musician. He had one of those type personalities.

"This is all court-ordered, Noah," Tripp whispered in my ear as he hugged me close. "They always side with the mother." The odor of his sweat cut with Gillette aftershave. His hand was on the back of my head, forcing me close. "I wanted you to stay with me. This isn't what I wanted for you—for us." He had promised an influential friend in the local music scene was going to help me get into Brother Martin on Elysian Fields where all the rich kids went. That would give me a leg-up in life.

"Just perfect," Angelia said as she turned and walked into the kitchen.

"Why Dad?" The bitter sting of tears was on my face. I didn't like crying in front of Ayanna, but this was almost too much to take. Still, I didn't want her thinking I was some little bitch. Ayanna glared in the direction of Angelina and walked out the front door. She pushed open the screen door so it slammed open and shut like Tripp always hated. He didn't make me call him Tripp that time. "I want to stay with you." Angelina's eyes filled with tears and she spun around so we couldn't see her reaction. I wasn't going to be a cool street musician anymore or go to Brother Martin. Instead, I was going to be stuck here with all the rednecks and racists in Satsuma Grove, watching my real life back in NOLA go down the tubes.

Tripp shook his head, earlier that same day in New Orleans, "My hands are tied." He dug some cash out of his wallet and put it in my hand but I didn't want it. I just let it fall to the floor. He knelt down in front of me with a groan, wiping away tears with the back of his hand, picked it up and stuffed it down in the front pocket of my jeans. "You're going to have to make the best of it with your mama for now. I'll get you back. Don't worry. I won't stop fighting for you." That was a lie.

Tripp stood and hugged me hard to his chest. I could feel his cigarettes and Zippo in his front shirt pocket. His wristwatch pinched the skin on my arm. He turned his back to me and told me to pack my things. Ayanna helped me pack. She sang an old-timey song called *Skylark* after she got over being mad at Angelina. It was a remake of an oldie she cut with a new arrangement by a local funk band called Galactic but she sang it the tearful, original way to me. Angelina didn't approve of Ayanna because she was black and too young for Dad in her opinion and we lived in an apartment over a Lebanese convenience store between Reggie's Liquor store and an Irish dive bar called O'Brien's. The difference was Tripp and Ayanna weren't rich, but they were happy. I was happy with them I'm almost ashamed to say. I felt like I had betrayed Angelina. I loved living in NOLA.

We sometimes went to Rock 'n' Bowl on Carrollton and listened to the live performances or even just bowled every so often, but music was the thing! Angelina liked to say that Tripp was in his "tragically hip stage" since he lost his real job. If we weren't going somewhere to hear it or they weren't working, they were writing songs and singing at home all the time. The place sure was a wreck, we had a good time. I was learning to play the used Yamaha keyboard that Tripp let me setup in my room near the stairs with a little divider area. It was a small studio apartment. The main room was open and the walls were red brick. He said I was a natural. I was learning to play some old stuff I had heard a few months back at the Po' Boy Festival down in City Park. It was just a completely different vibe there around people who were interested in having fun and things with real depth, instead of what should or shouldn't be done all the time. It felt like God was always watching and shaking his finger at us back in Satsuma Grove. Life's not about rules. Do's and don'ts don't make nobody happy.

My favorite time of the year was Mardi Gras, but I love all the festivals. I had a framed poster on the wall I had taken with my very own camera this past year of a dancing Mardi Gras Indian with a headdress and outfit made up of turquoise-colored feathers. We were positioned in our lawn chairs and a ladder right in front of Superior Seafood on St. Charles. The parade had started on Napoleon with the horns blasting Trombone Shorty and Galactic! It was good to hear so we jumped up and started dancing. An old white-haired King started things off early in the morning parade wearing a crown and holding a scepter, as he was tossing candy to all the kids. Tripp said he looked just like King Vitamin in his royal duds. There were kids atop ladders curbside screaming for candy and beads as the first of the elaborate floats started rolling past us. You had to watch the drunks on the parade floats who might take you out with a bamboo tomahawk or some other object just for shits and grins.

Tripp and Ayanna drove the old Honda down Oak Street and pulled up in front of the Maple Leaf so I could say goodbye to whoever was working today. I might have been born in another state, but I'd come to see New Orleans as my heart's real home. Maybe it was the party atmosphere and the crowds when Festivals were going on. The tourists, the musicians, and just the feeling that something good was about to happen. It was sometimes dangerous too but that gave an edge to everything instead of the fog I'd been living in Satsuma Grove where everything revolved around death or the possibility of death hanging over me like a hurricane warning.

"I bet I can tell you where you got your shoes for five dollars!" A black kid beating the shit out of a white bucket turned upside down with drumsticks hollered my way. His clothes were old but he had on a pair of blinding white kicks.

"What are those?" I asked. He frowned back at me.

"I bet I can tell you where . . ."

"You in the wrong place for talking that mess," Ayanna shook her finger in his face but her body was still dancing. "Take it on down to the Quarter and the tourists, sugar. We from here."

"On my feet!" I said.

"Oh, you in the know!" the kid said to me. He pointedly ignored Ayanna. "That's okay 'cause I got another one for you!"

"Jeezum!" Tripp shook his head. "We live here, bro."

"I ain't your bro!" The kid twirled his sticks with his fingers like a professional drummer and stared after us. He was about my age, maybe a little older, and gave me a dirty look like he wanted to kill me. Without another word he picked up his bucket and stalked back up toward Carrollton like maybe he was going to hop the streetcar that clattered down the avenue with a load of tourists and people who worked somewhere along the way. I'd never seen him before so maybe he was just checking out the action at the other end of the line.

"Hey hey! There's Noah! You going to make it rain up in here!" The bartender they called "Mother" shouted out to me. Since my name was Noah, there was always something about raining or the Bible he'd say to me. Mother was dressed like a Las Vegas showgirl with a bushy brown beard on his face. He had some kind of fake blue jewel in his belly button. "Sit over here, baby."

When I first saw Mother behind the bar I turned to Ayanna and said, "That's one tall lady!"

"Oh Mother?" Ayanna said. "She wishes she was a lady!" People sitting at the table against the window and on nearby stools at the bar started cracking up.

I sat at a stool where I always sat if I came by in the afternoon before Mother chased me out. I never thought I would miss Mother but just hearing him give directions to different places to eat on Oak Street and in the Quarter and hear music to a nice looking touristy couple made me realize I would miss him and his wildness. Last week he had been dressed up as a cowboy with white makeup caked on his face. I hated to go back to Satsuma Grove since it was kind of boring there unless you liked LSU football and just about everyone there did. LSU flags hung on porches, sometimes right next to Confederate flags. Even people who had never even thought about going to college were gung ho about tailgating and screaming for the Tigers like their son played quarterback. In NOLA, especially the Oak Street crowd, we were all about Drew Brees and the Saints!

Tripp refused to even go in the house with me. It was getting late in the afternoon and he wanted to head back to New Orleans before the rush hour traffic got too crazy. Blue dragonflies were flying all over the front yard hunting for mosquitos and no-see-ums. I had one foot in and one foot out of Tripp's old silver Explorer. He didn't want to have to talk to Angelina. Ayanna walked me to the door and even carried one of my backpacks for me. She sat my backpack on the front porch. She put her hand on my back and rubbed my shoulders before giving me a peck on the cheek. The door was unlocked so she nodded to me and danced all the way back to the vehicle. She shook her booty and smiled at me over her shoulder. She didn't want me to be so sad. She got in and sat next to Tripp. He gave me a forlorn wave and I waved back before pushing open the door. I knew he didn't want to leave me here but the judge had ruled in Angelina's favor, but maybe he was a little relieved too not to have the extra responsibility of me.

"Angelina?" I said as I walked into the murky house. The heavy curtains were all closed and it smelled heavily of garlic. "Angelina? Mom? You home?" No answer. I went to her bedroom to find her wrapped up in her blankets like a burrito. I wondered if she were dead for a minute but then I heard the rhythmic sound of her breathing. I decided not to wake her up and threw my stuff in my old room. It seemed smaller than I remembered. And they thought she would take care of me! It was pretty clear she was the one who needed my help.

I dug out a butt from Angelina's front porch ashtray and proceeded to smoke the rest of it. I sat there kind of stewing about what I was going to do. The house seemed so quiet. Here, Angelina wanted me back and couldn't even stay awake long enough to meet me at the door. I couldn't help but wonder how Jessica was doing at the old folk's home (what I called our grandparent's house) since the house would be pretty quiet with only the two of us here. I thought about playing around on the Yamaha but I didn't want to wake Angelina up. She could be cranky about being woke up from a dead sleep.

Just then a little Cooper car pulled up and a woman with a rockstar haircut and tattoos jumped out of her car and shut the door with the jut of her hip. She wasn't bad looking for an older lady. She was probably at least twenty-five, maybe a little older. Angelina said she was crazy and sold drugs but that didn't make a person all bad in my book. I didn't want to deal, some people did whatever they had to to get by.

"Hey!" the woman smiled. "Who are you, cutey?"

It jolted me the way she spoke directly to me like I was an adult. I noticed that she had a nice body. She was smiling at me like she wanted to know me. It was so straight-on that I stammered for a minute trying to figure out what to say. She laughed but like she was flirting instead of making fun of me.

"Where y'at?" I asked. She just kept on staring at me like she might eat me up. She didn't know what I was saying. So I said, "I'm Noah. I just come back up from NOLA."

"Oh yeah," she walked over to me, but didn't come up the porch steps. "I just got back from *making groceries* up at Albertsons."

"Making groceries, huh?" I said. "You in the know then." I laughed.

"You're Angelina's boy? Huh! You're a good-looking thang. I bet you broke some hearts down there?"

"Not really," I said. I was kind of used to people talking a little crazy like that in bars. I just kind of went off whatever they were saying. "I might break some here though." I'd heard someone in the bar say something like that before.

"Oooh, look at you then!" She laughed. "I could use your help tomorrow if you're going to be around."

"What kind of help? Does it pay?"

"It might," she said, "it just might. You come running when I need you, okay?"

"Maybe."

"Give me your phone," she said. I handed it over to her as obedient as a lamb even though I knew I shouldn't have. She pecked her number in. "Call me, anytime. My name is Heaven. Don't tell Angelina we had this little talk. She might not like it." She handed back my cell phone and touched my forearm and it burned something in me like fire. She patted my cheek. I flinched and took a little step back.

"Don't worry," I said. "We don't talk much."

"Gotcha," Heaven turned away and wiggled her butt a little in case I was watching, and I was watching, as she walked back over to her house. Just when she put her hand on the handrail leading up to her porch she turned and looked at me over her shoulder with an expression that said it all. I quickly pretended to be fascinated with my shoes and bent down to untie and retie them just to have something to do.

I felt something wet on my cheek. It was just beginning to rain and suddenly it started coming down in sheets. It had been raining off and on. We were a little relieved when the feared tropical storm began to break apart and was just dumping rain. In Louisiana we are used to buckets of rain. When you're local you know the streets that tend to take on water and the ones that don't. Like it usually flooded real bad off Pete's Highway, River Road, and Satsuma Avenue. Eden Church Road was usually safe. The old people said it was higher ground. It was the low-lying areas you had to watch out for. When the inevitable August and September storms and floods came, people usually tied their rowboats, canoes, skiffs, or fishing boats to their mobile homes and front porches just to get to the road when it became necessary and that could be just about anytime. All that water came rushing downstream.

I heard Tripp talking about levies being opened or closed despite how it might devastate the people living on the land in Mississippi for instance. It all rolled downhill and came to the Gulf one way or another. Flood water in Louisiana was just a way of life, you adjusted to it. You did what you could. The rain stopped just then. We were all expecting the storm to blow through like they usually did. The weatherman said it was an unorganized system, but the rain kept coming. No one panicked. It wasn't even a proper tropical storm, much less a hurricane.

There wasn't a thing to worry about until the flood waters came and began to fill our front yard. Angelina didn't want to but she reluctantly told me to go round up Miss Jamie Lynn and Presley since their house was a little wood house built on a concrete pad. Presley thanked us and said they'd get a few things together and come over in a little bit. When she opened the door, I could see an inch of water on the floor already. Miss Jamie Lynn was sitting cross-legged on a green couch and looked at me calmly smoking a cigarette like I had invited them over for a barbecue.

I knew Angelina hated Heaven but I thought about knocking on her door though I could tell nobody was home. Her "boyfriends" weren't home either. One was named Varnado and he had a big flaming neck tattoo and a gold tooth. I wasn't sure what the other one's name was but he was a bigger dude. Neither of them were around. Sometimes a house lets you know when nobody's home. It's like a vibration you can feel. It made me smile to think how she'd act if I showed up with the woman she claimed killed her husband right in front of her eyes. I didn't believe her though. I think it was just chemo-brain playing tricks on her. Angelina, Jamie Lynn, and Heaven were all three the kind of women who didn't really like other females.

When I got back to our house, the sound of a transformer nearby went *poof* and it got real quiet. You could tell who was home then because the loss of power made people come out of their houses and look around with dazed expressions. After Jamie Lynn and Presley showed up the water started getting deeper. The clouds in the wine-colored sky were a kind of pepper and sugar swirl like the angels had used a heavenly cake mixer. Jamie Lynn asked Angelina if she could invite her boyfriend Jack over since he didn't have no place to go. It turned out later he just didn't want to go home to his wife in Sherwood Forest. I wonder if he had walked all the way here. He had big green rubber boots up to his knees on over his street shoes. The rushing water cleaned out the crawlspace beneath our house. Angelina said it sounded like we were on a boathouse. We sat in the living room listening to the water slap beneath us. It was so hot and humid we wore as little as possible and kept the front door open. My cell phone couldn't get any service. No one else's could either.

## PRESLEY

They used to say Mama was the wildest girl in Livingston Parish!
I don't know if that's true, but I don't doubt it. She was still crazy
about men from what I'd seen. She was on the phone talking to one
of her boyfriends about coming over and "saving" her from the
flood. I was pretty sure it was Eddie, a real loser in my book because
he was still legally married to a Cajun woman who lived somewhere
in Jefferson Davis Parish. He read the meters in our neighborhood
and drank nothing but cans of PBR when he came around every
couple of weeks. Eddie thought he was real cool, bragged about his
parakeet yellow Corvette. Mama said he looked like Garth Brooks—
some big-boned yee-yee. He always gave Mama a big wad of cash
before he left. One time I counted it out and it came to one hundred
and seven dollars. Why the extra seven? IDK.

    *Oh great, Eddie's coming over! When it rains it floods, and it eddies.*
Eddie always talked real loud, made chili, drank cheap beer, and then
around midnight he would go into the bathroom and vomit it all up.
So gross. He liked to walk into my room without a shirt on and rub
his stomach like he just ate some delicious honey and creep me out
with his bulgy wanting eyes.

    "I'm sooo scared, Eddie," Mama said in her best sultry voice,
her cell phone pressed against her face. She winked at me. She just
doesn't have a clue. "Please come over if you can before it floods us
out. It might just wash us away. Yeah, just like the song. Come get us
and take us to a fancy Hampton Inn . . . oh, come on now . . . you'll
be happy you did . . . well, okay then . . . try . . . I miss your arms

around me." It was too cringey for words to listen to her.

"Mama! What are you fooling around with that man for? This flood is serious! We don't need him."

"Oh, you will understand when you're older," Mama laughed knowingly and went into the kitchen to eat leftover red beans and rice.

*I understand it just fine, you old horndawg.*

We ate red beans and rice every Monday night like Catholics eat fish for Lent. It was one of those traditional things we adopted when we moved here. We used minute rice and Blue Runner canned beans. Jamie Lynn was clinking and clattering the dishes around in the kitchen. I heard the sound of the clear round revolving plate in the microwave move slightly as she slid the bowl in. She started the microwave when all of a sudden the power went out.

"Shit!" Jamie Lynn shitted in the kitchen. "Shit! Shit! Shit!"

I hollered from the living room, "What happened? You blow the fuse again? You better go out and flip the switch!"

"All the power went out!" She started bawling in the kitchen. We both knew why the power went out.

"Maybe we better get out of here," I said.

I peeked through the blinds and the water was filling up the Laryisson's front yard now. Smaller trees partially submerged in the water strained against the current. Mr. Dixon started up his big blue Kenworth and was fixing to move it a few blocks over to the Carter's grocery store parking lot. I'd seen him do this a couple of times before because it was practically brand new. Miss Lynette said Blue Betty, the name of his diesel, was the love of his life even though she thought he should retire. He wasn't old enough to retire. He often told me had reached an age that, while not old, had rendered him all but invisible to other women except for Miss Lynette and Blue Betty. "Blue Betty" was painted white in cursive on the driver door of his powder blue truck decked out with naked lady mud flaps.

The Herberts were loading up their vehicles in a big hurry across the street. They said we were crazy to stay but they didn't say much more since they were in a hurry to beat the flood waters and take I-12 to I-55 North. They couldn't take Range since it ran next to the Amite the further North you went. They had family up in Jackson, Mississippi they could stay with if they made it that far.

"You better take the back roads," Dixon cautioned, "or you will end up stuck on the interstate. Take Range all the way up and around to 55." He walked back over to his driveway and searched the front pocket of his gray Dickies as he looked up at Blue Betty.

Miss Leah and Mr. Remy told me that we should put a few things together and go with them, but I knew Mama wouldn't do it. She was a contrarian. If a man suggested going away with him for the weekend to New Orleans she might do it but she didn't really like other women trying to tell her what to do even if it made good sense.

"Let's go with them," I said. She ignored me and started waving at them to beat the band.

"Goodbye Remy!" Mama called out to him from our doorway and tossed him a kiss. Miss Leah just stared at her and shook her head in disgust. Mama liked to get her goat. It was mean if you ask me since the woman would do anything for you.

"Take care of yourself, Jamie Lynn!" Remy's face was burning and he smiled like a Junior high school boy who had just had one of the popular girls talk to him. He held in his big stomach like a pregnant lady while he stared slack jaw at Jamie Lynn in her tight jeggings and a leopard print top she was just a little too curvy for. She made a spectacle of herself as usual. Old people shouldn't wear tight clothes if you ask me. She thought she looked good.

Miss Leah smacked him in the back of the head, "Hurry up so we don't get stuck here!" I couldn't help laughing behind my hand as he hitched into motion loading up his SUV. She hissed over her shoulder, "Put your tongue back in your mouth."

Dixon started up the Blue Betty. He let the Kenworth idle for a few minutes before pulling out of his driveway. His truck made all kinds of noise. The air seemed to vibrate with the noise of the diesel engine growling and grinding like a Tyrannosaurus. I could feel the vibrations climbing up from the soles of my feet and into my belly. I walked up to the street to wave him down and he gave a tug on on his air horn but then he realized I wanted him to stop. The brakes hissed at me. He'd given give me rides before so I put my foot on the step, used the bar to pull myself up, and managed to get the door open and stuck my head in.

"Can I ride with you, Mr. Dixon?" I said. Somehow I felt safer with Dixon around than I did with Mama. "Please?"

"I don't think I should carry you anywhere, hon," he said. "I'm just going to take Blue Betty and park her in the lot down to Carter's grocery store. I don't know how hard it will be to get back on foot. It might be dangerous if it floods worse, so I'm going to have to tell you to wait here. You know I love you, yeah?"

"Mama said I could go with you!" I pleaded and stuck my lip out so he would feel sorry for me and change his mind. I thought it might work since I knew he was soft-hearted toward Mama and me.

"Your mama don't have the say," Dixon said. "I should be back in the next 15 minutes. I hope. I want you to go check on Lynette for me. If I don't make it back for some reason, that is. She'll need you to keep her company. Take your little Mickey over to see her too. Sit with her until I get back. Can you do that?"

"All right," I said. "Watch out for the crazies!" I jumped down and slammed the door shut. Blue Betty shushed me with her air brakes.

He gave the horn a blast to tell me to make sure I was out of the way before he took off. I really wanted to go with him for some reason. The truck drove off down the street and it suddenly looked safer than our dumb old house that everyone on our street called "cottage style" and made me think of a house made of gingerbread like in the fairy tales.

"Don't go to the park. It's flooding real bad," I texted Olivia, but she didn't text back. I hoped she wasn't waiting for me at the park. I imagined she was surrounded by flood waters, her head barely above the surface, calling my name for help. My emotions got the better of me. I felt stinging little sweat-bee-tears in my eyes. Next, I imagined her stuck on the slide with water all around. I was so emotional lately. Mama said it was hormones because of my age. I slipped the phone in my back pocket. I stood there for a minute trying to decide what to do. Should I go home and pack up some clothes, my purse, and other stuff, or go check on Miss Lynette? I couldn't decide and that made me want to cry some more. I was so upset with myself I didn't know what the right thing to do was. Miss Lynette had been on some new medication and she slept all the time these days. It was hard to see her that way so I chickened out and walk over there.

The Herberts were already on the road. I didn't even see

their convoy of three vehicles pull out of the drive. It scared me to think of everyone leaving the neighborhood. Maybe we should leave too. Mama seems unconcerned but that's probably because she decided it was time to have a Bloody Mary. She put on her nicest bling jeans and a silver blouse that looks like a disco ball. Her hair was super blonde now because that's what Eddie liked. I guess I did enough worrying for the both of us.

She was putting on makeup while I was filling up the tub and every container I could find with water just in case we ran out of drinking water like when Hurricane Isaac walloped us. I filled tea pitchers, canisters, every big plaster container, even the vases that different men had sent to Mama with roses in them over the last couple of years. Some of the vases were clear, red, green, blue, white, and a few were so cheap I was afraid filling them with water might crack them. I even found a couple of old coffee pots to fill. We had them because when the Mr. Coffees had quit working it seemed like a shame to throw the pots away.

"Mama!" I hollered over her little clock radio. She was one of the few people I knew who actually still listened to the clock radio in their house instead of iTunes or Spotify. She was so retro! It was like the Nineties all the time to her because that's when she had been young.

"What do you want? I'm trying to listen to my music."

"Fill up the bathtub with water just in case we need it for flushing the toilet while you're in there!" I held my breath and listened for her to answer but instead she was singing "Dolla Diva" by Galactic who she'd heard at a festival in New Orleans. "You're a dolla diva! You're a dolla diva! You're a dolla dolla diva!" She couldn't sing good like Maggie Koerner and didn't know her voice was off key the whole entire time. I don't why I always had to be the responsible one!

"I guess I've got to do everything myself," I said to no one in particular. I wiped at a tear in my eye. Mickey was following me around and kept staring at me and backing out of my way just before I stepped on him the way dogs will do. After all this flood business was over I decided to get a nose ring and maybe a tattoo like Ashley Madison in my Art class. Sure, she had to take out her nose ring in school but I saw her put it in while looking at herself using her cell phone camera after school. It made her look so much older.

After I filled all the containers I could find I ran down the street to check on Miss Lynette. The water crept up the street. The couyons in the boat from the school were gone now. I just burst through the front door and went straight to Miss Lynette's room because I knew she wouldn't hear me if I knocked anyway since she was deaf in one ear.

"There's my girl!" Miss Lynette started with a hand to her chest, but then threw her arms open wide. The backs of her arms wiggled from the gesture. It was so easy to fall into her arms almost like a relative instead of just a neighbor. She surprised me because she was sitting up in the little wingback chair at the foot of the bed with a blanket over her legs. Her hair was wispy, salt and pepper, and made her look like a tiny, good witch. Mama said she'd certainly never let herself look so haggard. She went to a rough Croatian lady who did hair by working out of her apartment in Baton Rouge. She talked like Natasha from Rocky & Bullwinkle cartoon reruns. She dyed Mama's hair platinum blonde about every six weeks. Mama stopped for a little while when it started falling out. "Girl, you better go into the kitchen and get something to eat. You're just a skinny minnie!"

"I ate a donut from Mary Lee Donuts," I said. "We had them leftover from yesterday."

"Mmm hmmm," she said doubtfully. "Ya'll doing okay?" Miss Lynette asked. "Your mama all right?"

I knew she didn't approve of the blonde lady or her men. She was trying to be nice. I didn't tell her what I thought about Mama calling gross Eddie to come over so I just shrugged away her question.

"Mama's mama. The blonde lady does what she does."

Miss Lynette rubbed my back, "Honey, could you go to Skelly's convenience store and me some Aleve or Motrin? As long as the water ain't come too far down that way. I hate to ask you this, but Arthur is after me again." She rubbed her knobby fingers together as if to illustrate the pain. She called her arthritis Arthur. Her thumb looked bent at a crazy angle just below the nail, but she said it was a side effect.

"Okay," I said. "But I don't think Mr. Dixon wants me to

leave you all by your lonesome."

"Awww shoot," She waved her swollen fingers at me. She handed me a ten out of her little cigarette snap purse. "Get yourself a Red Bull!"

"Okay, Miss Lynette!" I snatched the money out of her hand and ran out the door.

"Be careful, wild girl!" She called after me.

I wanted to tell her I was actually pretty scared about the flooding but everyone else just acted like it was normal. It was kind of normal. The old people would just say, *Oh, it's nothing compared to Katrina!* Or, some other old storm name. Maybe they thought pretending it wasn't going to be so bad would make it easier to deal with but there was a part of me that just wanted to hide in my closet, eat Takis, and draw Sailor Moon in my notebook all day until it was safe to come out again. I bit my tongue as usual and just thought I'd try to act as normal as everyone else.

I grabbed an old skateboard left out by the Herbert's yard and skated all the way to Skelly's convenience store. Before I even got there I saw that crazy rooster who liked to hang out in front. It marched up and down on the strip of grass in front of the store or like he was standing guard near the double doors. The rooster belonged to an old man who lived in the trailer behind the store and had a battered Confederate battle flag waving from the flagpole in his front yard. The rooster just refused to stay in his own yard.

"Get on out of here superchicken!" I hissed at the rooster. He strutted away from me with a look that said I was beneath his dignity to run from.

Skelly's sold all the regular stuff you'd expect: Cokes, energy drinks, chips, candy, candy bars, bags of ice, beer, and gas. They also cooked ribeye and baked potato dinners on Fridays in the add-on connected out to the side like a screened-in porch. They sometimes had the most spicy red crawfish steaming on the food bar inside behind an old glassed-in meat counter, and they even made their own boudin. It was just about every kind of boudin you could possibly imagine. The smell of all that fried food would hit you and make your stomach growl as soon as you pulled the door open.

The bell dinged to let them know you were there and the Mexican cashier would usually greet you with *Hola ¿qué tal?* And then

Daren Dean

she would quickly say, *Hi, how are you?* If Skelly was behind the counter he would shout, *Who dat?*

Ash Madison worked at Skelly's and I wondered if she was at all worried about the flood. I heard Ash lived with her boyfriend and was going to marry him even though she was only a Junior. She was skinny and ultra pretty but she had an edge to her. You know? I mean, the way she looked. She had blondish hair normally, but she dyed it maroon or green or gray. She was about to quit school so she didn't care about the school uniform or rules about hair color. Her makeup made her face look pale, but then her black eye makeup was like an Egyptian. Her eyes already had that doe-like, baby doll look that could hypnotize you. She hypnotized all the men who went into Skelly's. Some men found themselves going in and out of there several times a day when she was working and everyone one of them knew why and so did their wives.

The doorbells clanged as I went in with my skateboard in my arms. Ash up and downed me as I came in, but she didn't say anything at first but give me a sly grin. I waved my fingers at her. I suddenly felt shy about her noticing me. I kind of stood there and an old man with a Vietnam Vet cap pushed passed me with a growl. Still, I just stood there thinking that maybe the skateboard might make me invisible or something. A heavy black lady dressed in a cheap purple track suit nudged me accidentally with her arm as she came in.

"I'm sorry," she said but it didn't really sound like it. She was kind of gasping for breath from walking in from the pumps.

"That's okay," I said. I took a few steps forward so I was out of the way a little bit more as the doors were awkwardly positioned right in front of the cashier. Ash stepped up to the register like she was going to wait on me. She opened her mouth as if she were going to say something, but nothing came out.

"You need some help there little lady?" Skelly himself said. I'd been coming there for years with Mama but I guess he didn't recognize me without her.

"I need some Advil or Aleve or something, Mr. Skelly," I said.

"Do I know you?" He wiped his hands on the barbeque stained apron.

"My mama is Jamie Lynn," I wasn't afraid to admit it.

Ash made a look like she smelled something bad when I said Mama's name.

"Oh! Why of course you are! You are Presley, right? You look just like Jamie Lynn when she was your age! My ain't you a pretty thing? I don't remember seeing you? Must have been awhile?"

"No sir," I said. "Not really." I went in there at least once a week.

He didn't seem to know what to say. Neither of us did. He grabbed his tongs and snatched up a couple of shrimp boudins and put them in a little white sack and threw them in my direction.

"Them's for you," Mr. Skelly said. "Better get what you need and get on home before that storm catches you."

"Ya'll going to be open tomorrow?" A man by the restroom doors hollered.

"Gonna try to be!" Mr. Skelly said.

I bought some Aleve and Ash put it in a little plastic bag and winked at me like I was a dumb little kid. I wanted to tell her that I was in high school too, but I couldn't feel my tongue. It was like it was glued to the bottom of my mouth. I felt myself blush bright red because Ash was so cool and I wasn't.

"Let's hang out sometime, Presley," Ash said, "when all this flood stuff is over."

"Okay!" I said a little too loud. "You could come over to my . . . I mean, cool."

Just as I left Skelly's, I saw Dixon walking by on the side-walk. I hollered and waved the bag of boudin at him. At first, he didn't hear me and kept walking. Old people just don't always hear you when you talk or they talk louder than you so they don't have to listen. I'm used to it so I don't take it too personal. They always seem distracted when you talk to them.

"I got the pills for Ms. Lynette," I said. I held the bag up and rattled it. "And some of Skelly's boudin. It's still warm."

"Oh good," Dixon said. He took the pills from me and put them in his pocket. "We'd better get back quick and check on Lynette. I'll take one of those boudin off you. What flavor is it?"

"Shrimp," I threw the skateboard down, jumped on it, and started skating down the bumpy sidewalk.

"How much he charge?" He took a big bite and he smiled

with his lips, but the rest of his face forgot to smile along except his crows feet went deeper. He started walking a little faster to keep up with me.

"It was a lagniappe, I guess . . . for buying the pills. Mr. Dixon looked at me funny. I guess because he knows Mama."

"Everyone knows your mama," he said, but not unkindly. He closed his eyes and laughed for a second. I wondered if he was thinking something nasty and felt bad for thinking it.

"One time your mama took Lynette to Baton Rouge General when I was out on the road," he said. "You was just a wee little thing. Don't listen to no one who talks bad about your mama. You get one mama in your life and when she's gone, she gone."

"What was wrong?"

"Wrong?" He seemed incredulous.

"Yeah, Mr. Dixon, what was wrong with Miss Lynette? How come Mama to carry her to the hospital?" I put my hand on his shoulder so he pulled me along on the skateboard as he walked, but then he stopped all of a sudden and looked at me.

His gray bristly mustache quivered. His eyes filled with tears and he wiped them away with the back of his hand. He turned back to stare straight ahead like he was looking way into the past or maybe the future and began to walk with a little more purpose than before.

"We take care of each other on Eden Church Road. That's all." He didn't say anything else about it.

I stopped thinking about what we were talking about. I couldn't help wondering why Ash wanted to hang out with me. She was pretty and cool. Me? I felt like a big dud. A dead head. I had brownish-red hair (Mr. Dixon called it auburn), freckles, and lips that were too big for my face. I was definitely an ugly duckling compared to Ash. Did she know how cool she was? I was starting to feel bad about myself but then the sun came out and beat down on our heads. When I got home it was only to find that Mama had let Mickey out and he had disappeared. I looked all around calling her name and then I sat on the back porch and cried like a little baby. I stayed out looking for him until the blood-drunk no-see-ums chased me inside.

## JULE

He did not want to leave his home. He was proud he had never run from a hurricane or even any kind of rougarou weather in his entire adult life. Eden Church Road had never flooded since they had moved onto the street back in 1983, so he hadn't thought it would happen now but he heard Davey Baby's big Dodge Ram pull into the drive waiting to take them to a shelter like he was an invalid. The old man was so pride-hurt he would not speak to Hope for calling Davey Baby to come take them away even though their home was in serious danger from the flood waters. The water had flooded the north end of the street, just beyond the stop sign, in front of the elementary school. In protest, Jule was up out of his Hoveround and hacking, black-handled machete in hand, at some especially stubborn kudzu growing along his back fence trying to devour his storage shed.

Davey Baby was an electrician in the area who was born and bred in New Orleans. He was known to call everyone "baby" all the time, it sounded more like *bebe*. He had an old-fashioned, almost laid-back, way about him everyone seemed to like. He dressed in a gray Dickies work shirt and blue jeans covering the tops of his Wolverines. His hair was salt and pepper on the sides and, despite his age, he still had plenty of thick black hair to spare on top. His skin was made a permanent reddish-tan color from working out in the sun doing construction ever since he was a young man. His dog paced back and forth in the bed of the truck watching her master's every move. But she wouldn't leave the bed of the truck unless he gave her the command.

Daren Dean

Jule slung the machete down on the ground where it shuttered in a piercing gesture of hopelessness and disgust. He turned and backed up into his chair where it seemed to embrace his backside as he coughed a scoffing disgusted growl. He drove around the corner of the house and onto the paved driveway in dread of the electrician's smiling face.

"You going to get old too one day!" Mr. Jule said, "I hope you know. Then, I'd like to see your face, padnah."

"I got other people to help out today, baby," Davey Baby said with a Swisher Sweet cigarillo burning between his lips. "You want one of these, Mr. Jule?" Jule almost imperceptibly shook his head no and waved his hand in front of his face as if he smelled a foul odor. He just said it to be polite since Mr. Jule couldn't smoke anymore. He was stewing, ass-burnt over the indignity of running from a storm and still too angry to talk even to Davey Baby who he considered a good friend. The electrician was generous and had a strong work ethic that caused older men like Jule to admire him even if their pride would never have allowed them to express the sentiment out loud. He allowed himself to think he was still the electrician's age and capable.

"Up we go!" The electrician swept Hope off her feet suddenly and she hollered with delight. He carried her to the truck since water was already up to his ankles. He didn't want her to get her feet wet. He already wore rubber knee-high boots himself since he liked to be prepared. He had already put their little suitcases in the backseat of his Ram truck. It had big wheels so it could still travel the roads unless the water became too deep. "There we are," he said, once she was situated like a child in the front seat.

"Just take us up to the . . . whatever . . . across from Carter's, Davey Baby," Hope motioned impotently, searching for the exact words, with her hands in the direction she wanted to go as she sat forward in the backseat so the electrician could hear her. "That's where they put the shelter."

"Where is it, baby?" Davey Baby squinted at her.

"Oh, you know!" Hope's eyes rolled back to look up over her head. "It's that church . . ." The electrician noticed that today her hair was so white it seemed to glow almost artificially like cotton candy at the spring fest.

"The Catholic Church over there?" He pointed above the

dashboard in a northern direction.

"Naw!" Mr. Jule said, and then clamped his mouth shut and covered it with the hollow of his hand. He hadn't meant to say anything for the whole trip. He then crossed barnacled arms, crisscrossed as they were with welts and bruises from his various physical ailments, to demonstrate his protest. The doctor had once said his body just wasn't able to recover like it had when he was a younger man.

"What's the name of it, Jule?" Davey Baby smiled magnanimously in the old man's face.

"No sir." Jule shook his head like a pouting toddler. He put on an old pair of heavy gold sunglasses that reminded him of glasses Elvis Presley wore in the seventies.

"Awww now," Hope purred. "He knows, he just won't say. It's called . . . you know, whatever-whatever. You caught me in an old-timer moment. Haha!" She pointed a finger to her head to indicate her inability to think of the proper name. ". . . I lost it."

"Okay," Davey Baby said. He put the truck in reverse to back up carefully into the street as water was pooling up between the paved driveway and where it met the macadam of the street. "So we're heading over to the Carter's across from that Baptist Church then? That's the shelter."

"Yes! But the other way around. We going to the church . . . the . . . designated shelter. Somebody designated it!" Hope said. "See, you don't remember no name either. It ain't so easy when you start gettin' old, is it?"

"Old?" The electrician pumped the breaks. "Old, you said! Why baby, I ain't but sixty-two years old. I ain't all that old. I'm just hitting my stride!"

"No no," Hope agreed. "You a young boy still. A, um… teenager compared to us, Baby-Baby." Instead of calling him Davey Baby, it was her habit to call him Baby-Baby because it was easier for her. She had a habit of changing people's names as it suited her but no one seemed to mind.

"Now you're talking!"

"Would have liked to have my Hoveround is all," Jule sniffed. "It ain't so easy getting around with a cane."

"I can put your walker in back real quick," Davey Baby said. Jule shook his head, "Naw sir. I ain't no invalid. I got my hick-

Daren Dean

ory cane." He patted the cane resting against his leg with his gnarled hands.

"Ah now!" Hope said. "Don't be so prideful! Baby-Baby will throw his back out trying to load that big electric thing in his truck."

"I ain't talking 'bout it no more," Jule said. "It hurts my leg being up walking all the time. I got to *thug it out* like the youngbloods say."

"Ha ha! I like dat!" Davey Baby said.

"Doctor told you to start walking more! I remember 'cuz I was there when he told it. It was that day when we went to the farmer's market and I got those good peppers!" Hope gave him a crazy look with her eyes. Her bottom lip trembled when Jule didn't say nothing back but just looked at her with hurt, stoney eyes.

Davey Baby pretended not to notice their fussing at each other and started humming an old Jazz number he liked. They reminded him of his parents or maybe what they would have been like if they had lived as long. He had adopted them as his own and liked to visit them when he could. He worried about them when he started hearing reports about flooding.

Later, he dropped them off and said, "Call me on my cell phone later," Davey Baby said. "Let me know y'all's okay."

Jule set in a sturdy wooden chair with faded, orange leatherette upholstery, fastened in place with antique, hammered brass, and Oxford nails. A small detail but the old man's fingers were drawn to them. Hope would have sat next to him but since he was still huffing at her about making him come to the shelter in the first place so she walked around and talked to everyone instead of watching him pout. She made sure not to stray too far from her husband in case he needed something. She worried and fussed over him so. His gnarly cane was allowed to rest against his leg. It was made from a piece of hickory that an old friend of theirs who lived in French Settlement made by hand as a gift.

A little boy was weeping and sucking in his breaths the way little kids do when they are very upset. He held his little balled up fists in the air, a little above his shoulders, and cried out his frustrations. The boy's eyes were wet and filled with tears. His skin was dark brown from the sun and his lips were chapped and bright red. His nose was snotty and he was skittering away from one of the church lady's who was helping out until he found himself in a corner under a purple banner displaying a golden crown of thorns. It was clear he had recently been out in the elements for days at a time. His clothes were torn and dirty.

"Hey there," Jule called. "You boy!"

The little boy looked up with his wet eyes and slid the back of his forearm against his snotty nose. He paused for a moment as his dark eyes lifted toward the comforting low voice of the old man. "Qué quieres?" The boy hiccupped and crossed his skinny arms in front of him.

"Come sit next to an old man," Jule said. "I need a good boy to keep me company."

The boy seemed to understand. He obeyed and presented himself to the old man. He stood before the old man expectantly, hopefully. The old man took the boy by his hands as if he had known him all his life and the boy submitted to it.

"You alone? Where's your mama?" Jule asked. He took out a red bandanna out of his back pocket, wadded it up, put his left hand gently to the back of the boy's head, and the bandanna he put up to the boy's nose. "Blow. It's okay."

The boy nodded that he was alone. "No lo se, señor." Then he raised his head up and commenced to wailing.

"Here now," Jule said. "Listen to me. You like candy?"

The boy nodded though his bottom lip still protruded. The old man folded over the kerchief and replaced it in his back pocket.

The old man suddenly made a funny face at the boy. The boy grinned but then just as quickly shook his head and stuck out his lip again. Jule sat back so he could reach into his trouser pocket and came out with two pieces of Werther's in their golden wrappers. He offered them up to the boy who immediately took one and unwrapped it expertly and popped it in his mouth. The other he put in his little pocket for later. He made some happy sucking noises. The caramel candy made a clicking noise as it glided over his teeth and he turned it expertly in his mouth with his tongue to get at all the sweet.

"Is it good?"

The little boy nodded. He sniffed. He inhaled and his tiny body spasmed with hiccups of feeling better. He understood the old man, if not the words, his kind intentions.

"Good," The old man said. "Sit on this bench next to me. You can be my buddy. Stay here with Hope and me. We need a good little boy to talk to. I'm Mr. Jule and this is my wife, Hope."

The boy nodded, "Don Jule y Doña Hope."

The boy looked with wide eyes at Hope who had just walked back over to stand next to them from across the room where she had been talking to a woman who was busily setting up little cots in the church's large foyer. He was still standing in front of Jule.

"How are you, little boy?" Hope said. "Como te llamas niño?"

"Filipe," the boy said and nodded.

"Siéntate a mi lado," Hope said.

"Gracias dama," and he sat on the bench between them sucking happily on his candy for the moment.

"That lady said Filipe got separated from his family some- how," Hope said.

Jule gave his normal baleful look, "He's okay. He can sit with us for a bit. Ain't that right?" He patted the little boy's bony knee. He was the size of a doll compared to the big man himself. Looking at the little boy made him remember his own eldest son when he was little and then the car wreck on I-12 just outside of Baton Rouge that took his life in his early twenties. He put his thumb and forefinger up to his tear ducts to keep from weeping at the still painful memory.

The boy nodded.

"He's a smart little boy," Jule said to his wife. "You thirsty?"

The boy nodded enthusiastically. He clapped his hands like a sophisticated children's toy made for just that purpose. The boy was so tiny it made the old man want to protect him. He felt his chest constrict with emotion. He didn't know why he felt the way he did since the boy was no relation of his. It didn't matter. He would do for the little child if he could.

Jule leaned back and reached into his pocket and pulled out his money clip. He peeled off some bills and gave them to the little boy. "Young blood, take this to that woman over there and see if she'll give you a Coke and a candy bar. You look hungry."

"Gracias Grandpa," the boy smiled and leapt to his feet.

"Espera un minuto, pequeña!" Hope said. The boy turned as

if frozen to look over his shoulder with an expression of dread. "We have to clean him up first, Daddy. Look how dirty he is. I'm going to take him into the bathroom and wash him up."

Jule shook his head gravely in response. Hope held out her hand to the boy who took it. He could tell that she was saying something to the boy as they walked past the information booth and toward the restrooms but he didn't have his hearing aids in. He leaned forward and stared down at his hands. Now that he had started thinking about the death of his son he couldn't seem to put the thoughts away again. Tears streamed down his cheeks. He looked around but no one was looking his way or paying attention to him because he was old and all but invisible to them. He allowed the tears drops to fall down his rough cheeks. They could do whatever they wanted. He couldn't stop them. Then, he imagined the little boy coming home with them. He could have one of the kids old bedrooms. They could wake him up in the morning with hugs like he had never done with his own children. He had been too tough, too mean, and it was much too late for those kinds of regrets. But this boy, this Felipe, he had no one. They could keep him and love him. Do it right this time even if he and Hope were old.

As they walked across the room the church lady walked briskly toward Hope and the little boy. She seemed to be making an announcement of sorts. She held out her hand to the boy and now the boy took her hand and she led him away. The boy looked over his shoulder and waved goodbye with his little muppet hand. Jule could tell what had happened just by observing the interaction. They must have found the boy's family. Maybe they were going to take him to be reunited with them now or soon. Hope walked back with mincing, tired steps before she sat back down in the chair next to his with a deep sigh. They did not look at one another.

A master sergeant with the National Guard walked into the entranceway with a commanding presence flanked by two young privates. He seemed to survey the room as though he considered them all some foreign race of troglodytes. Everyone sat up straighter under his harsh gaze. Something was about to happen. The shelter, he announced, wasn't prepared with enough food or water to support such a large group of misplaced people. No one was prepared for this kind of emergency. They were to be taken to another shelter. After that, they would even be taken to yet another shelter, only to find that none of them were able to handle the sheer numbers of people who needed help.

# HEAVEN

I was actually glad the storm came, in a weird way. I thought maybe the cops and everyone else would forget about me. If I left now no one would come after me since everyone was leaving if they had any damn sense. I was planning on going back to Okeechobee, Florida where my mama is from. I was raised down around Jennings but I moved up here with Jeff. Long story, short. Don't ask. I always thought about moving away from here permanently but something always pulled me back. Mama has a new husband and lives in a really nice doublewide in a half-ass retirement community called the Pink Palm Mobile Estates and she said I could stay with her if things didn't work out with Jeff. It even has a hot tub and a swimming pool, Mama said. I mean, a swimming pool just right out from your front yard! All I have to do is get off the crank.

I figured crazy cancer lady next door called the cops on me. I caught her spying on me through the window the day Jeff passed. He was my reason for living. I saw her talking to that big cop parked on the street, she saw me too. She knew what I done. I didn't care if she did see me either. The thought crossed my mind to go over and kick her ass! At least, I could scare shit out of her.

On day one, she thought she was better than me when I first moved in with Jeff. She made everyone call her Angelina when I knew there was no way everyone where she was from didn't call her plain old Angie or maybe Angel. Wouldn't that be funny, to have a Heaven and Angel right next door to each other. What are the odds on that? Some people put on airs so bad. She had the prettiest long

Daren Dean

dark hair then but then that snob got some kind of cancer and it all fell out. It serves the bitch right. You reap what you sow!

She invited me and Jeff over once we first moved in and she made barely enough food for the four of us. Yes, I said four because her daughter lived with her then. Her boy was already living with his daddy down in the French Quarter from what I understand. Neither of her kids live with her anymore. Now that should tell you something right there. The woman made us something weird, little stuffed green peppers with beef and cheese and a salad, and I was still starving after we left. We went to McDonald's over on Florida Avenue and I had a Big Mac, fries, with an apple pie and a Shamrock shake. I love McDonald's. I'd eat there everyday if I could but it's getting expensive to do that anymore. People say it ain't healthy. It might not be, but I still like it! In America we got freedom of choice! If I want McDonald's, Cane's, or Popeye's chicken every-damn-day–can't nobody stop me!

Daryl and Varnado didn't want me to leave. They come over to score some redneck cocaine but with everything going on, all bets were off. Bowtie man wasn't cooking. They were waiting on my green light and decided just to show up even though I never turned the porchlight on. They said it was on, but it wasn't. It was a case of wishful thinking.

Those boys were getting all googled-eyed when I told them I didn't have nothing for them. I didn't need them trying to get violent with me. Varnado thought it was okay to treat me like his bitch because we got high and did some sex stuff together. It wasn't no big deal to me. He was just my boy toy. Only good for one thing. He was young, dumb, and full of cum like they say. The first time I did it with him he was so soft and tender to me. I could barely feel his lips on mine and on my body. Later on, he turned mean. That's how it always goes. I just turned off my feelings long ago.

The three of us smoked shit together like always. This time I let him take me in the back room and gave him head, that way he would cum faster. I gave them some of my stash to get them by. I got the two of them out the door while they were still feeling the rush.

He slapped my face on his way out to show off for Daryl. I spun around and fell on the old green couch to make him think he was a real man, but I also wanted him to keep going. If he only knew what I done to Jeff, he wouldn't be so quick to treat me that way. He didn't know it, but he just made my list! The next time he showed up tweaking, his ass was mine!

When they was about to leave I noticed they were pulling a brand new red and orange speedboat that they must have stole right out of somebody's driveway with their shitty truck. The cops would be on their ass normally but with everything going on they might not notice if they got rid of it quick. The cops were busy now probably out saving their own. When a hurricane or a tropical storm was looming, this was the best time to steal anything especially since rich people usually left their homes in times like these. Perfect time to rip 'em off. Poor people had to stay and ride it out. They didn't have a second home in another state to go to. Staying at a nice Hampton Inn up in Mississippi in the meantime ain't an option for just everybody.

"Before you leave, I got something to say!" I leaned into the truck to kiss him but he didn't kiss me back so I bit his bottom lip hard enough it drew blood.

"Damn bitch! What is it?" Varnado laughed through slitted eyes. He rubbed his lip hard and looked at the blood in the palm of his hand. "Why should we listen to you?"

"Stupid whore," Daryl muttered and looked away. He couldn't meet my eyes. They was both just dumb little boys.

"Don't ever fuck with me again!" I smacked his face for him. His hand went to his cheek and started rubbing the sting out. "You forget I'm the one with the drug connection! Bowtie Man won't even talk to you but through me. Get it? You ain't got no idea how shit works!" He grabbed at me, but I jerked my head back out of the window.

That got their attention real good.

"We can get our own shit!" Varnado snarled.

"Who shit? Bull–shit!" I put my head back and laughed hard. "You ain't got the balls or you wouldn't have to *aks* me to get it for you. I tell Bowtie Man you ain't cool no more and he'll put your lily white asses in the ground. If I told him you was a narc, it be all over for you little motherfuckers!"

Their eyes got real big then. I could see the fear on their faces. They didn't know for sure what to think. I loved yanking their chains. Serve 'em right. "I been having to hit licks for drugs when you two were still jacking each other off in middle school. I been out running the roads since I was twelve years old. You think you can hit me and be a big man? You seen what I done to Lazy Jeff, didn't you? I done that! He didn't just die. I killed his ass. You could be next!"

Varnado shook his head. I could tell he was afraid again. I had him now. It was written all over his little boy face. He didn't have no poker face like me. I had them both right in the palm of my hand. They were my bitches whether they knew it or not. Daryl had probably pissed himself a little. I'd bend them both over the couch one way or another the next time they crossed me.

Varnado stuttered, "I jus—"

"Don't say nuthin' more!" I said to his face. "I tell Bowtie Man you two are narcs, you'll be another shit stain on I-55! So you better stand next to my fire if you know what's good! What I want you to do is bring me back some shit we can fence easy. I know that's what you was going to do anyway but you're doing for me. We'll all get what we want then!"

Varnado caught a smart look in his eye like he still had a brain cell. "What if we just don't never come back, Heaven? What then?"

"Oh? Ain't you been listening?" I ran my hand in his blond hair like he was a child. He jerked his head back and started eye-fucking me hard, "You gonna come back to Heaven when you start needing a fix? You know you will, right? I'm just saying, you work for me and I'll take care of you, baby boy."

The streets were like rivers. I knew Varnado and Daryl would be up to no good but they'd be doing for me this time. This time it was me sending them out into the world like my own little demons. I could tell they seen the light. And, if they didn't, I'd just have to drop a dime to the Po-Po, what with them driving around with all that stolen shit. They drove down Eden Church Road in water almost up to the floorboards of their jacked-up pickup. That crazy-ass storm was over us again and it started raining, not a heavy slant rain but just a teasing drizzle out of the gray sky to add insult to injury. The storm was still alive and letting us know she ain't dead yet. I called her "she" because she was acting all passive-aggressive raining, but not hardly storming-like.

I was putting stuff in the car even though the water in the driveway was so high it was starting to get over the tires. I was trudging in water going back and forth. When I opened the car door the water was already in the floorboard. I sat down anyway, stuck the key in the ignition and prayed under my breath: "C'mon, Gawdddamnit." Wrong prayer, wrong god. The engine wouldn't even turn over. I beat the steering wheel with the heel of my hand. I should have parked out in the street in front of Cancer Lady's house since there was a strip of pavement on the street there. I guess it was higher there, but you couldn't tell it by the naked eye. It was flat just like everywhere else around here. There was already four cars parked end to end. I cried but more pissed than sad. I didn't even unpack the car. Screw it.

I jumped around in the water for a minute. There was a lot of shit floating in the water. I started imagining snakes and alligators swimming around. I freaked myself out. I ran up and sat on the bench back seat from someone's SUV on the screened-in porch. I was stuck here in the Grove. I'd probably die here now. About that time, I saw a man driving by. His truck was loaded up with his stuff. He had a yellow lab pup, probably less than a year old, six months maybe, kind of jump-fall out of the truck. It yelped pathetically when it hit the ground on its chin and limped like it broke its foot.

"Hey!" I yelled at the man. "Your dog just fell out the back, boo!"

The driver slammed on his brakes. He looked in his rearview mirror and then his side mirror. He had something on his face. Maybe it was a tattoo. I knew he could see the dog. There was no way he didn't see it. He had a guilty look as he came around the truck rubbing the top of his bald head like he was shining it up. He had a pink birthmark like a jelly stain on the top and running down one side. I knew that look well. Every methhead and tweaker I had ever known had that look on their face until they didn't give a shit anymore, and that didn't take long.

"You ought to take your dog with you!" I said. I don't know why but I felt really pissed off about how he was treating his dog. I always loved animals maybe even more than people, yeah.

"I don't really have room for him!" the man hollered back. I wonder why he gave a shit what I thought. He could have just kept driving. "You want to keep him for me. I'll come back and get him when I can."

"Hell no!" I yelled at him. "I don't want no fucking dog! Man, what are you? Some of kind of sorry asshole!"

He didn't answer but he got out of his truck and pitched a box of shit out in the watery street so the dog could sit up front with him. The man petted the dog and felt at his paw the dog held up in a pathetic way. When he squatted down I could see the crack of his ass. He opened the truck door, scooped up the dog, and stuck it on the seat like just another box. He went back around to the driver side, flipped me the bird straight up over his head without looking. When he got behind the wheel he bellowed, "Happy Now?" I wanted to say I really don't give a shit, but I guess I did or I wouldn't have given him such a hard time. He didn't deserve that pretty yellow dog. He drove down the street and into the deep water in the same direction as my bitches, Thing One and Thing Two.

## PRESLEY

The wind was whipping the branches of the trees. It made me more worried than ever to see all the yards up and down the street looking like a river was running through. The Spanish moss hanging from the ancient live oak in front of our house was whipping like a trashy woman's greasy hair frizzed up due to the stormy humidity choking everyone out.

Bijou, a little third grade girl, was running barefoot back and forth from her house out to her grandpa's little burgundy-colored Mercury parked in front of our house every ten minutes. Her grandparents had parked their vehicles in front of our house on the street because it was the only area that didn't seem to be flooding at the moment. It was weird because you couldn't tell from looking that one part of the street was any higher or lower than the other. When we took trips and drove up north on I-55, I was always happy to see the rolling hills of Mississippi. It was flat as an ironing board around here. Daddy liked to say that the only hills around here to speak of were the Indian Mounds on the LSU campus.

Bijou lived with her grandma and grandpa at the end of the street. A lot of kids I knew were being raised by their grandparents. Half the time they acted like they could care less what she did. She ran up and down the streets in our neighborhood barefoot most of the time. One summer day she disappeared. Her granny came looking for her all frantic and raccoon-eyed. I passed the word up and down the street and everyone was on the lookout some two streets over.

Daren Dean

Bijou and me had cheapo flip phones so I texted her, *Where u @?*

*Ice creem man.*

That was all she texted back. I felt a tingling jolt run down my spine. A literal tingle. The reason? Our ice cream man drove an ice cream truck that was only decorated or identified or whatever on one side. That alone was pretty sus. The music he played sounded like ice cream music but like hip hop turned into that tinkly come-get-your-ice-cream-treats music. He always cruised through the neighborhood a little too fast so sometimes he was gone by the time you could find someone to give you some money. Then you'd have to take a shortcut through the neighbor's backyards and try to cut him off on the next street over. His voice would come over the loudspeaker like an O. G. '80s rapper and he'd say, *Oh yeah, boyyy! Get ya ice cream, yo!* He looked Rastafarian with his long braids and he always had on the same Jamaican lion t-shirt, green-red-yellow with a crown on its head.

When I told Bijou's grandmère her hand flew to her mouth and she squeaked, *Oh my poor baby!* Then she started hollering up and down the street like a human bullhorn, *She's with the ice cream man! Find the ice cream man! The ice cream man got my baby!* Everyone freaked out then because in their minds they thought she said he's going to rape my baby because some weird kind of group think took over in the heat of the moment.

See, I really didn't want to tell her about the text because here in Satsuma Grove "we have REALLY GOOD schools" (wink, wink) and "it's a great place to raise children" (big smile, eyebrow raise) and if you're still not getting the picture in high def or CGI then you should know this town is hella racist. Let me put it this way, even if you tell any black person who lives in Baton Rouge you're from Satsuma Grove or Denham Springs they look at you like *OH SHIT!* I was too young to know why but I heard Mr. Dixon and Mr. Jule talking about how the former Imperial Wizard of the KKK used to live right here in town back in the day and was buddies with David Duke! This is what they call common knowledge, yo.

The ice cream man hella wisely let her out over by the elementary school. Needless to say, we didn't see him for the rest of the entire summer. The whole thing sounded like an episode of

Dateline. Jamie Lynn's favorite show. I told her a good title for the episode would be "You Scream! We Scream! We All Scream for the Ice Cream Man!"

The blonde lady shook her finger in my face, but then she got tickled and burst out laughing, "You ain't right!"

Jamie Lynn said Bijou's grandparents were just old and tired. Bijou's mama was strung out on opioids and was an unfit mother who lived in Lafayette with her boyfriend. Mr. Jule call them *dope-o-roids*. I tried to correct him by shouting "OPI-OIDS" real loud after he said it because I knew he was nearly deaf. Mr. Jule said he was *deef*. His wife liked to say he was *death*. "You mean, DEAF?" She didn't say a lot of her words right or sometimes she was just too lazy to say them proper. I found out later that Mr. Jule knew all about opiods and called them dope-o-roids for his own funny.

Bijou's mama seemed crazy when she would show up out of the blue with her eyes bulging. She'd disappear for weeks or months at a time. Then she'd show up trying to act proper and tell you, "I am Bijou's actual mother." Like everyone didn't know who really took care of the poor girl. I felt sorry for Bijou. She ran around the neighborhood like a little barefoot heathen. She reminded me of how I was at that age. It was clear to me she was going to grow up to be a bad girl if someone didn't start caring and keeping an eye on her. Something bad was going to happen to her. The human traffic people was going to get her, yeah.

Jamie Lynn swore Bijou was going to end up *pregnated*. She bobbed her head listening to an old Dr. John song on the radio. "As soon as she hits Junior high they better put that girl on birth control." But that was Mama. All Mama ever thought about was men's attention. When she looked at a man it seemed like she was thinking about doing the deed with him. The men could tell it too. Her eyes lit up at every half-decent looking man she ever saw. She was one of them kind of women. Men loved her, married women hated her. She couldn't help herself. Sex was all she thought about.

"What's that girl doing? Is she cray-cray?" Jamie Lynn asked, lighting up a ciggy.

"I'm not sure," I said. I wiped the tears in my eyes away with the back of my hand.

"You okay, Presley?"

"It's just my allergies bothering me," I said.

"You sure?" Mama looked at me closely. Normally she ignored me so having her stare like this annoyed me. I wanted to tell her to take a picture, it would last longer but I kept my pie hole closed for once.

"I think their little cat is in the car." Kids don't always know how to explain everything they think and feel to their parents. It's not always so easy just to answer just a random question when there's an emotion close to the surface.

Jamie Lynn put her hand on my shoulder and it was all I could do not to shake it off, "Maybe you should ask her what's she doing?" She is wearing a long t-shirt that extends down past her waist. It's hot but she's wearing LSU purple and gold short shorts. She's always complaining about being cold, even in the summer. Mr. Dixon said maybe she needs to take some Geritol for iron.

"What are you doing, Bijou?" Jamie Lynn hollered through the screen door.

"MA'AM?" Anytime an adult said something to Bijou she always said it real loud like she couldn't believe she was being asked a question and like maybe they was little bit deaf. But, after I thought it about it one time, I think she heard her every time it was just her way of buying a little extra time while she thought up an answer.

About that time I heard the whirring of a big helicopter and ran out on the front porch to see the National Guard flying low over-head, surveying the devastation like they always said on bad storm reports. They were probably trying to save people off their roofs. I'd heard of many people who had to be cut out of their roofs with chainsaws during floods. I hoped that didn't happen to us.

I'd been up in our attic once but you had to go out on the front porch to get to the attic. You needed a ladder to get up there. A funny place to put the attic access according to Jamie Lynn since anyone could get up there from the outside if they wanted to bad enough. It was completely empty up there. Just some left over pink paint from when a past tenant had gotten a wild bug to paint the exterior of the house pink, without asking the Arceneauxs first. Mr. Jule told me that old story. It was when Old Man Arceneaux himself was still alive. I didn't know the old man and I imagined he looked like Nick Saban, the now Alabama football coach, or Nick Satan as he was better known around here for leaving LSU. Whenever I think of evil men I can't help but picture Saban or ole' Bobby Jindal. Mr. Jule said he about had a heart attack when a man who once rented our same house decided to paint it pink without telling the old man. It tickled him plumb to death to tell the story. I think he had told it to me three times already!

Daren Dean

## CODY

In the side mirror he could see the mudmilk water behind his silver F-250 rushing to push him down the flooded road near the Amite River. It was coming at him relentlessly in sync with Tab Benoit's blaring *Shelter Me* over the speakers. He had gone tubing down the river earlier in the summer with some old friends from Live Oak High and plenty of cold *Purple Haze* but now the water was over its banks. He was pulling a load of Watusi cows in the trailer behind him, hoping to move them from his pasture north of Watson to his PawPaw's pasture down in Satsuma Grove as a precaution but now it looked like he started too late. He pounded the steering wheel a couple of times with his fist at the futility of it all.

Suddenly he realized with a sick feeling in his stomach that not all of his tires were on the highway. It was like he was in a terrible waking nightmare as the waters rushed across the road, causing the cemetery across the street from the Baptist church to disappear under murkish brown water except where a small island of stone crosses and family mausoleums stood high and dry. As he floated and listened to the terrible grating noise the truck made as it rubbed against something just beneath the surface, Cody had a premonition that this was going to be bad. The flooding looked worse than it had been in the area during Katrina.

To make matters worse his truck was now more of a boat than a land vehicle. It looked like he could get pushed up into someone's yard just up ahead or if the water got a hold of him it might divert the pickup into the river itself. The engine quit but the air still blew from the vents while Tab Benoit was going at it on his guitar as if even a flood couldn't stop the blues, until it did. Sweat was beading up on his forehead as the heat and humidity filled the interior of the cab. His stomach cramped with anxiety like going on a crazy, herky-jerky Six Flags ride. He had gone with friends to the Six Flags in New Orleans before Katrina hit and closed the park down permanently.

The trailer was jackknifing and he could see the Watusi swing next to him with their enormous horns and looking at him now as if to say, *What did you do?* He might have laughed but he was as much annoyed as scared to death and now his rig was banging and clattering into God- knew-what under the surface of the polluted waters. He white-knuckled the steering wheel to keep his hands from shaking. He tried to think what his daddy would have done if he were still alive today and the thought made him attempt to will the fear away. He could tell he wasn't exactly heading the right way down the road anymore, but not too far off of it either.

The trailer became disengaged and the cows were sucked into the strong rapids of the little river and the last he saw of them the trailer capsizing and dunking the cows hard under the water's surface like some comic carnival ride for bovines. He half expected them to come back up again like a special oil rig that pumped cattle instead of oil, but if they did it must have been beyond the new oxbow the flooding had created, and further downstream. It hurt him to see their demise since he had raised them from calves, his PawPaw would have said something sardonic with a straight face like, *Money down the drain.*

"A damn shame," he said out loud, "damn shame."

After days of the strange no-name weather system circling and crying all over them, it was beginning to rain again as his truck bounced like a pinball machine off other cars, an old shed, and a grove of citrus trees. He adjusted the cowboy hat he wore by pushing it up to see a little better as his truck began to do a 180 and now he was looking back up the direction he had come from. He quickly rolled down his windows before they lost power for fear he'd become trapped in his new-to-him pickup and then drown or maybe not even drown but have to kick out the windshield to escape the cab.

Now wouldn't that be a hell-of-a-thing!

Daren Dean

The truck was sent hurtling into the bruised arms of a horizontal live oak, but the truck inched its way down the limb for five minutes or so until he was once again spinning uncontrollably and smashed into plastic mail boxes where driveways met the roadway. He noticed the first mailbox he took out had its little red flag up and he wondered if it contained important letters to loved ones, bills, or just plain old junk mail and return to senders. He imagined important correspondence, perhaps even heartfelt, that would now never be delivered.

*Communicating with people is hard enough without all of this.*

The mail delivery in the parish was already questionable as it was. It was strange to have thoughts like these given the circumstances, but he couldn't control his brain. He couldn't help thinking about his four-year-old daughter Emma. He hoped she was safe with her mama in Baton Rouge. He didn't see her much since the divorce even though he was supposed to have custody on the weekends, but it didn't often end up that way. The words didn't always come out right in the heat of the moment with his ex and the little one had to suffer for it. It suddenly hit him he might never see Emma ever again. Jen would probably like that just fine, he thought ruefully, but at the same time he didn't think she would want him to die like this. Besides that, there was the question of alimony to consider.

The truck became espaliered against a rather large outcropping of wrecked and twisted trees and brush along with the odd assortment of objects the river had picked up along the way, giving the impression of a giant's bulletin board. To make matters worse, now the truck's cab was pointed up out of the drink. The angle created a new outcrop for water to rush around like a boulder in the midst of a mountain stream. The water began to pour into the truck through the windows and his jeans and workbooks became quickly soaked. Without another thought, he took off his seatbelt and reached up to pull himself into a sitting position in the truck's window. He sat there and surveyed his position. It appeared to him that he was still in the road. Not far from where he was stranded, a line of cars were parked facing him. There were plenty of people out of the cars talking and milling around. He was so close to safety he ground his molars with anxiety. Children pointed him out to the adults and a man with a hand to the side of his mouth was hollering something at him but the water was too loud to make it out.

"Call 911!" He yelled back at the heavyset man.

The man gave him a thumb's up and walked away pressing buttons on his cell phone.

Cody didn't have time to mourn his cattle though they were a big loss to him. Instead he was beginning to wonder if he was going to make it himself. The water here was much deeper than he had first thought. The debris coming down the river might push the truck under like it had the trailer full of cattle, dislodge him into the current favorably or not, or possibly even impale or crush him. He made his way gingerly out of the cab and onto the truck's roof where he had to hold on to the sides of the truck with his hands like he had been crucified since he couldn't seem to grip anything with his boots as they just slid impotently off the truck.

The front end of the truck was beginning to sit up in the water as the bed began to fill. This caused the water to spray up a bit. He didn't think he would go under since the debris of old trees and other flotsam and jetsam appeared to lodge the truck in place. But he didn't know how long he could hold on like this either before he might have to let go out of sheer exhaustion. The people in the middle of the road, not more than thirty yards away, were gathered near the water's edge and pointing and talking about how to help him. He was grateful for this but at the same time no one looking on seemed to know what to do.

Daren Dean

## PRESLEY

When Jack drove up in his carpet cleaning van he bounded out of
the driver side and scooped Presley up almost like she was his own
daughter. Her daddy had died when she was a baby and she pressed
her eyelids together tightly in an attempt to remember something
about him, but nothing ever came. So when big Jack picked her up
and twirled her around she closed her eyes and pretended the stubble
on his face was her daddy's, his aftershave was her daddy's, and his
embrace was also her daddy's. He carried her into the little house
she'd heard her mother call a cottage, strangler vines creeping up the
trellis, and he ducked so as not to bump his head on the door frame.
Oops, he said and they both laughed together. She even kissed him
on the cheek and that made him roar with laughter like the big bear
he was. He was a grown man who actually loved kids, and kids knew
it.

  "Here's my Jamie Lynn! My kitten!"

  "My big man!" She said and tipped her head back and
laughed like she was the happiest woman in the world. She looked
like a child next to Jack.

  When her mama, a plump bleach-blonde in her early thirties
with a pixie face beginning to blur, saw him she squealed and literally
jumped into the big man's arms. Presley clapped as he carried her
mama into the bedroom like they were just married, but when they
shut the door all the excitement was gone. She stared blankly at the
door for a full minute while she listened to their excited whispers and
groans. Presley wasn't sure if she were mad or just bored. She wished

someone was crazy about her like that! She knew if her daddy was still alive he'd be crazy about her.

She turned on the television to watch Arthur on PBS and turned up the volume several bars with the remote so she wouldn't have to listen to the bed's headboard banging against the wall like something was being built by a carpenter who was maybe in a big hurry to get his work done. She was too old for cartoons, she watched them just the same. This was Jack's date with her mama, but tomorrow she might have a date with Terry, Tim, or Rick.

She turned off the television and through the remote at the television screen, but it just bounced off into the carpet. She looked at herself in the dark screen of the television. It was old. It had an almost greenish-black swirling quality that made her think she might be able to see the future like the man, the wizard, looking into the crystal ball to tell Dorothy her future in The Wizard of Oz.[italics] She saw her own reflection like in a funhouse mirror that stretched her body so it appeared longer. She touched her long, brunette hair just to make sure her reflection would follow suit. Strangers told her she was a pretty girl all the time except her teacher and the kids in school. She heard people behind her back say she was too saucy. She liked to think of herself as a little-little girl still. She was small for her age so people thought she was as young as she acted.

Presley picked up what was left of a bottle of Mike's Hard Lemonade and drained the contents. She went outside and picked up a fistful of loose gravel in the driveway and waited for a car to drive by and tossed it like hail at the random driver door of a passing Landrover.

"Hey now!" The driver, a fat woman with a bunch of kids, called out to her in surprise but she kept driving.

No one expected a pretty girl to do something bad like that. She so pretty. Such a pretty, pretty! The woman's face when she cried out made Presley laugh quietly to herself. She looked around to see if anyone saw her, but the only person outside of their house on the entire street was Cancer Lady, three houses down but she wasn't too worried about her because everyone knew she was crazy. Crazy Cancer Lady. She even saw her smoking an occasional cigarette on her front porch. She looked like a zombie meth head with her hollow eyes. Presley waved to her, but the woman just looked straight through her. Ghosted by the walking dead, Presley thought.

Presley's younger friend, Olivia, was roller skating down the street and waving to beat the band. They were close, like two peas in a hull. She was carrying her My Little Pony collection in a hot pink carrying case to come and play. Presley might be able to talk her into letting her have one of her Pinky Pies or Shutterflys, if she gave her something exotic in turn. They were both way too old for this baby stuff according to her mama but neither of them could stop loving the toys. Presley was a whole two years older than Olivia but that didn't matter. Neither of them were yet full grown and they were firmly in the grips of a neon pink nostalgia. She might give her one of the fancy European cigarettes her mother had taken to smoking after she dated a guy named Igor from Belgium who she met at Live After Five in downtown Baton Rouge.

Olivia was her best friend because her parents were rich and that made Olivia rich and that made Presley rich too because they were friends. She overheard Olivia's parents talking about her in their expensive kitchen in their grand house on River Road where all the fancy people lived if they were anybody. Olivia had the largest collection of Manga she had ever seen on bookshelves in her huge room. The room itself took up most of the second floor. She basically had the run of the second floor. Olivia's parents felt sorry for her because her mother was a slut. *Such a pretty girl too,* Olivia's mother tsk tsked right in front of her once and then went back to combing her lava red hair in front of an ornate mirror that presided over the woman's hardwon beauty.

She waved to Olivia like a maniac. Presley met her out on the street in front of her house and Naruto-ran down the sidewalk before grabbing her friend by the shoulders to help her stop. She would do anything for Olivia to like her and think they were best friends. They air-kissed on both cheeks like French people like they'd seen the girls do on one of their favorite Disney Channel shows called *Cherry's Chocolate Surprise,* which featured quirky looking girls overacting to a studio audience laugh track. The girls dressed so cool and they could sing like grown divas. Presley knew the show was dumb but Olivia liked it, so Presley liked it.

She hoped Olivia brought her brush and other girlie stuff because she did like brushing her ash blonde hair with the brush. The color of her hair just hypnotized Presley. It was exotic to her and Olivia liked her hair too. It was like they they were sisters with different color hair. Presley sometimes called Olivia, Miss Clairol. Even their moms both said it was like they looked into mirror when the girls looked at each other. Uncanny, Olivia's daddy said. Olivia jumped on her father's lap. He kissed her cheek and Presley felt like Olivia had stolen something from her so she jumped on his other knee but he looked slightly uncomfortable and did not put his arms around her or kiss her cheek as he had Olivia. Instead, he very deliberately patted her shoulder like you would a dog that might bite. She felt her heart break a little on the inside.

"I brought the Ponies with me!" Olivia said, she was drinking a Red Bull but Presley liked Monster drinks better. Red Bull tasted like melted down SweeTARTS to her. "Put your roller skates on and we can skate around the neighborhood! When we come back, I'll show you my new Pony! You will love her."

Presley squealed with delight, "Okay!" She tried to make herself sound just as happy and stupid as the girls on *Cherry's Chocolate Surprise*. She opened the door and grabbed her white skates with the bright pink shoelaces and put them on the porch. "Oh, let me show you something!"

"What is it?" Olivia said in her high-octane voice.

"It's this!" Presley went over and grabbed an empty Mike's bottle out of the trash, walked across the gravel in her skates on her toe stops, and spun in a circle in the middle of the street. Then, she raised the bottle dramatically high over her head and smashed it on the ground.

"Oh Presley! You're so wicked! I think I love you!"

Olivia was always scandalized by everything she did because her parents were so strict and Presley's mom could have cared less what she did. This was part of the charm for Olivia to get a taste of playing without supervision. Olivia went out into the street and the girls locked hands and began to spin like a whirling dervish in the center of the street. Even when a red pickup drove by and honked at them, Presley wouldn't allow Olivia to go. When they finally collapsed on the front lawn they were sweating and laughing as the man in the truck cursed at them and then drove over the broken glass.

A few minutes later they thought about going to Albertsons'

grocery store and buying some candy and energy drinks with Olivia's money but then Presley remembered the storm. They roller-skated down to the end of the street where the elementary school sat with several feet of water sitting in its slightly sunken parking lot.

"I forgot to tell you," Presley said. "I just wanted to pretend it wasn't happening."

The girls were both a little afraid and held hands as they looked out over the encroaching waters. They had never seen anything quite like this before in their neighborhood though they were both used to seeing flooding around town. The water seemed to be climbing before their eyes as they watched Dixon offloading the Blue Betty II into the water creeping down the street. The water shimmered in the sun like normal water on a lake and looked like it was laughing. The temperature had climbed to the mid-90s, while the humidity in the air smothered the girls in its sultry embrace.

DIXON

Some days the air outside smelled sweet as a lilac dryer sheet, other days there was a chemical stench of benzene emissions, and sulphur dioxide from the ExxonMobil oil refinery in north Baton Rouge. The refinery itself looked like something out of *Mad Max* with its towering stacks and a yellow torch of flame erupting like an evil spirit, belching a fiery tongue-lashing ectoplasm, doing an aerobic dance at its zenith.

You could drive west from Satsuma Grove to Baton Rouge on the I-12 and smell it all day long. Nobody talked about the horrible stench or even bothered to mention it. If you complained about the odor, the most you would get is a disinterested shrug of acceptance or a kind of *it is what it is*, a shake of the head from the BRPROUD. It's the price you paid for being front-and-center of the Petro-Chemical industry, and don't forget about the millions they donated to keep on the good side of LSU and to placate the black community at large as a necessary penance. They take advantage in Baton Rouge and up and down cancer alley as far south as New Orleans. Luckily, the smell of the neighbor's confederate jasmine was strong today as I backed the trailer with the Blue Betty II into the muddy waters.

Some of my buddies, other truckers I've known, used to call me the King of Ohio! Then, it was King, which then got downgraded to "Ohio" when I started driving cross country. My CB handle was "Midnight Rider" when I was young just like the song. I'd answer to Ohio if someone on the radio noticed my rig and the company I was driving for. I was a different guy then. I was in my prime. That was when I was still in my 30s and 40s. I've driven all over the country, but I never felt at home anywhere for long except with Lynette. Her elder sister lived in Satsuma Grove back then and that explains why we decided to hang our hats down this way. Even long after Elenore passed and was buried in an ancient New Orleans mausoleum, an above-ground crypt, that belonged to her husband's people, we decided to stay in Satsuma Grove. We went on a tour of the "Cities of the Dead" in New Orleans, one particularly sweltering summer, of St. Louis Cemetery No. 1. The tour guide told us about how every so often they shoved a ten-foot-long stick down inside the vault and pushed the old bones out the back to make room for the family's recent dead as needed. It seemed barbaric to me, but I suppose it was practical given the fear of yellow fever back then.

Everywhere I've been, I can't help asking myself, *What am I doing here? I don't belong.* At my age, I don't expect to do anything big or important. I'm in a holding pattern just waiting. One day I'll look up and this giant red Chuck Connors shoe will fall flaming right out of the sky. That's the sign I dreamed about, so that's the sign I'm looking for. I only ever believed in luck or destiny but I'm also smart enough to know you can't rely on either one. Everyone around here calls me Mr. Dixon. I guess I done went and got old. It's funny how that comes up on you all of a sudden. People down here don't tend to call me Mr. Richard but using a last name like that is something Yankees do. It took some getting use to at first. I learned to go with it.

The water was rising fast. Lynette noticed it first. She was doing dishes and saw it from the kitchen window. *Oh Dixon! It's flooding down the street! Come lookee here! The Cajun Navy is driving a boat in the school parking lot!* A friend of mine from the grounds crew at LSU's Death Valley warned me by text I'd better get out quick but Lynette and me argued back and forth. *Hell, it's not like it was a hurricane.* I reminded her that Achilles fought the river god; she reminded me that I was no Achilles. *The Iliad* has always been my favorite. Now, don't take nothing from me just because I'm a Trucker. I like to tell everyone I'm a Roads Scholar of the Dwight D. Eisenhower's Interstate System. While everyone else is liking and LOLing in their free time, I'm up in my bunk reading so as not to end up like the rest of the unwashed masses dying slowly every day, white-knuckling their cell phones.

They should just as well attach a teat to the end of those things.

I hoped the no-name storm would blow over, but it did not. It dumped rain north of central Louisiana for days and refused to move on. On the news they were talking 12 inches, then 20 inches, and close to 30inches in some places. Now, we were stuck and had to make the most of it. I told her to be ready to go upstairs and to stay up there just in case it looked like the water was going to seep into the house. Going upstairs always depends on her *Arthur*. I got the chainsaw, an umbrella (it can get hot on a roof with or without shade), and a sledgehammer out of the garage. I put it all up there too just in case we had to cut ourselves out of the attic and sit up on the roof until we are saved by a chopper. It don't look like fun. I hope it don't come to that.

My neighbors, Jule and Esperanza, bugged out when a man came and packed them up and talked them into going to a shelter. On the door of the truck it said, *Davey Baby's Electric*. The old man was none too happy about it. He was about as tough as an old cob. He wanted to ride it out at home as usual with a bottle of Old Crow for company in his shed out back of his house where he could listen to his records and play along with his Martin guitar. Their grown daughter's little blue pickup was still parked in the driveway with water climbing the wheel wells. There was no mistaking it since it had a bumper sticker that read, BIG BOOTY JUDY. And there was no denying that the woman did have a sizable derrière, but hell that was popular again! How did it ever go out of style? I like women with a little meat on their bones.

It had never flooded on Eden Church Road before but the Amite wasn't too far away and that dirty whore was raging. She had filled and spread out from River Road. There was a little float business where you could pay $25 to rent an inner tube, drink beer, float with your friends, and I wouldn't have been surprised to see entire families floating by on a rubber raft now. People needed help. I was going out to find them even though Lynette wasn't crazy about the idea. I told her my conscience wouldn't allow me to do any different.

When I saw Angelina's boy, Noah, out in his yard, I cupped my hands and shouted him over. He heard me and his head popped up like a turtle poking his head out of its shell. What I was most shocked by was just how tall he'd become. My God he was tall! I remembered the boy from when his family had first moved in and he had been a real cute little guy then. He was almost as tall as me now but he was as skinny as a yearling calf. His reaction made me laugh to myself but I didn't want him to think I was laughing at him. I waved my hand high over my head back and forth so he'd come over.

Water was beginning to fill his front yard. The street was a little higher up and people on our street, the ones who hadn't packed up and hit the road, had started parking on the street between the boy's house and Jule's since it appeared to be the high ground but there was precious little of that around here. It was so flat in this area you really couldn't tell by looking where the high ground was, but the water would tell you. As I looked further down the street you could see the one newer build in the neighborhood, two houses down on the left, already had water a foot or so up one side of the house that young couple lived in. I never learned their names, but he was a great big ole boy who drove a Ram pickup and she was a cute little redhead. I could tell from the blue scrubs she wore what she did for a living. They had already left because they weren't from Satsuma Grove to begin with. It was no skin off their nose to leave for higher ground. Nobody could blame them. But then right across the street, ole' Frank and Colleen, who had the perpetual garage sale under their carport, didn't even appear to have water in their yard. I need-ed to remember to go check on them later since neither of them got around too well.

"Hey, Mr. Dixon!" Noah sloshed over from his yard down the narrow dry part of the street. He was a good boy. It was sad him being pulled like taffy between his parents. His mama got the cancer and his daddy was living like he was a kid again, shacked up with that pretty little singer according to Lynette. Too bad he got stuck in this flood with us. It was only going to get worse before it gets better.

"How did you like living in NOLA, son?"

"It was a blast! I've been playing—y'know, making music with Tripp on the streets from Canal over to Esplanade and Decatur on Jackson Square. We can make a lot of money every day just from the tourists without even an actual gig."

"What do you play?" I asked him. I really didn't like hearing him call his daddy by his first name. To my way of thinking, it just ain't right. It's disrespectful too but his daddy probably encouraged it.

He ought not allow him to do it either, but I learned a long time ago live and let live. His daddy was a fair-to-middlin' musician at best. His true calling was as a welder, but hell if we don't all got dreams.

"We play classics. Rock. Nola-flavor music. Ayanna, Tripp's girlfriend, writes songs so she plays originals. When I go back, I might get to play on their CD. Tripp calls us *Tripp and The Light Fantastiks*, that means I get to be one of the *Fantastiks*."

"Long name," I said. "Ayanna, that's his black gal? Yeah?"

The boy looked at me uncertainly, "Yes sir . . . "

"Anyway," I said. "She's real pretty. Your daddy's a lucky man."

The boy just looked at me without expression.

"Uh, what instrument you play?"

Suddenly, he broke out in a grin, "I play bucket drums, but I'm better on the 'bone!" The boy laughed and then he blushed real hard for some reason, maybe he thought it sounded like bragging. "I have a Yamaha keyboard. I can play a bunch of songs by ear." He whipped a mouth harp from his back pocket and started playing a few riffs. He said it was a song by a dude that went by the moniker, Trombone Shorty.

"Very nice! You're tearing it up, son!"

He laughed bashfully and hung his head to the side. He must have known how good he was. The boy hadn't learned how to take a compliment.

I clapped him on the shoulder, "Listen, the Cajun Navy is about to set sail if you're up for it? I might could use your help. You could be the Entertainment Director."

"Shoot! Really?" Noah stuck the harmonica in his side zipper pocket. "Let me tell Ang…um, my mom. If she's awake. If she's asleep, I'll leave a note for her." He turned to run off back to his house. I noticed he had on some beat-to-hell clothes, an old Tulane University t-shirt, and green cargo shorts. He was wearing a brand-new pair of black Converse. Those were popular when I was a kid. Guess some things never go out of style.

"Hold up! Think you could move my pickup back in front of the house for me?" I tossed my keys, where they hit him square in the chest, though he managed to get hold of them before they dropped on the ground.

Daren Dean

"Sure thing, Mr. Dixon!"

"Hey! Now take it easy with her!" I said. "Don't wreck it."

"Yes sir! I mean, no sir!" He turned and jogged over to the truck. I waded out to the boat in my thigh highs.

He drove the pickup to my driveway about five miles an hour. It was funny but he got the job done. While he was doing that, my Fox Terrier mix, Slash, came over and jumped right into the boat, shook himself off, and sat on the front bench seat like he was coming and there wasn't going to be no discussion about it.

"Welcome aboard the Blue Betty II," I said. The dog turned and looked at me with a noble expression on his face. His little van dyke tuft blowing in the breeze. "Too bad this boat ain't blue, it's green. It would make more sense, huh?" Blue has always been my favorite color. I bought this boat on the cheap for fishing but really because flooding is so common it's a good and practical thing to have. I eventually ordered Slash back to the house. He ignored me at first until I raised my voice, so he knew I was serious then. He sneezed and grumbled into his beard. Eventually he jumped back in the water and swam back to the dry part of the street. "Go on now! Go!" I pointed at the house. Slash sneezed back at me one last time and went back to the porch. He liked taking boat rides but it made him dauncy if he rode too far. That's why I didn't want him along. Besides that, we might need the space.

Out across the field between South Side Elementary and where the neighborhood began was a field just past the second-growth cypress where it was quickly filling with water as the land drowned down in a little soup bowl. A contractor had been trying to build an upscale housing development in a little cul-de-sac. He had put down the street, concrete foundation pads for several houses, including the plumbing and electrical infrastructure. This flood probably made the man sick to his stomach at the loss of the investment. The development was only about 40 yards from our street in what was, until recently, an empty field. It was the only unobstructed view from Eden Church Road where you could see how we were trapped by water. If you could escape, where could you go and where would you make it to? Even the local radio stations were confused. We couldn't even make or receive calls on cell phones. I was going to find a new cell provider first chance I got.

About that time a Black Hawk helicopter flew by overhead. The noise of the engine and the whirring blades stirred the branches of the live oaks on our street. I could see one of the crew leaning out of it like he was looking for something. He gave me a wave and I waved back, and then it banked up hard and away. That was when something heavy slammed into the boat. I guess they were trying to signal me instead of waving. It turned out to be a black and red sign with the word LAGNIAPPE on it in giant white letters. The word itself, so full of promise, but so rarely realized at the restaurants that advertised it throughout Louisiana.

"Lagniappe!" Noah said, just beyond the water's edge. "That's a good sign." A nimbus of angel light from a break in the clouds emanated briefly from him like a signal from a minor saint.

I agreed, "Signs and wonders." I laughed and coughed at the same time.

I didn't know at the time, but he brought his mama's Ruger with him in his school backpack amidst the Monster energy drinks and protein bars. I moved the boat with a long pole where it could still touch the bottom so he wouldn't get wet walking out to me. The air was too stagnant and humid for getting your clothes wet, if you could avoid it.

"Man, that's crazy!" He was looking at the sign and shaking his head in wonder.

I ain't going to lie, it would have been nice to have another man in the boat since I had been going out in the boat for years when flooding happened in the area. You never knew what you might run into when you went out after a hurricane or tropical storm. Sometimes the situation required a little extra muscle.

I started up the boat and we were rumbling up and down the streets going straight through the stop lights at the intersections that were still cycling red, yellow, and green despite the fact that Entergy had already shut the power off to Eden Church Road. I wasn't sure how that worked. Maybe the power wasn't off everywhere in the area or it was a different company or power grid. The next street over didn't look too bad since the water wasn't as deep there. Whole families were out on porches and waving to us trying to catch a breeze in the ninety-plus degree temps.

"Hey there!" An elderly man sitting in a white metal lawn

chair on his porch. "How high's the water on I-12?"

"That's something we're going to check," I said, "if we get around to it. It sits up higher anyway."

He nodded and spat an amber liquid into the water. "Could y'all check on my son and his family over on Oak Street? He's at 105 Oak." His eyes were red and rheumy like he had been crying, or drinking.

"Yessir," I said. "I'll let you know on my way back. Help me remember that address, Noah."

Noah nodded.

"Thank you," the old man waved. "Ya'll be safe." He tried to smile, but he was struggling. His face looked jaundiced. A gnarled hickory cane leaned against his knee.

After we had buzzed down the street a stretch, Noah said, "Was that man blind?"

"I believe he probably was," I said. "Maybe he could see a little still. Why?"

Noah shrugged and looked up the street as we cut a swath through the water in the street. You could tell he thought real deeply about things if they affected him a certain way. That made me like him a whole lot. I could still see the cute little boy he used to be riding his big wheel up and down the driveway.

Oak street, just a couple of streets over, had water almost to the top of the door frames. These houses were even older than the ones on our street. Nobody was out. The people on this street had had to abandon their houses. No one was out up on their roofs either. I guess someone could have drowned. I had the sense they just got out when the time came. The water had come up so fast. It was like someone was filling a swimming pool with water, but in the streets instead of a pool. I couldn't see the house numbers either.

"Dixon! Dixon! You got your Walkie Talkie on?" It was Lynette calling to me. "Pick up, hon'!"

The static shushed us each time we clicked our buttons, "We're just over here on Oak Street, baby. The water is up to the tops of the doors. Those houses are a complete loss over for these people."

"That's so sad to hear," Lynette said. "I just heard there is someone in their attic over on Shiloh! Do you think you can get to them? Yeah?"

"We'll try but that means I have to go across the big road."

"Someone with you? I heard you say we."

"Noah's with me! Angelina and Tripp's boy. You should see him, he's about all growed up!"

"I did see him when his daddy dropped him off out front of the house!" Lynette said. "Hi there, Noah! You be careful now! Help the old man. Don't let him over-do. Yeah?"

The walkie talkie shushed when I clicked the button and held it out toward Noah. "Thanks Miss Lynette! I will!"

Her words were clipped off, "—trouble."

"Yes ma'am!" Noah shouted back into the receiver.

"Tell Dixon I'm really running low on oxygen. I don't know if the oxygen man that drives the van —not. I'm having trouble breathing."

Noah looked at me for clarification. I shrugged. I didn't know what she said either, but it didn't seem important.

"Okay, I'll tell him." Noah said. He stared at the radio in his hand for an extra second or two before adding, "Over and out." The shushing sound was all we heard.

"She knows I can't do nothing about that," I said. "It's the Lung care people who bring the oxygen to her. I guess they have an office or something in Baton Rouge somewhere. I doubt I could even get out of Satsuma Grove today. It's not as easy as picking up a loaf of bread at Rouses. Them people are shysters. They love to bill the hell out of your insurance. You can't hardly stop them, once they get started."

Noah turned around to survey the flooding and make sure we don't run into anything just below the service of the brown water like submerged cars and other smaller debris. "Look!" The boy pointed to a cottonmouth, its head up and mouth open, shimmying on the surface of the water the way they do.

"You going to see lots of snakes today, son," I said.

We zipped on down Florida Avenue and turned in an easterly direction down Range. The street itself appeared to be as wide as any of the small rivers in central Louisiana. There were also other people driving boats up and down over the road in four or five feet of water, maybe a little deeper, looking for the basics or helping neighbors and loved ones. I could see the boy was taking everything in with big eyes. We passed the flooded buildings squatting in the dark water: *Anytime Fitness*, *Satsuma Grove High School*, a sign that read "the home of the Panthers," *Gary's Automotive*, a Westlake's hardware store, the MFA pet store, and the *Whistle Stop* coffee shop by the railroad tracks. There was some high ground in a parking lot of a church called *The Way* where a red fire district truck sat as people with shovels and of all ages gathered around a mound of sandbags on one side and a mound of sand. The flooded Mary Lee Donuts parking lot made me remember how hungry I was. I would kill for a half-dozen donuts and some Jamaican-Me-Crazy flavored coffee. I had a thermos of Community Coffee and two homemade Shrimp po' boys Lynette had made for me. I normally liked those roast beef po' boys dressed, but that would have been too messy for the boat. I didn't want to eat them until later in case we got side-tracked too far from home.

I waved to boaters whether I knew them or not. It never ceased to amaze me how complete strangers pulled together when storms hit even though they might not have much to do with each other otherwise. Some were just sightseers cruising around town to see what they could see. I had made a half-dozen good friends just from helping folks out from hurricanes over the years. The flooding was bad. Many people would lose everything they owned only to start over again. Even people with good insurance had a hard time getting their insurance company to actually make good on their policy. The agents were always acutely aware of their own self-created loophole policies. I had seen more than one local insurance office lock their doors, even during business hours, to keep out outraged customers who had vowed to kill their employees when they wouldn't honor their policy. It's funny how you have to have insurance for everything, even when it turns out to be completely worthless to you. Sometimes people from up North like to say, "That ain't right" like they don't believe how they do down here and I always say, "No, it ain't right, but shit happens."

As we went further toward central Livingston parish, Noah thought the water looked even deeper but it could be because the land was lower there too. There were a couple of times I wasn't sure even where I was since there weren't as many landmarks now that so much was underwater. Finally, we turned down flooded Shiloh Road where we ended up in a D. R. Horton subdivision. A pair of pink roseate spoonbills fished several feet apart on a roll of chemically green lawn turf. You could even see the template the grass seed clung to. There was a two-story house where a man with a walrus mustache threw open his upstairs window and waved at us like he was having the time of his life. A flagpole was sticking up a few feet out of the water in the front yard with a flaccid Confederate flag attached to it.

"These must be the folks Lynette was talking about!" I hollered so Noah could hear me but the boy didn't say anything. His annoyed gaze was locked on the man at the window. I'm sure it had everything to do with the flag, but I was busy checking out the house itself. It was a real shame too because it looked like a nice place although the people coming out of it didn't look like they could afford such a grand manse. Even if I could afford it, you wouldn't want the heating bill as a great man once said. A power line that ran to the house had been knocked down by a tree limb so we had to maneuver carefully around it. The sound of an exploding transformer in the distance made the white noise of the civilized world go quiet on the street.

Noah looked over his shoulder at me, "I thought the power was out already?"

"We're on DEMCO in Satsuma Grove," I said, "here they're on ENTERGY, I think."

Now a woman stuck her head out of the window next to the man.

"Hello! You the folks called for help?" I held my hand next to my mouth to improve the sound though it carried easily over the water.

"Yes! Thank God you're here! I got my wife and son. We also got our two little dogs in a cage," he hollered down from the window at us. His voice echoed between the houses.

"I believe we can handle that!" I said.

As the boat docked against the house, just below the roof line Noah tied off the boat and pulled it tight around the upper branch of a Dogwood. Without being given instructions, Noah seemed to know what needed to be done. He pulled tight on the rope and secured it close to the house with a sailing knot. I nodded appreciatively at the boy's resourcefulness. I wondered who had taught him that. I allowed the boat to coast to a stop where it loudly bumped against the house with a thud.

"I'm Bear Gatlin, bubba," the redheaded, mustached man of about thirty-five called from the window he was halfway in and halfway out of. He was cradling a deer rifle in his arms like a favored child. As you might have guessed, he was a pretty good-sized man. He had a big beer gut on him that pushed out the waistband of his jeans.

"Nice to meet you, Bear!" I said. "I'm Dixon and this here boy is my neighbor, Noah. Are we going to take you to the nearest shelter?"

"Where might that be, sir?"

"At the First Baptist Church across from Carter's," I told him. "That's one of the closest designated shelters. It's the one near the Petro Mart. You know, the one where they make their own boudin? The church has food and water and the basics. They even got homemade jambalaya and gumbo. It's the kind made by church ladies, so you know it's good! I just ask that you leave everything but the essentials or we'll run out of room in a hurry."

"Sounds good! Everything else is ruined. We tried moving everything to the top floor we could, but it was a losing deal." Bear was a husky guy who wore black wire-framed glasses with what I guessed was a lazy-eye eyepatch and his facial expression seemed determined but resigned at the same time. He wore a green and blue plaid western shirt with pearl snaps and jeans with black tennis shoes. He ducked back into the window and disappeared from view. When he appeared again, he was shoving a cage through the window with two toy poodles and a fat gray cat all huddled together. He slid the cage down the roof by a dog chain so that Noah could grab it like a box while one of the poodles barked at him.

I asked the boy, "You got it, son?"

"Yeah, I think so," Noah said, grunting as he strained to lower it down into the boat.

I carefully stepped to the front of the boat as it rocked with my movements and took the metal cage from the bottom until I could grab the handle on top and carry it all the way into the back of the boat so there would be more room for some belongings and the family itself as we loaded the boat.

A hatchet-faced woman in an old-fashioned house dress, who

looked too old to be Bear's wife, came out of the window wearing a leopard print robe with a battered blue suitcase and pink rubber camo boots first. Maybe it was his mama. Either way, the woman's atomic-alcohol breath was about as shocking as Godzilla's to Tokyo. Noah took the suitcase from her and handed it back to me with a little grin on his lips. I turned my back to the lady and gave him a wink. I sat her suitcase next to the pet cage for safe keeping. It felt extra heavy. It could have been full of Pabst Blue Ribbon, bottles of Jose Cuervo, or children's toys for all I knew. The lady slid on her bottom down the shingles and made some grunting noises and I caught her as she slid down into the boat like a newborn fresh from a stork. Her robe flew up over her head, revealing a dirty white house dress with a peach thong I really didn't want to see, but it was either catch her or watch her land in the boat like a box of rocks. She smoothed down the fabric and I pretended not to have noticed. She gave me the eye just the same. Even if I were single, I wouldn't want to be the man in constant sorrow with her witch fingers at my throat. It gave the willies just to think it. Bear was quite a man in my inestimable opinion.

"Sit back there by the pets, Miss . . . ?" I said, as I helped guide her carefully around me as the boat rocked, waiting for her to answer.

"Ashley," she leered at me. "This is my son, Ethan." Her skin looked like it had been hung to cure in a tobacco barn.

She looked way too old to be an Ashley without teeth.

*Your grandson, you mean?*

"Miss Ashley," I repeated and gave her a nod. I did no leering myself. When I turned away from her, I could see Noah trying not to laugh. I shrugged. I've always been irresistible to a certain strata of women, usually older. Even when I was young and purely invisible to certain other females of my own tender age.

A sullen, teenaged boy with the same flaming orange-red hair as the father stepped out of the window, not wearing a shirt with cutoff shorts, and his red-pimpled skin looked as if it had never seen the sun. *What manner of lowborn vampire is this?* The boys, Noah and Ethan, were roughly the same age and each nodded their heads and exchanged *Sups*. This Ethan boy had on a pair of head phones attached to an iPod with music buzzing around his ears like invisible, angry bees.

Daren Dean

We were busy securing the family's belongings in the boat. I grabbed a green tarp, tossed it down over their cans and foodstuffs, and unfolded it like a table cloth to protect everything from the sprinkling rain. It fluttered slowly down about the boxes and lashed it down with nylon rope. Miss Ashley chattered the whole time in her mushmouth way about everything she had seen and heard on television, but her monologue was difficult to parse. She was scarecrow thin and her cheeks were sunken. How had she lost her choppers? This was what made her look so much older than her husband. I wondered if it was just bad luck with her family genes or the result of meth. That stuff was pretty big throughout the parish.

"This just reminds me so much of Katrina," Ashley mumbled. "What Katrina taught me was suck it up and take care of business. We move here from New Orleans . . . I just can't believe God did this again to us."

"It's just terrible," was all I could think to say back.

"God's in control," Bear said. "What I've been telling her."

*God had a lot of explaining to do.*

The water was apparently still rising back at the entrance of the subdivision, which surprised me. The water wasn't just setting there getting hot in the sun like in recent floods. This water had a current due to being pushed by the Amite and the no-name storm rain flowing down from the north. The geography of the land was playing a part in it since we seemed to be witnessing dramatic shifts in the current and water depths.

Someone had staked out a homemade stick with water levels on it. According to this guage, the flood waters had risen from about four feet to just over five in the last thirty-forty minutes. I knew that back on our home street we were at thirty-nine feet above sea level but up here, closer to the river, it was closer to sixty-five feet. I couldn't help wondering what the Mississippi River was doing in Baton Rouge and what it might possibly do in New Orleans after all this water made it down there.

"There's probably not another way out of this subdivision, is there?"

"No sir," Bear said. "There's a big sturdy wooden fence running along the property line for the subdivision in back but that's because there's an ugly junkyard and an old pole barn that the owner uses as his office. You can kind of see it."

"I see mostly kudzu and toothache trees out that way," I said.

He settled down onto the front benchseat. Kudzu has about taken over and growed up all over the junkyard office. I put the fence up so I wouldn't have to look at that eye-sore.

"But could we get out that way?"

"We might could," Bear said.

Bear's son spoke up, "They still burn their trash in a barrel and it . . ."

"What he means," Bear said, "Is—"

Ashley interrupted with something muffled and indistinguishable.

Ethan pinched his nose with two fingers.

"Right!" Bear said to her and then deadpanned over his shoulder at me from where he sat in the boat as though I understood any of that. "It's pretty rough that direction. After you made it over all those old cars and trucks in the junkyard it backs up to a pretty dense forest and bayous. There's really nothing out that way. I think we'd be better off going back out the entrance. I'll keep an eye out for anything in the water."

"All right, good!" I said. "Take this long pole down in the bottom of the boat. It has a sharp end on it too that you can use to push or cut anything that gets in the way. I sometimes have flipped it over and use it to push off the ground if we get hung up on any debris."

I fired up the boat, backing carefully up, and turned back toward the street. The current pushed us toward the entrance but at the same time it was pushing us toward the little guard house, more for looks than security, so Bear used the pole to keep us from crashing into it. Noah was filming our journey out of the subdivision with his cell phone a couple of minutes at a time. His blondish hair riffled in the breeze. He filmed all of us including me. He took some pictures too but I was mostly focused on the task at hand. He had some cell company I had never heard of before, not from this area so it explained why his phone worked and mine didn't. The water situation wasn't as bad as I thought it was going to be and we made it back over where the main road I used as my own little highway but so were other people. A big-boned family in a 21' Gator boat, yellow with a checkered racing design, fit for Lake Pontchartrain blew past us as we idled at the edge of the road.

"People out joy-riding in a flood," Bear said.

It took us about thirty minutes to travel what might have been ten minutes by car. I took her slow, not like the Gator boat family, I thought I should err toward discretion and take it a bit slower. It was hard to know what might be submerged just below the waterline. We navigated streets, fields, the circle drives of machine shops, and even a fence of pleached beech and hornbeam. We sped by what was left of Swamp Ice SnoBalls just off 190. Half the building, including the ICE machines, were missing but what was left was still its normal maroon and mint green walls on a yellow deck. All the popular snowball shacks in the area were painted bright garish colors and sat crouching on the sides of the twisted lanes and cracked macadam throughout the winding roads of the parish. I used to take Lynette there to cool off in July and August but we hadn't been yet this year. They might be out of business for good. I didn't know the man's name who ran it but he was Greek and had a debonair mustache. He especially loved his female patrons and never failed to exclaim, "Beautiful ladies!" He made an inappropriate show of giving select women a cherry sucker for free. He had Saints posters up on his walls. He always wore a Drew Brees, No. 9 Saints' jersey, except on the weekends when he wore a white oxford shirt with a black sportscoat.

"There's Carter's!" Noah said. "We're close now."

As we drew closer to the grocery store, I could see a National Guard truck being loaded up with a ragtag group of people aged from babes-in-arms to senior citizens who were straggling out of the Baptist church across the street carrying their personal belongings in back-packs, suitcases, and black trash bags forming a line for the transport truck. The guardsmen were dressed out and some were carrying M16s like they expected to come across a faction of armed Al-Qaeda any minute but instead all they got were refugees from the flood. Just over in the church cemetery, the hallowed dead played peek-a-boo with the living. A herd of coffins, obviously from disparate centuries, were corralled together with orange rope and awaited parousia.

"That don't look good," Bear said over his shoulder to his wife.

"I guess this is as far as I can take you," I said.

"This will be fine," Bear said as if to assure his family. "We're much obliged to you and your son for helping us out." I didn't try to correct him. It was kind of nice he thought Noah was my son and the boy smiled and kind of fell forward at the shoulders after he said it.

"He's a good boy," I said with a nod toward Noah. "We were happy we could help. You don't know what all is in this water. You wouldn't want to have waded too far from home. It wears you out too, besides not being safe. There's all kinds of raw sewage and other chemicals in the water."

Bear pulled out a wad of cash and thrust it at me, but I held up my hand, closed my eyes, and solemnly refused it. "What goes around comes around," I said, "some day someone will help me out and that will be payment enough."

"You reap what you sow, huh?" Bear said. "That's what our preacher says too."

"I kind of think it as keeping the good vibes going," I offered since I wasn't all that religious.

"I could take your name and address and send you something?" Bear offered.

"It's okay," I said. "I like helping people. I'm just glad ya'll are safe. I've been doing this Cajun Navy thing for years."

"All right then," Bear said. "But . . ."

His wife suddenly hollered at him as though he were hard of hearing, "He said he don't want no money!"

Bear looked kind of hangdog then. Pushed his bangs out of his face and jumped out of the boat and into the water. He then carried his wife like a new bride over the threshold and stood her up on the rise leading to the street. I passed the suitcases and the pet cage up to the front of the boat and Noah then handed them off to Bear and his son. One of the little dogs began to bark at all the people congregating in front of the church. The family stood up on the road like they were posing for a picture and Ethan made a strange movement like a double-handed salute.

Noah laughed, "Ethan dabbed!" I'd seen kids in the neighborhood doing it all the time. We watched them walk over to the church where they stood for a while until one of the guardsmen told them something and then began helping them up into the troop truck with the other people who had just come out of the church.

"Should I dab back?"

"No," he snorted. "You think they'll be okay?" Noah asked.

"I reckon so," I said. "I don't know for sure."

Noah tapped his leg. Took another picture with his cell phone. "I heard the soldier say the church was out of food and water."

"I expect they will probably take them to another shelter."

The air felt still and overwhelmingly humid as we sat in our boat. I could feel the heat reflected from the midday sun. It was in the 90s and with the trembling heat it might have been close to 100 degrees. Noah stripped off his shirt and he was so thin I could count his ribs. He was staring off into the direction of the Carter's grocery store where a long line of people had begun to gather. Some people carried backpacks or gripped buggies they had found in the parking lot so they could stock up. I could see the Blue Betty I sitting high and dry out back where the store manager had let me park her. That made me feel very relieved. She was my means of making a living. Without her I didn't know how we could recover, especially if our house flooded. We had been lucky so far.

I sent Noah over to talk to a man standing in line with a blue heeler on a leash to ask what was going on. He talked to the man and his daughter for a few minutes. The man was wearing a cowboy hat and well-worn boots that looked like they could have been made from the earth itself and he seemed to instruct the girl to dig a couple of cold Ozarka bottles out of his camo backpack. The girl, a little younger than Noah and very tan and pretty, handed the waters to Noah, and I could have sworn she curtsied. Noah talked, turned his head and looked in my direction and just about everyone in the line did so at about the same time. I lost the spotlight when a rumpled, hungover-looking police officer came out of the store with his hand resting on his holstered sidearm and gestured toward me like he was shooing the boy away. Noah walked back across the parking lot very slowly with a pained expression on his face. As he began to walk toward me, I could see the cop talking to the crowd and a collective groan went up.

"What are we supposed to drink? We out of water up to the house!" A wide-shouldered man with a goatee and pockmarked face called out above the heads of those standing in line.

"What was that all about, son? Looks like that officer has his hands full."

"Oh, I don't know. I think they aren't going to open now until tomorrow. Maybe they're scared of the people." He handed me one of the cold waters. I waved a thank you to the man with the dog. He looked like he was probably in his mid-thirties or so. A muscular guy who looked pretty tough. He stared at me from under his hat brim, turned his head and spat on the ground but I didn't think much of it. His daughter waved back almost as if the father had prompted her.

"I was talking to that Cajun man and his daughter and their dog," Noah explained.

"I seen ya," I said. "And?"

Noah blushed and placed the cold bottle of water on the back of his neck before getting back into the boat. "Well, the Cajun man only talked Cajun, yeah? His daughter had to translate everything he said but I'm pretty sure he understood. She said, he's old-fashioned. He's keeping his heritage alive or something. She said her daddy's name is Jourdan Broussard and her name is Genie. At least, I think that was her name." He smiled then but was quick to put his smile away. "She said he's a meat man with a boucherie in Lafayette but they got trapped by the storm on the I-12 going home. They heard Carter's was going to open up so they could pick up some things."

"What did the cop say? He seemed pretty mad?"

"He said they weren't going to open up until Noon tomorrow, so everyone has to come back then if they want anything."

"Why did the boudin man give you the waters? We got bottled water by the way."

He laughed. "I was kind of afraid not to take them."

„Didn't want to offend him?" I asked.

"Yeah, I told them we were trying to save people who were trapped in the flood."

"Did the girl say where they was staying?"

"No sir," Noah said. "Didn't have time. That was about when the cop chased me off."

"Hmmm?" I said. "He's probably just worried they'll bum-rush the store. Hop back in the boat. I got a couple of shrimp po'

Daren Dean

boys and some bags of Zapp's Gatortators. There's some bottles of Mexicoke in the big blue cooler. The kind made with real sugar."

We ate our Po' boys on paper plates with our knees closed together for a table. We washed our hands in the flood water and wiped them dry on the thighs of our pants. Our boat was still hitched to the pole of the signal light. The grocery store was beginning to empty and some people were loath to leave the dry lot since many had nowhere to go and the off-duty cop acting like he was going to shoot somebody didn't help matters. Eventually, someone came by in a vehicle and picked the people in line up one-by-one or they just walked on the white line down the middle of the road while the brown water boiled in the sun.

## PRESLEY

I got tired of walking through water in the house with galoshes on. At first, my boots made imprints in the carpet that popped back up when it filled with water but now the entire floor was underwater by a couple of inches. The frogs went crazy the night before from their hiding places in the ditches. Some made sounds like sheep, others sounded like old-fashioned bike horns. They were so loud, it was hard to sleep. There was one with a deep, bass voice that made me think he must have been a whopper. The water gushed through the little crawlspace under the house along with the filth from everything imaginable upriver. Washing away all the sins of Louisiana in a great-big gulp. I was too scared to sleep. I couldn't help worrying the water would rise up into the house and we would all wake up drowned.

None of Jamie Lynn's men came and saved us like she thought they would. They wanted her when it was convenient for them or when they could get away from their wives or girlfriends. I didn't try to know their business. They didn't care about me; I didn't care about them. We're even. But Mama, for her part, didn't let it bother her that none of her "beaus" came to save her. She thought it was funny to use old-fashioned words like that. It just seemed sad to me. I felt embarrassed for her. She didn't need no beau, she needed a man.

She dressed in a faded pair of Levi's and a sleeveless, floral print top. She had to lie down on the bed and suck her pudgy tummy in to get them on. She leapt up, standing in the middle of the bed,

Daren Dean

like a monkey-child bad to jump on the bed. She looked like a little girl for a second in the morning light in our house without power or lights. I would have told her to wear old clothes to walk in the flood water but she wouldn't listen to me. She was always looking for love. She probably thought she was going to meet a new guy, the perfect man, at some point during this disaster. Tall, dark, and handsome shows up driving a bucket truck or a boat and saves us while holding a hat with a feather sticking out of the band like a hero from a black and white movie.

"Get down off that bed!" I said in a faux authoritarian voice. "Just what do you think you're doing?"

"Oh shoot!" She laughed at me. Even with the house flooding, she was still cheery. Maybe she had smoked a joint in the bathroom earlier or ate one of those edibles she didn't think I knew about. Her eyes were rheumy-red like she was high. Her face was always a little puffy with pillow creases on her cheek in the mornings. She thought I didn't know she smoked pot in the bathroom, but I did. "I just don't want to get the cuffs of my jeans wet when I'm getting dressed."

"Let's be serious, lady," I said. "We only have 6 bottles of that water left we got from Dollar General. I'm getting worried we won't have nothing to drink. And if we are stuck here for another day . . ."

"What do you want me to do about it?" Jamie Lynn jumped up and down on the bed. "We're trapped by the flood, honeybunch. Is anything even open? Oh, I'm so hot!" She pinched the front of her blouse to grab her bra with her thumb and forefinger and pumped the material up and down.

"The good twin said he'd ride us up to Carter's," I said. "They're going to open today at Noon. His pickup is parked over there on Hyacinth. I think it was the good Twin anyway."

"Which one's the good one, boo?"

"The nice one!"

"Don't yell at me," Jamie Lynn scolded. She almost sounded like a real mom. "Of course, the nice one is the good one. What's his name?"

"Cameron is the nice one," I said, "Cal is the evil one." Even his name sounded mean. Sometimes he wore a baby Fu Manchu that gave him away as a jerk.

"Sounds like the Bible," she plopped down on her butt with her feet hanging over the mattress like a little kid.

The twins were teenagers with jet black hair that lived with their grandma on the next block up. The bad twin was always getting in trouble in and out of school. I saw him in his backyard teaching his pit bull, Sissy, to sic a little first-grader who lived across the street from him and then laughing about it. I only ever saw the good one in school—in regular classes. Cal took most of his classes in the new Vo-Tech building. You could tell it was Cam anyway because his school uniform was always neat and clean and he combed his hair with a part over to one side. I wondered if he was just pretending to be good because whenever someone told a story about his brother doing bad stuff, his eyes smiled all crafty. The bad twin acted like a wild cat waiting for a bird to pounce on.

"Who's their mama?" Jamie Lynn asked.

"Who's their mama?" I repeated. "How am I supposed to know that? I think their mama's dead or runned-offed. They live with their grandma up on the next block. And before you *aks* me her name, I don't even know! She's an old lady."

"He's going to give us a ride then?" She asked suggestively with her eyebrows. "The good one?"

"First of all . . . gross, Jamie Lynn!" I power-rolled my eyes, "And that's what I just said."

Mama clapped her hands together and jumped back on the bed with her shoes on. "Hot damn!" She forgot she didn't even want to go in the first place just thinking about the twin boys.

"Quit jumping up and down on that bed! And watch your language!"

"Why?" She bounced even higher now. "All this furniture is going to have to be thrown out to the curb now anyhoo! Look at me. I'm going to put my head through the roof like Charlie and the Chocolate Factory!"

I couldn't help laughing and shaking my head. Sometimes I think the Blonde Lady is full-on nuts. Nothing bothers her except not having what she wants. What she calls the necessities: cigarettes, coffee, sugar, sweets—men to worship her. As long as she had those things, she was happy. This flood was nothing to get upset about to her. We'd been through hurricanes, tropical storms, and floods before. Flooding was just part of life here but that's not to say I liked it. It was just temporary. When she was young, she said it was an excuse to have a party. But now she is old! Now no one was inviting her to any hurricane parties. Not as much as they used to.

"Come down here and let's go! I'm serious or we're going to lose our ride." I was standing there in my rubber boots, shrugging on my old Bratz backpack. I threw my fourth grade Hello Kitty backpack up to her.

"What's this for?" She pouted like a little kid and even stuck her lower lip out. "Don't you love me anymore?" She was trying to jump and do her hair in side ponytails and chomping on Dubble Bubble, she didn't even share with me. *Ponyhairs* looked ridiculous on someone her age. She already did her fingernails in pink *paint-o-polish*.

"It's for the bottled water and food!"

She acted like she was hard of hearing, or she was ignoring me. She didn't look at me half the time. Do you have any idea how hard it is to talk to someone when you know they ain't even listening?

"We're going to have to walk halfway."

"We got plenty of food." She was doing something with arms and hands like she was a cheerleader. "We got all that stuff in the freezer. We got to cook it up on the grill before it goes back."

"Goes bad," I said. "Before it goes bad!"

"What?"

"You meant before it goes bad," I said, "not back."

"I know, boo!" Her face was all polka-dotted red when she got piqued. She never got mad—she just got piqued. That was her word. Life was too short for getting mad she liked to say.

"What are you doing, lady?" I imitated her arm and hand movements.

"I'm vogueing," she said, continuing with her movements. I had no idea what that meant, and I didn't like it when people knew things I didn't. It was so embarrassing.

"Well," I said. "It looks stupid." Actually, I thought it looked kind of cool but I didn't want her to know that.

"Put that backpack on and let's go! Like, today! Believe me! You don't want to have to carry it all the way back in a bag."

"Oh honey," she stopped jumping and walked in postholes

across the bed to lean on me and balancing by holding onto my shoulders. "I don't want to walk in that dirty ole water. Who knows what's in it. Everything from snakes to poo and who knows what all! It gives me the *frissons* just thinking about it."

I caught her looking at herself in the mirror on the wall. She was sucking in her cheeks and making duck lips. Last year we read a bunch of Greek myths in Miss Harbourne's English class. I loved reading them. Mama reminded me of Narcissus who fell in love with his own reflection and turned into a flower. She was no flower, but I think she saw one when she looked in the mirror. She had been pretty when she was young in a campy-trampy kind of way. I hated to be the one to tell her she didn't look like that anymore. In her mind, she was still smoking hot. It is so gross when old people think they are still young when they're not. In the summer, she still wore two-piece bathing suits even though she had the muffin top going on. Those walking dead yee-yees over at Lazy Jeff and Heaven's hooped and hollered at her whenever she laid out in the front yard.

"I can't carry it all myself," I said. "Let's go! Don't forget your purse!" I tossed her purse at her.

"Oh shug!" Mama caught her purse against her tummy. She put the strap across her body like a teenager. She dropped down on the bed on her rump like it was a trampoline in PE class and bounced back up with both feet in the water seeping from the rug.

I hollered then, "You're getting me all wet!" I put my hands on my hips. "Let's go!"

"Presley," She leaned toward me real close. Her lips were so close I thought she might kiss me. "You're already wet!" She gave me an air kiss near my cheek with a loud smooching sound.

"Oh yeah," I said looking down at the flooded bedroom. I grabbed my red and blue ball cap with the word "MEOW" on the front and put it on since the sun was out so strong. The sun rays tried to burn against my skin when I wasn't under the live oaks. My skin is extra pale and I get eczema if it's too hot or too cold.

We stood outside the door for a minute and looked up the street to the twin's house for the best route to walk up there in the least amount of water. It seemed like hardly anyone was still at home. Either that or they were hiding out in their house. About that time the twins both came out onto their porch. Cal looked at me with that smirk of his. He didn't even pay attention to Mama because she was old. His greasy black hair stood up like he slept on his head. He didn't have a shirt on but he was wearing a pair of green cargo shorts. His chest had a patch of dark hair on his chest and made a sick narrow trail down to his belly button. He was so gross! Cam stood behind him. They really didn't look that much alike when they were together. Cam wore a green t-shirt that said, "Baton Rouge St. Patrick's Day Parade." It was his favorite holiday, he'd confided to me during school lunch. A clean white t-shirt and a pair of black and white striped Adidas shorts. His pale legs were covered in gross black hair.

"Pres-lee!" Cal hollered using the v between his thumb and forefinger like a megaphone. "You're looking good, girl, damn! Even in a disaster!"

I flipped him off with my ring finger and mouthed the words to him so Mama wouldn't know since she was a little in front of me and off to my right. He threw his head back and pretended to laugh like a sarcastic mime who had just heard a hilarious joke. His face suddenly went expressionless until he shot me a snarly look. He was so sarcastic! Ugh! How did his poor old granny put up with him? She probably thought he was an angel. Mr. Jule said Cal was bad, sure, but at least he wasn't an Eddie Hassle like Cam. Honestly, half the things old people said made no sense to me. Who the heck is Eddie Hassle? I guess it was some old guy Mr. Jule knew from back when he fought the Indians in the Wild West.

Cam said something to Cal, and the good twin responded by nodding his head and twirling his finger in the air over his head and went back into the house. As he disappeared through the doorway Cal yelled, "YEAH? BIG WHOOP!" He slammed the door shut behind him. Cam walked toward us alone with that funny little smile of his. Was he embarrassed or amused by his brother? It was hard to tell. Everything Cal did had a bad taint to it.

"I'm sorry about that," Cam said as he slogged through the water on the street about halfway between his feet and knees. "Cal's mad all the time! It's his hormones or something. He needs to take his meds. I think when Mom took off he kind of lost it! He always thought she was mad at him. He can't, you know, just get over it."

When you got off the road and went into someone's yard the

water was much noticeably deeper. I had never thought about any difference in the level between the street and our yards before but the muddy water made it difficult to ignore. I just thought it was all pretty flat. Now, you could see some houses weren't going to get much water in them unless the stream shifted again. Other houses had a few feet of water. Even before the flood you could see most of the brick houses with their discolored bricks up about a foot above the ground.

Jamie Lynn talked over me, "Don't worry about it, hon!" She put her hand on Cam's shoulder in a flirty gesture. It made me blush just watching her doing it. *He's just a kid!* I wish she wouldn't act like a *thot* but I knew there was nothing I could say to make her change. "We just appreciate you giving us a lift so we don't die of thirst, shug! Ain't that right, Prez?"

"Yeah, thanks Cam!" I sassed and rolled my eyes at Cam so he would get the full benefit. He smiled that secret smile of his to let me know he understood. He didn't need to tell me his brother embarrassed him each and every day of his life.

"WHAT ARE THOSE?" I yelled at Cam, pointing at his shoes. It was the latest joke.

"My lawn mowing shoes," Cam said. "Why waste your Vans on walking in bayous and the filth of the parish?"

"Damn Daniel!" Cam said and smiled at me. His eyes sort of crinkled when he smiled. I had never noticed that before. It made my stomach do a flip. He had nice teeth and lips too. When I caught myself thinking that I told myself to shut it up. "So gross," I whispered to myself under my breath.

"How's your grandmere getting on?" Jamie Lynn asked even though she didn't even know her.

"Oh, she's all right," Cam said. "She takes it in stride. We didn't get as much water in the house as y'all did, sounds like. We got some in the kitchen. We'll have to replace it when this is all over. Might have to throw out most of the drywall, carpet in the living room, and replace the lower cabinets in the kitchen."

"Make me wonder how Austin and his grandmere are doing in Baton Rouge," Jamie Lynn said more to herself than us. We hadn't seen Austin for a couple of months now. My brother seemed like a completely different kid. He wore expensive clothes. He went to the special grade school for the arts not too far from LSU. It was hard to get into it unless you were connected or rich. Maybe they just felt sorry for him but he was especially good at art and music. He'd probably become famous one day and forget he ever knew us.

We were all walking down the street. I let Jamie Lynn and Cam walk side-by-side and I followed from behind. I couldn't help noticing that there weren't any birds, squirrels, and the usual neighborhood dogs and cats roaming around. I hoped people's pets were shut inside and not swept away like we thought Mickey was. I was going to go looking for him as soon as the water dried up. I said a little prayer for him every day. I could see his little puppy dog eyes begging me for table scraps and it made me want to cry.

Next thing I knew Jamie Lynn had put her arm across Cam's shoulders. She had a way of taking unsuspecting people and making them her buddies. His head was turned toward her as they sloshed through the water. I wouldn't have been surprised if they had started holding hands. His eyes were watching her lips move. It was as if he was totally engrossed in what she was saying. It made me jealous because no one listened to me the way Cam was listening to her. To be fair, he was a born listener. It occurred to me that he was born second. Cal must have been the oldest since he did all the talking. Cam was used to listening. I remembered when they were still in Junior high, and I was a lowly grade schooler, they were still dressing alike. That was when their mama was still alive, before Cal had turned to the dark side. Mom had her hands wrapped around the straps of the backpack I'd given her like they were bib overhauls. Her boobs looked enormous. She kind of stood straighter when she knew someone was looking. She was so embarrassing. I still barely had anything up top, but Jamie Lynn swore my life would be transformed (her word, not mine) when my boobs finally came in.

When we came to the end of the street, just before the parking lot of the elementary school, we stopped and looked out across the field that had been in the process of being turned into a cul-de-sac. They made a residential street, built two big houses, and the rest were undeveloped lots though you could see they had concrete slabs and the plumbing and electric ready to go for several more. Cam was pointing at his pickup parked up by the stop sign at the other end of the residential street but it was clear the water was much deeper and roiling around like water moccasins in the center of the street where the water was deepest. We would have to walk down the small rise in much deeper water just to get up to the truck parked by the stop sign. The heat reflected hot and shimmery off the water, just another deterrent to actually making the walk.

"Will we get electrocuted?" I asked out loud. "I'm worried about those electrical box thingies out there." The butterflies in my tummy were about to rip out my guts.

"Naw," Cam said, "I've already been across the field a few times now. It's fine. All the power was turned off by the power company. Ain't nobody got any power."

"I'd sure hate to get a shock!" Jamie Lynn said.

"Oh well, lady," I said. "We've probably been walking in raw sewage up 'til now anyway."

"Nice one, Prez!" She looked back at me like she was deeply offended.

"I'm just saying it's not any worse!" I defended myself from her hip-jutting stance. I couldn't get her to be serious and now she had to put on a big act of being the responsible one for Cam's benefit.

He pointed at a little metal post standing up out of the water, "Now see where that post is? You've got to be careful along there. There's a narrow little trench dug in the ground for the water pipes or electrical or something. It runs up that way. You probably want to try to avoid stepping in it. Other than that, we'll be fine."

As the water got deeper, Mama got all scared acting. "Oh my Gawd!" She said. "I hope there aren't any alligators in this water?"

Cam looked over his shoulder as he led the way and smiled his sneaky smile, "I don't think so."

The water was up to our waist. It looked like we were walking in spoiled chocolate milk. I was following behind Cam. Jamie Lynn was behind me holding her purse on top of her head like those topless African women in *National Geographic*. I kept a sharp lookout in the water for snakes or anything that might be dangerous and swimming around. My heart was skipping around in my chest. I had to give myself a pep talk about how we didn't have any choice. We needed more bottled water. I was thinking how we needed to buy an outdoor camping and cooking set for when the power and gas is out just after a hurricane when suddenly I heard Jamie Lynn scream.

"It's got me! Oh Gawd, it's got me! Help!"

"What is it?"I screamed.

Cam looked back with almost a look of concern but I don't think that was really in his repertoire for facial expressions. I'm sure Cal had beat it out of him a long time ago. It was his regular, uneasy *smizing*. The sound of her distress made my insides seize up like I was being squeezed at the waist by a powerful hand. Maybe there were gators in the water after all but I knew enough to know it was unlikely.

"What is it?" I asked. "Tell me!"

"It's got me by the foot! Oh my, Gawd! Help me!"

Cam turned and started splashing toward her like he was trying to run in the water but it was hard going so he was trying comically to get his knees up higher than the waterline. "I'm coming!"

"It's okay, Cam," Jamie Lynn said. "I think I stepped in something. When I try to pull my foot out it's trying to suck my shoe off. My clothes are all wet now! Just great. I'm going to have to go back home and change clothes."

He stopped trying to run on top of the water and stood there, staring at her. "Oh!" He said. Cam shook his head with that uneasy smile of his. His eyes crinkling in that way I knew I adored, though I wished he was someone else, I wished he was someone famous on the internet instead of Cam, the good twin.

"What, oh?" I said.

"It's that trench I warned ya'll about," Cam said. "Did you step in it?"

She nodded like a wide-eyed little girl who was trying not to pee her pants as she tried to work her foot loose. "I can't get aloose."

"Oh Mama!" Oh, how she could exasperate me sometimes! She was worse than a child. She glared a me for calling her Mama. "I mean, Blonde Lady!" I honestly felt like she was doing this just to get attention. I wanted to tell her that Cam wasn't a real man, he was a kind of species of half-man. He wasn't *trying to talk to her* like the high school girls said. But we had to go through this if we were ever going to get across this flooded cul de sac and eventually to the supermarket and pushing a buggy down the aisle. It wasn't but maybe half-a-block, I guessed but with the heat and water it looked like a mile.

Cam made his way over to her. He grabbed both her shoulders and pushed at her—like that was going to work! She just smiled at him like he was trying to dance with her. She let out a laugh and snorted. It was funny but then she started crying. She was always so emotional. She thought she was the star of a movie. Cam saw what he was doing wrong and he suddenly knelt and grabbed her by her leg and felt down it with the water halfway up to his face. His eyes looked very blue now reflecting the blue of the sky and his black hair. Blue eyes like his were interesting but there was something disturbing about them too. I couldn't look in a blue-eyed person's eyes for too long before looking away. I felt more comfortable looking brown-eyed people in the eye.

"Well Cam," She gave him an amused smile, "I guess we're getting to know each other today."

"I'm sorry Miss Jamie Lynn," Cam said. "Don't mean nothing by it. I'm just trying to get your foot out."

"Mmm hmm," She said with that flirty grin of hers.

"He's just a high school kid!" I knew she'd get mad at me but I really didn't care. It was too hot to care. I could feel beads of sweat popping out on my forehead. Lines of sweat were running from my underarms and down my back too.

"I've got an idea," Cam said. "I'll get you out but I have to go underwater for a sec! Hang on!" He plunged down forward into the water like he was baptizing himself. His whole head disappeared. Mama was looking down at where he disappeared with her mouth hanging open in an O shape. A few air bubbles came up. Was he drowning? Why didn't he come back up?

"Oh, oh my!" She said.

"What is it?"

"He's . . . doing . . . something . . . oh my!"

"Is your foot out?"

Jamie Lynn shot up out of the water and fell backwards. She threw her hands in the air over her head like she was doing the backstroke because one held the strap to her purse. It looked funny but I knew she did it to keep her cigarettes and lighter, cell phone, money, and other stuff in her purse from getting wet, and it did a little anyway. Cam didn't have any pockets. I wondered where his cell phone was but his keys were on a lanyard around his neck. I just had a cheap-o dumb phone—the opposite of smart. I couldn't even go online with it now anyhow. Nobody's phone worked now.

Cam broke the surface like the swamp creature from a deep dive. He was sputtering and wiping his hair and the water out of his eyes. He seemed to be surprised to find himself above water again. Mama bobbed back up out of the water and her cheeks filled up with air and she blew out. I was afraid she might be mad but she just started laughing with her hands still upraised in the air like she was at a Baptist tent revival.

"Well! You got my foot unstuck!" She said. "Woohoo!" She did a little mom dance right there in the water.

"Oh, I'm sorry!" He said but he was *smizing* again like maybe he yanked up on her leg extra hard just so she would go underwater. Maybe it was an accident. You couldn't tell with Cam. It was probably why he never got into as much trouble as Cal. They both probably had 666 etched on their heads somewhere. "Didn't mean to drown ya, just tried to get your foot out."

"You can make it up to me," She gave him the eye. So mega gross, I thought. "I didn't go completely under so it's okay. Does my hair still look okay?"

He gave her a thumb's up and she glowed in his direction. "Why thank you?" She did the motion of pushing a non-existent strand of hair into place. The material of her soaking wet blouse was making her big milk monsters stick out and Cam was staring at them. It wasn't all his fault. You couldn't miss 'em.

"C'mon!" I said. I hoped I could distract them both.

We looked up into the sun-bleached light and summer heat reflecting off the surface of what had become a new lake. The silence was so strange to me as we started wading in the pee warm water up to our waists toward the newly paved street of the new development rising out of the depths like it led to Atlantis. Cam's old Silverado was parked up by the stop sign. We all walked a little faster as our feet found the concrete, except for Jamie Lynn who was fanning her hand at her face. Tears formed in her red eyes when I turned back to see what was taking her so long.

"C'mon on Jamie Lynn! We're almost there now."

"I was just thinking about something you said earlier . . . " her lower lip protruding like a little kid. "You don't seem to ever like my hair, my makeup, or my clothes. You don't like the music I listen to or the men I date. I wonder if there's anything about me you do like?" She had stopped splashing forward and stared at me. "Are you embarrassed of your mother? Is that it? The one who gave birth to you and raised you and kept you?"

At first, I was stunned to silence. That bit about being embarrassed by your mother junk was rich. Was she really going to get into all of this now? After everything I had been through, I was immune to mother guilt. What we really needed to do was get into the truck and go to the Carter's. She was worse than taking a couple of toddlers on a grocery run.

"Well?"

"Are you for real right now?" I put my hand on my hip with one foot slid out a little extra wide like a mother who is about to lose her patience. "C'mon Mama!"

"I want an answer or I'm not taking another step!" She touched her hair like she does when she's primping in front of a mirror and then she crossed her arms in front of her like a little kid. "Well?"

Cam had already made it to the truck. He stood next to the driver's door with a funny expression on his face. He didn't know what we were talking about. He waved at us to come on.

"Mama!" I said.

"Jamie Lynn."

"Ma—Jamie Lynn!" I huffed. "We don't have time for this now. We've got to get to that store before all the water's gone or you're going to be sorry then! We both will be. I promise we can talk about it later. I love you and all that good stuff!"

"Really?"

I couldn't help but smile then. I didn't really want to, I promise you, "Geezum! I LOVE YOU! Is that what you want to hear? You know I do! You drive me crazy is all! Would you come on!"

She smiled big then. She was so moody. One minute she was all euphoric and the next she was crying about losing her keys or her cell phone. She was ADHD before they even thought of what that was, only she didn't know it. I thought about trying to buy some Adderall from Connor LeBlanc at school, so I could slip it to her when wasn't looking.

"Okay sweetie,'" she said in her fake sounding sing-song

voice. "I'm coming if you promise we'll talk about why you hate me so much. I love you, my little Muppet."

"Cross my heart!" I said. "Move your big badonkadonk!" I stuck my finger in the air straight over my head and made little circles. "Let's head em up and move em out!"

"Don't call me a heifer!" Jamie Lynn said. She was on the road now and splashed out of the water onto the dry concrete of the new black road. "You're the heifer! You just ain't growed into your size yet, but you will. Then, we'll see."

The three of us squeezed into the front seat of the pick-up. Just before Jamie Lynn got in I put my hand on Cam's hand. "Thanks."

"You're welcome." He smiled at me for real. I didn't know how to take it and then I did the unthinkable and blushed and turned my head away as Jamie Lynn was sliding in.

"What? Why don't I get to sit by Cam?" Jamie Lynn asked.

## NOAH

The pretty Cajun girl and her daddy walked over to us from where
they stood in front of the ICE machine of the grocery store after
the security guard waved his gun around and told everyone to move
along. The two of them just kind of stood looking down at us on
the concrete lip of the parking lot since we were basically in a ditch
filled with dirty brown flood water. They didn't say anything at first.
The daddy wore a backpack and he was holding the leash to his dog
wound up around his fist like brass knuckles. I think it was one of
those Louisiana Catahoula dogs. The dog looked like a creation from
a graphic novel in the shadow of the Carter's sign with spots like
giant chocolate chips and disturbing, almost human, brown eyes. I
half-expected it to start talking. It stared at me like it was going to say
something any second.

Father and daughter were dressed Cajun I guess, like
they bought their clothes at a western boot store. I guess he was a
good-looking guy like from a movie almost. He looked stout with
broad shoulders although he wasn't any taller than me and his cowboy hat and roper boots were expensive. I could tell her daddy wasn't
exactly poor, even if he was traditional. He also wore a nice brown
belt with silver stars on the side and a big silver rodeo championship
buckle. I figured there was a story behind that buckle. The girl's dark
hair was combed and she had a braid down her back that I would
almost bet her daddy had done for her even if he was a tough guy.

"Ask them if they want a couple of Cokes?" Dixon scratched
his stomach. He was usually holding his stomach like it hurt him all

the time or he was holding something terrible in on the inside.

The girl laughed and said in a Cajun accent, "I speak perfect English and so does he. He just don't want to. He's mad because he wasn't raised traditional." I noticed the girl had high cheekbones and almond eyes.

"*Ta gueule*, Eugenie," her daddy scoffed.

"*Meh*," she said with a grin, "you make me talk English for you all the time."

He was probably in his thirties. He was pretty old really. Half the older generation before him didn't even learn French because of the government suppression of French. Back then it was considered a bad thing not to speak English. I read about it in our social studies unit on Louisiana history. It's hard to think how dumb people used to be. Her daddy probably wished he was one of those old seventeenth century Cajun dudes from Nova Scotia. He looked like a pretty solid guy and I gave him a nod. I liked that he was old-fashioned. It was like he was a throwback to an earlier time.

"What's your daddy's name?" Dixon asked the girl. I guess he needed a formal introduction. Old men were funny about things like that. You know? Shaking hands, looking each other in the eye, and all that stuff they thought was so important. It sorta reminded me of the way dogs sniffed each other's butts.

"*Mo pele* Jourdan Broussard," he started to stick out his hand to shake but he was up too much higher up the little bank where the parking lot for that to be practical, "*Sa tchob byen? Sa-ki to non?*"

"Papa aks—what is *your* name?"

"I'm Dixon and this young man here is Noah," Dixon placed his hand on my shoulder.

"I'm Genie," she nodded and looked at me with big doe eyes. It felt like someone stabbed my heart with a knife. She was that beautiful.

"Dixon and Noah." Jourdan nodded formally.

"And who's this?" Dixon asked after the dog. "Looks like Huckleberry Hound."

"This is our dog, Banjo! I've had her since she was a puppy!"

"That dog is something else!" I laughed.

Genie laughed a little. "She's part blue heeler and something else, we don't know."

"Well, that's the finest looking merle-dog I've ever seen!" Dixon declared. He repeated himself after a good laugh. "Yes, that's what I call a Huckleberry hound!" I had no idea what he was talking about or why he said it twice. None of us did. Old man stuff.

Genie stuck her lip out and the rocked back from her heels forward, "Oh, Papa said we both like Coca-Cola." I would have given her a case of Coca-Cola if they were mine to give. I could feel my face turning red just thinking that. If it were up to me, I'd make sure she never ran out. I'd get her the good Coke in the glass bottles from Mexico, the kind made with real sugar.

Dixon scratched the back of his head, "You sure are a cute little gal, you know? Your daddy is a handsome man too. I guess the apple don't fall far from the tree. Y'all hungry I bet? I don't have anymore po' boys but I can give you a couple of bags of Gator-tators."

I was pretty sure her daddy hadn't said anything about Cokes but then I got two cans out of the cooler anyway and they were sweating. The man had to adjust the dog's leash so that the loop was up by his elbow. He opened one of the cans for the girl before he handed it to her. She tipped the can back and drank deep and even said *aaahhh* after like they did on commercials. Her skin was smooth and tan and I could hardly keep myself from reaching out and touching her cheek. I couldn't take my eyes off her red lips as they met the lid of the Coke can. I looked away quickly when she glanced at me.

The next thing I know they agreed to help us save people since they don't have nothing else to do anyway. We really were the Cajun Navy now. I whispered that to Genie since she was sitting right next to me and she smiled like she thought I was sort of a dope and leaned into me with her shoulder just a little. The day wasn't a total loss now that I had Genie to look at and talk to. Her daddy sat on the bench seat behind me and mean-mugged me every time he caught my eye. Every so often he would turn around and say something in Cajun and Dixon would just nod or say "right" in response. Even if her old man did speak Cajun, we couldn't hear half what he said over the motor as we we tried to make our way back toward our neighborhood.

The walkie talkie crackled. Lynette told Dixon about a woman trapped in her car, which was floating in the water, just a few blocks from our house. She heard about it on Facebook. I was amazed that she could get the internet since my own phone was useless now. She said the water was getting up on the front and back steps at the house.

"How's the generator going?" Dixon asked.

"It's going."

"I love you, Lynette," Dixon told her. "Keep us posted." He didn't blush or anything when he said it.

"I love you too, honey," Lynette said back to him, her voice sounding like it was in a big echoing room, and then the static *shhh* was the last sound we heard.

"Awww, that's so sweet!" Genie said and pulled on my arm.

"He has her name tattooed on his shoulder," I whispered.

"I wish someone would tattoo my name on their shoulder," Genie said. "I think someone would have to love you good to do that."

I couldn't disagree. I wanted to kiss her but I knew I couldn't with her daddy sitting there waiting to beat the hell out of me if I did. I heard his deep, baritone voice say some stern cajun stuff to her.

"What did he say?" I asked.

"He said to tell your boyfriend how old you are."

"Am I your boyfriend?" I waited for a couple of seconds but she just smiled back at me like it was a big joke. "Well, how old are you?"

"Guess?"

"You better tell me, so your daddy doesn't get mad," I said. "How old do I look?"

"I don't know," I said. "Not too old. About my age? 14-15?"

"I'll never tell!" Genie smiled and blushed so I thought she might be younger. "Besides it's not polite to ask a lady her age or her weight."

"How much do you weigh then?"

"I told you that's not polite." She *tsk tsk'd* me in mock disappointment. "You must not have been raised right."

"You're pretty skinny," I said. "You don't sound Cajun when you talk to me but when you talk to your daddy you sound super Cajun."

"Meh, that's what he is! Super Cajun! I can talk the talk but I don't always have to—my real name is Eugenie by the way. It's so old-fashioned, I know."

"Eugenie—"

"Just call me Genie."

Thunderheads rumbled by high and loud in the dark swirling clouds overhead. I'd seen so many storms over the years but there was something truly wicked about this one. It just wouldn't leave us alone, it was like it was stalking the parish for someone in particular. It was mad at someone. Out for revenge. Bad juju. The heads of the shelter people jerked up toward the sound echoing above as if to say it wasn't quite done yet. I saw an old woman with wet, gray hair down to her shoulders with a green blanket wrapped around her shiver even though it was blazing hot. Maybe she had been in the water before they found her? Who could say? The National Guard trucks lined up and pulled out of the church parking lot and onto the road.

"Where do you think, they're going?" Genie asked.

"Honestly, don't know," I said. "I heard the soldiers saying they didn't have enough food and water at the shelter. Nobody was prepared for all of this. I guess they'll take them to another church or a Salvation Army, or before I moved to New Orleans with Tripp they used the gym at the Junior High. I don't know much about this stuff really."

"Who's Tripp?" Genie asked but before I could answer Dixon interrupted.

"I think I saw Miss Esperanza and Mr. Jule get on that second truck," Dixon said. "I swear it was them."

"It could have been," I said. "I pray they're all right."

"You care about them? That's so sweet," Genie moved a little closer to me on the bench seat. "Who are they?"

"Our neighbors, across the street from us on Eden Church Road. They're real nice people. They're kind of like my grandma and grandpa."

"I love my great grandmère and grandpère. I'm not not sure I could go on living if anything ever happened to them. They raised daddy like he was their son on account of he didn't get along with his parents growing up. They taught him how to be traditional."

"Untie the rope from the post, Noah," Dixon said. "It's time to motorvate!"

The sun peeked out from behind rimlit clouds. The boat was slicing through the water. There were people walking around in the water like zombies, only this was real life. I saw an old woman walking slowing between two trailers like she was looking for a lost cat. Should we stop and ask her if she's okay? Dixon was on a mission now when I turned to look at him. He was smoking one of his American Spirit cigarettes. At the same time, Jourdan was smoking a Swisher Sweet. I could smell the cherry sweetness of it whenever we slowed down to avoid a parked car or something else that was floating in the water. The dog was just sitting there as pretty as could be smiling into the wind but it looked like it might have some bird dog in it due to its face and ears. It had kind of puppy dog ears that reminded me of Snoopy. Genie pulled on my arm to get my attention and when I turned I could smell the flowery perfume of her hair.

We were passing flooded houses, drowned buildings, and all makes and models of cars and trucks sucked up by the river. Mr. Dixon said, *Today, Louisiana is a giant toilet.* I had never really thought of Satsuma Grove as my home with air quotes before now. I would never have told anyone I was from here. At least, I wouldn't have said so recently. I mean, I liked to think of myself as from NOLA but looking around the words popped into my head: *Home is destroyed.* I hoped Tripp regretted leaving me here now. I wondered if it was flooding down there?

Genie pointed at a yellow dog with a pink nose balancing it-self on the cab of a white pickup truck. It looked at us like it thought we might save it the way it kind of tap-danced in a circle. The old man blasted on by. We were on a mission to save people now; even so, my heart sank a little for the poor old thing.

Ten minutes later, Dixon cut the engine and flicked his cigarette and we sputtered to a stop though the boat kept moving forward with the momentum it had built up. There was a sporty red car mostly underwater now. It had a convertible roof with a little plastic window in back. Jourdan stood up and leaned with a hand on Genie's shoulder and indicated that we both needed to change places and sit in the back of the boat. He wrapped the purple leash to the dog around Genie's wrist. She nodded wordlessly and her face went pale. She gave Banjo a couple of quick pats on the head, but I could see she was worried. Dixon was coming forward and I ended up sitting in the back of the boat with Genie and the dog. I didn't know what to do. Genie's daddy picked up the harpoon and tested its heft.

"Help me!" An old woman's muffled voice called from inside the car. "This water is about to drown me and I *cain't* get out! I still got my seatbelt on. I have Freddie in here with me too. We're both stuck."

Dixon was leaning over Jourdan's shoulder, "We're going to get you out of there ma'am! So don't you worry! We just have to figure out the best way to do it!"

"Well, Hurry up!" She hollered. "I don't want to die!"

Dixon had the machete in his hand and I could tell he was thinking about slicing into the back window. Jourdan stood on the trunk of the car and was trying to puncture the little plastic window with the harpoon but incredibly it just kept glancing off the plastic.

"I'm drowning! Get me out of here. It's filling with water!"

The Cajun tossed his cowboy hat toward us and Genie put it on for safekeeping. Jourdan kicked off his boots into the bottom of the boat. He dropped the harpoon and reached to his belt where he had a case knife in a sheath, flicking the blade open with his thumb he jumped from the boat to the top of the car where he balanced precariously. His leap caused the boat to wobble and move several feet from the red car. The car bobbed up and down before it sunk into the brown water a few more inches. Genie gasped into my ear. She grabbed my hand with both of hers. Her daddy fell to his knees and slid into the water and plunged the knife down into the rag top of the convertible and made several more stabbing motions. I hoped the woman was further in the back so she wouldn't be cut. The back end of the car was sitting up out of the water while the front end was now completely submerged. Jourdan dove under the water and we all held our breath for what seemed like minutes. When he finally emerged, he held the elderly woman in a tight embrace as they broke the surface. He still had his knife in one hand.

The old woman gasped, "Oh my Lord! You saved me! I thought I was going to die!" What hair she had was plastered to her head and her scalp was visible through the strands. Her face made a perfect circle of terror and the water streamed down into her eyes and she gave her head a shake.

Jourdan let go of her and she dog-paddled toward us.

Dixon hollered at her, "There we go! All right now, swim to the boat! Swim to the boat!"

"I can't!" The lady said. "I can't do nothing without Freddie! He's still in the car! Save my little baby!"

"You got a baby in that car!" Dixon hollered. "Jesus H. Christ! Can you get it, Jourdan?"

"It's hard to see down there!" Jourdan shouted in perfect English. He pinched his nose a couple of times and he blinked the water out of his eyes. "Don't see no baby." Flecks of water splashed us in the boat.

"A baby!" Genie squealed. I had to keep her from jumping straight into the water herself by pulling her back down on the bench next to me. "I've got to save the baby!"

"Your daddy's gonna do it!" I said. "Don't worry! Your daddy's gonna get the baby." I hugged her around both arms and her body squirmed against me with stress. I loved that she wanted to just jump right into the water herself.

The current was pushing them both away from us and I started to worry they were going to be carried away to the next parish if they didn't both get into the boat right now. Jourdan seemed to be struggling to stay where he was and the current seemed stronger than it had a moment before.

Much to everyone's surprise, the old lady raised her arms up out of the water and into the air and then drove her fists down onto Jourdan's head and shoulders, "You gotta save, Freddie! He's still in the car!"

"Who's Freddie?" Jourdan asked. He moved away from her so she couldn't pummel him again. "Is that your baby?" She was having a fit the way drowning people do when they panic.

"He's my little dog! Get him out of there!" She started to go under again herself.

"Dog!" Dixon exhaled loudly in relief. "I'm sorry, Ma'am. I think he's gone. Swim to the boat now before we lose you too!"

"NO!" The old lady wailed. Her face was wet and leathery and she looked like was probably going to die soon even before this flood came along. What little white hair she had was plastered on her head. "You gotta save my little baby boy! I can't go on without him!"

Jourdan bobbed up out of the water, taking a deep breath

and plunged straight down below the surface again with his legs kicking like a frog's. He wasn't down there for long when suddenly he popped back up with a little runty white dog. His little feet were doing the dog paddle even though Jourdan held him by his underside and high up above the water's surface. His little paws swimming in mid-air still.

"*Kyoo!*" Jourdan said! "Here he is!"

"Awww, he so cute!" Genie clapped her hands in delight. "Don't you think he's cute?"

"I guess so," I said.

"We got him! Now swim to the boat ma'am!" Dixon beat the side of the boat. He wasn't in any kind of shape to be jumping into the water after her but he could pull her out.

Jourdan put the little dog into the boat and Banjo looked at it funny and then gave it a little lick on the head. Genie and me laughed. Genie didn't hesitate to scoop up the little dog and hold it in her lap. Banjo came over and started sniffing the little dog like she wasn't sure if she approved or not.

"You almost drowned, Freddie," Genie said to the dog. "Dat something you don't want to do."

"If cats have nine lives," I said, "I wonder how many lives dogs have?"

"You heard dat, bébé?" Genie said. "Don't listen to him."

Dixon reached out and grabbed the old lady's hand and pulled her into the boat. Jourdan got up and under and heaved her into the boat by her bottom. It didn't look appropriate but it got the job done. The old lady laid in the bottom of the boat gasping for breath and began to moan and cry as she recovered from almost drowning, trapped in her car. It hit us all, that if we hadn't come along when we did this woman and her little dog would be dead about now. Probably nobody would have ever found her body either. Jourdan pulled himself back into the boat and managed to sit up on the plank in front of us and the water streamed off of him. He looked exhausted.

"You saved me! Thank you for saving me! Oh, thank you for saving Freddie too! I would have died! I would have died!" She started sobbing now and her tiny frame shook with the effort. She was bawling like a child but I could see her face since she was facing the front of the boat. She took one of Jourdan's hands in her tiny ones and covered the back of it with little kisses.

"Come on now, *sha*," Jourdan looked a little alarmed.

"There's a blanket in that box," Dixon pointed behind me. "Put that on the lady so she don't go into shock."

"Yes sir," I said. I had trouble getting the wooden box open but once I did I pulled out what looked like a green Army blanket and draped it over the woman's shoulders but she didn't even look at me. She stared at her savior with a kind of religious intensity. I gave her a bottle of water too. She cracked open the lid and took a big swig from the bottle.

Jourdan rubbed the lady's arms through the blanket, "You don't wanna get the *frissons*, sha." He sat and stripped his western shirt off since it was soaking wet. The humidity made wearing wet clothes almost unbearable.

"What's your name, Ma'am?" Dixon asked the lady. "My name's Dixon and this here is Jourdan. The kids back there are Noah and, um . . . Genie. Right?"

The old lady stared at him but didn't say anything. I could see Mr. Dixon's face change expressions and I knew the old lady was not responding to the question and not just because she hadn't said anything. His face went from trying to be extra friendly to a smile that disappeared into a grim line across his face. She wasn't in her right mind. Was she normally like this or did the accident make her this way? It was hard to say.

"It's okay," Dixon nodded to her. "It's okay. You can talk to us when you're ready." He started heading back toward us in the back so he could get to the engine. The boat swayed in the water and he steadied himself on Genie's daddy's outstretched hand.

"Where's Freddie?" The old lady suddenly screeched? "Where's my Freddie boy?"

"Here he is!" Genie said with a smile in her voice.

The old woman turned and raked Genie with her eyes. "Give me back my baby! You trying to steal my little boy from me!"

Genie looked uncertain and a little helpless. I saw tears form in her eyes. Dixon took the dog from her and put it in the woman's lap. The dog gave a little uncomfortable yip. The old man gave Genie a reassuring look to let her know she shouldn't take what the woman said personal. The woman had almost died after all. Genie's eyes seem to dry up almost instantly. She looked at me and I gave her the same kind of look that I hoped was reassuring but I wasn't very good at showing anyone how I felt since I spent more time trying to hide my emotions. People in school and in the French Quarter were always looking at you and sizing you up so I tried to give them nothing to work with except when I was playing music on the streets or at the festivals. Everything flowed naturally and I didn't feel so self-conscious when I was performing.

"That was very brave of you, Jourdan," Dixon shook his hand. "I'm too old to be jumping in after anyone like that. It was lucky you were with us."

"Awww now!" Jourdan waved the compliment off. He went to sit in the front of the boat and took his backpack and boots with him. After he got situated up front he took out a box of Swisher Sweets and tried to light one but his Zippo wouldn't work. Dixon tossed him a little pink lighter. "Rose?" he said. The smoke from the little cigar was sweet and comforting somehow.

"What are we gonna do with the old lady?" I whispered though I knew the crazy lady could probably hear me.

"We're going to take her to the Fire Department over there," Dixon pointed as if I knew exactly where he meant. "The one not too far from the Dollar General. I think that's the best we can do for her if they're taking folks on. First, I gotta get back there. If that don't work, we'll take her to the church."

Genie and me got up and let Dixon sit in the very back so he could start the engine and steer the boat. As Dixon turned the boat around he went slowly at first and had to steer around a dump truck that was parked on the street. He went around it and into someone's front yard where the water was up about eight foot on the side of a brick rancher. I could probably have pulled myself up on the roof from the boat. We started buzzing down the wide street-river and the chocolate milk water was everywhere now. The current moved as if it had a purpose, like a watery snake, doing its dance of bad juju trying to find it's way down to New Orleans.

## DIXON

It looked like Eden Church was an isle unto itself the way it was surrounded on all sides by the muddy waters. Pastor Rob was coming out of the front door of the chapel like he was expecting us. He was a young man, maybe mid-thirties, with light brown hair and he wore a thin beard of the same color with red highlights that glinted in the sun. His eyes were a disturbing pale, turquoise color.

Word was his boss, Preacher Bledsoe, or just plain "Preacher" had been rushed to the hospital when his parsonage flooded. They had to cut through his roof and airlift him by chopper to Baton Rouge General. The young pastor wore a short-sleeve, white Oxford shirt, and jeans with tennis shoes due to the nature of the work the disaster had brought upon him. Normally, he was dressed in either his brown Dockers or a three-piece gray suit for weddings and funerals. His casual dress made him look even younger and more approachable. Despite his youth, I respected him as a man of God, even though I'm not much of a church-going man myself, due to the serious expression he always wore. It must have been all those altar calls that had instilled that tone in everything he did. The church believed in speaking-in-tongues, laying-on-of-hands, and rolling around on the floor and even though I didn't necessarily believe in all of that holy roller business, I could respect the spiritual experience. Still, no one could deny the presence of God (even if you want to call him the Great Spirit or whatever) was in that building when it was going on. It was a great spectacle and a part of me like to spectate instead of praise His name. I didn't go regularly but I had seen enough to have an opinion on the matter.

I met Pastor Rob originally at a fish fry fundraiser. He gave a brief sermon from the Book of Mark about Jesus feeding the people with the loaves and fishes and then he gave the blessing before the fish eaters were allowed to partake. Lynette once drug me there to see if these gormandizers could save my soul. She started going to the church about six months earlier in the hope they could pray away her physical ailments. Pastor Rob introduced himself to me while I was drinking coffee spiked with a bit of amber intoxicant and smoking a cigarette, minding my own business. Even from that first meeting, when he shook my hand I could feel a kind of spiritual warmth and power coming off the man. Even though I had my doubts about his brand of Jesus, we ended up becoming friendly. Afterwards we would meet for coffee and pie at the Down Home Grill on Saturday mornings when I wasn't on a haul and talk God, politics, sports, philosophy—all the usual verboten subjects. Usually, a couple of geezers and some church ladies would show up to pass the time as well. They plainly worshipped the man and hung on his every utterance, which struck me as a lonely byproduct of his vocation. He talked more straightforward one-on-one, in a no bullshit way, until the old biddies showed up and then he hammed it up a little to make them feel comfortable with his appropriateness. He had a million dad jokes that I imagine any preacher worth his salt needs. He was a smart cookie and a tough guy who had served 3 tours in Iraq and Afghanistan as an Army medic when he was no more than a boy. Pastor Rob had my respect.

The church was surrounded by water on all sides. It looked like a spectacle on a par with Jesus walking on the water. Only faith itself could be holding the waters back from the house of God on this little island and it seemed improbable given the floodwaters. Men, women, older children, and teens were drafted into service furiously filling white sand bags to place around the perimeter of the church in an effort to keep the waters at bay. Smaller children were running near the water's edge like sandpipers hunting the waves on a beach. I didn't believe too much in anything supernatural but thought our current situation left the subject open for debate.

"It looks like you're all prayed up, Pastor Rob!" I shouted at him with my hands cuffed around my mouth and then grabbed the til again before I lost control. "What do you think is holding the water back?"

"God moves in mysterious ways," Pastor Rob called back, "his wonders to perform."

"He plants his footstep in the sea," I said. "And rides upon the storm."

"William Cowper!" Pastor Rob laughed, "I can never stump you, Dix!"

He knew I had some serious church in my background, plus I was an avid reader. Some of my fellow truckers thought I was some great philosopher reborn! Forget that I am fluent in both kinds of music: country and western as well! I got no special credit for that.

Pastor Rob opened his arms as if to say come and see but at the same time it was clear the church was brimming with displaced people and would run out of food, water, and other supplies in short order. There were green, yellow, blue, and red tents erected on the dry lawn near the church. A couple of shirtless men were smoking cigarettes and cooking meat on a Weber grill toward the side of the church probably because everyone had to empty their freezers due to the sudden loss of electricity. Young children lolled about inside the tent, some eating snacks and others playing with dogs. There were more than a few crying babies and mothers attempting to comfort them. The people there were in remarkably high spirits despite the face-melting heat. I knew part of it was Pastor Rob's calm but he would claim it was a gift of the Spirit. There was something about the pastor that was born to give comfort.

"That was an easy one for an old man like me!" I had reached into the special pocket in my wallet as we pulled up and palmed a folded Ben Franklin to surreptitiously place in his hand to help support the cause.

Pastor Rob suavely pocketed the bill and gave me a wink without even looking at the color of my money. "This will help." He swatted me a good one on my shoulder and gave me a little shake. He was the kind of preacher you wouldn't want to get into scrape with. Before he got religion he had been the Sergeant-at-arms, aka the chief security officer, for the Booze Fighters MC in some eastern state after his military stint. Simply put, he was highly skilled at kicking your ass, should the need occur.

Once we were all out of the boat, Noah and Jourdan helped me pull the bow of the boat onto dry land to keep it from floating away. I tethered it to one of the pole's of the church sign. Genie and her merle dog walked around the water's edge and looked at the people there like they were from another another planet. I'm sure the girl was overwhelmed by everything that had happened and being away from home. I figured she must be missing her mama. Noah gave me a look and I nodded to him to go talk to his crush.

"Good to see you, Pastor Rob!" I reached out and shook his hand.

"Likewise!" He clapped me on the shoulder and gave me that small, wise smile of his. "Who's your friend?"

"This is Jourdan," I said. "He's been helping us. You should have seen him jump in the water with a knife and save this woman here about to drown in her car. It was almost totally underwater. If he hadn't done what he did . . ." I shook my head. "Jourdan here is from Lafayette and don't speak much English, but he can when he needs to." I turned and gave Jourdan a wink and he came forward and crushed Pastor Rob's hand.

"*Ravi de vous rencontres,*" Pastor Rob said, much to my surprise. He was a wonder.

"Nice to meet you," Jourdan shook Rob's hand with a manly nod. He seemed bored with the entire situation he was already getting some looks from the people there because of his muscular physique or because they thought he should put his shirt on.

"Now this young lady here," I said. "Is someone who needs some help. Maybe you could put her and her *baby* up for the night?" I took him by the shoulder and led him toward the church so I could speak frankly. "She's the old lady we saved but she's not right in the head. I mean, it could be she has meds she hasn't taken or she's in shock. She calls that little dog there her baby. I can't get her to answer any questions. She wouldn't even say her own name once she was in the boat."

"Don't worry, Dix," Pastor Rob said. "We'll see what we can do. We've seen a few elderly folks like her and some not so elderly who are struggling. I'll make sure she's taken care of. We'll do the best we can."

With that he peeled off, walked back and put his arm across

the old lady's shoulders and began to speak to her in a comforting tone I couldn't quite make out. She smiled at him like he was her favorite grandson. All her combativeness from earlier had evaporated into the humidity and she was walking strong. I stood helplessly and watched him lead her and her little dog to the church.

Jourdan looked at me and gave a shrug. I knew how he felt. I didn't like standing around feeling useless. I suggested he help folks fill the sandbags if he was bored and he seemed happy to have something productive to do. He clapped me on the shoulder and went over to do just that.

The volunteer firefighters were there helping out and it looked like a command center of sorts at the church under the live oaks dripping Spanish moss, which was probably because the local fire department was now under water on St. Paul's Highway as we moved away from Satsuma Grove and toward the city of Walker. Their walkie talkies cackling on and off like an exotic breed of bird. Another Black Hawk helicopter flew relatively low overhead and no one could hear anything until they flew by. Each time I saw one, it made me feel a little relieved and that maybe we hadn't been completely forgotten by the outside world.

The whole scene was being filmed by one of the Baton Rouge TV news affiliates. Dawn Danielsen, who used to be a fresh-faced college kid when she first started doing news in the area about twenty-five years ago, was staring intently into the camera talking about the flood victims. She didn't look so pert today in the wilting heat. It looked like she might be wearing a blonde wig. Her caked on makeup was already running down her face in rivulets. It almost looked like her face was melting, but she was still pretty as ever to me. She was about to interview one of the firemen who stood to her right shoulder waiting self-consciously for the first question as the camera man adjusted a bright white light attached to his camera.

I had to clamber back into the boat, pick my way carefully among bags and other items while keeping my balance, and find the walkie talkie. I kept calling Lynette but she didn't answer. I wondered if maybe the batteries were used up. I sure hoped she was okay and wasn't having any issues. As long as the generator was working she'd be cool. She knew how to gas it up. She'd been having so many health problems the last few years I couldn't keep up with them anymore. One day it was endometriosis and then she'd be okay for a couple of months, only to be followed up by a painful bout with her rheumatoid arthritis or "Arthur" as she called it, like it was a person who had come to conduct an especially painful visit that even Vicodin and her other *dop-o-roids* didn't seem to touch. Her knuckles had become bulbous knobs of pain with no relief in sight. That was the frustrating thing, you went from Tylenol straight to Opioids. There wasn't anything in the middle for relieving pain. Opioids never did nothing for me or Lynette anyway. Her doctor laughed at me when I suggested marijuana.

I kept hoping they'd make weed legal but some of the religious nuts believed Jesus didn't approve of pain management. I wish to God He would have let his son smoke a little doobie in the Garden of Gethsemane or maybe when he came out of the tomb and showed himself before he ascended to heaven, just once, so people had an alternative. Then Luke could have written about it in his book or in Acts, "Jesus said it was cool, man." Talk about your good news!

Back when she was feeling herself, we would travel around to festivals all across Louisiana when I wasn't on the road. One of our favorites was Tab Benoits's "Voice of the Wetlands" down in Houma—Cajun country! She loved his song *Shelter Me*. Lord, it seemed appropriate now given our current situation.

That first time we went Tab even came right up to where we sat in our lawn chairs,wearing his dark sunglasses out in the street that hot afternoon in front of the stage with a local group singing and playing traditional Cajun music! It was a real treat, particularly for Lynette who was always talking about how handsome she thought the Blues guitarist was. Later that night he was on the main stage and he said, *This one's for my friends Lynette and Dixon!* We waved our hands in the air like we were celebrities. *He* broke into *Shelter me*, following it up with *Medicine* and *Darkness*. Lynette got teary-eyed and leaned her head on my shoulder.

I couldn't remember the last time I'd seen her so happy. Driving on the twisting roads out of Houma we saw where a full sugarcane truck flipped over on its side on an unusual curving embankment. The roads along here were curvy and narrow and maybe the driver had just driven off onto the soft ground, there was no shoulder to speak of, and lost control as the weight caused it to tip over like a wooly mammoth on its side. A cop car was already on the scene with a big tow truck and locals trying to lend a hand. Another cop waved us on by. Despite the accident, Lynette was chattering excitedly about returning to the festival next year.

I wasn't too worried about the flood waters because Eden Church Road had never flooded before. Even during the big flood in 1983, Jule said our street stayed dry because it was at 46 feet above sea level I'd read in *The Advocate* years ago. I could imagine her just getting caught up in doing what she could for folks in the neighborhood like pushing her wheelchair into the downsized kitchen I'd remodeled just so she could still cook. She loved baking breads, pastries, brownies, cakes, and pies for our friends and neighbors. She could still walk but standing for long periods was difficult for her. She was not one to sit idly when things needed doing so I decided to put the worry out of my mind for now.

I talked to one of the fireman since he seemed to be sending out other Cajun Navy members out on little missions. He gave me an address of a family to check on who were trapped without food and water and they needed help moving livestock. I didn't know if that meant cattle or sheep or just what exactly. He asked me if I knew about where the place was and I knew the area very well even covered in water. The scary thing for folks was now they didn't have water to drink unless they had plenty of bottled water. There was no longer any electricity and the temperature, humidity, and the water everywhere was beginning to take its toll.

It wasn't long before I talked things over with Jourdan, Genie, and Noah. We were all going to stay the night at the church. I had a firm rule about not bringing strangers back to my house with the kind of shape Lynette was in. Experience had taught me a lesson on being too generous and this was where I drew the line. Jourdan and his daughter seemed like good people, but I had been wrong before. We filled sandbags for the next couple of hours in the hopes of saving the church. Noah helped carry the bags to the perimeter. Every so often he stopped and stared lovestruck after the church hoping for a glimpse of the girl. We were going to be sore tomorrow. I could already feel it in my bad knee from standing too long. As a trucker, my ass was used to sitting for hours and hours but standing and bending like this was another thing entirely.

Genie gravitated toward an elderly lady, a Yat named Rose, who had moved here from New Orleans after Hurricane Katrina caused Baton Rouge to double in size almost overnight. It was a hard blow to people who had already been through something so devastating and believed they were safe here being some eighty-ninety miles from New Orleans. Genie's dog seemed to put up with the old lady's little dog, but she had to keep a firm grip on its leash since it seemed to hate miscellaneous dogs though it loved people. The dog seemed very agitated and Jourdan chalked it up to the dog's breed.

Later that night, I tried Lynette on the walkie talkie but again there was no answer. I gave up after 15 minutes of attempting to contact her. I took out my old emergency flip phone and sent her a text, something I rarely did just on the off chance it would be delivered and she might text back an answer. I still couldn't make a phone call with my cell phone. It was frustrating to say the least. I told myself she was probably okay and I was just being a worrier. She once scolded me by saying, "It's hard to look sincere with a cell phone in your hand." She was right too.

Genie slept in the church on a cot next to Rose but the church was filled to capacity. Pastor Rob had a generator so they were able to run lights and air to make it possible to sleep for those who were lucky enough to have a pallet on the floor of the church. It was a great relief for all. Even I walked into the church and stood in front of one of the AC vents in the fellowship hall for a few minutes and gulped down a bottle of Ozarka water. Pastor Rob handed over a blue nylon tent to erect out on the lawn. Jourdan and Noah helped me put the tent up after much discussion. It was nice to sleep in the tent since it kept the mosquitoes from eating us but even with the mesh windows open, the August heat made it almost impossible for me to fall asleep soundly. I knew I'd pay a price for sleeping on the ground, but it couldn't be helped since I hadn't learned to hang from tree limbs and rafters like a bat. I managed to rest my eyes and body for a few hours.

## VARNADO

Varnado had been off his bipolar meds for almost six weeks now. He knew he didn't need those antipsychotics anymore! The doctors just wanted to drug you up for the kickbacks from the pharmaceutical companies. Besides, he felt fine. Meth worked much better than any prescription, as far as he could tell. There would probably be a study on it from the Mayo Clinic eventually. He unwrapped a carefully folded bit of aluminum foil and ate some of the shrooms he'd been saving for a special occasion and then folded what was left back into a little square to squirrel away in his breast pocket before Daryl caught him. He didn't like to share.

He was glad to finally get shut of that crazy bitch, Heaven. Her name should have been Devilwoman instead because all she ever did was lie and hold out on him. He and Daryl were going to get rich now that this flood had come along. The cops would be busy with flood emergencies. They couldn't watch everything and everyone in Livingston parish twenty-four seven.

Their plan was to gather up as much shit as they could and put it all in the pole barn on Daryl's daddy's land. He was all crippled up with rheumatoid arthritis and kidney problems. He was about two doors down from death to hear Daryl tell it. The old man never even left the house except when Daryl rode him to the store each week or took him to his doctor. They had already fenced anything of value that belonged to the old man, from tractors, to the old brush hog, tools, and even the ATV and four wheelers he had. Hell, they had even sold the last of the firewood the old man had cut himself on the back end of his sixty acres. Daryl even laughed that his daddy might freeze in the winter now.

Varnado had been best friends with Daryl since fifth grade at South Side Elementary. Daryl was a new kid from San Jose, California, and a little bigger than most of the other kids like maybe he had failed a grade. Back then his long hair had been blond and his skin was tanned. At first glance, he looked like one of the rich kids but he had a street smart way about him that made him different from the rednecks despite the same crappy Rustler jeans. He pushed other boys around and Varnado was quick to buddy up to him. Not so much because he was afraid of him, but he was drawn to the boy's blue eyes and quiet confidence.

By the time they were ninth graders, Varnado found himself gazing at Daryl when he wasn't looking at lunch while he ate his Reuben sandwiches wrapped in aluminum foil. He noticed his tan skin tone was just about perfect. His lips were full and red and even though he had crooked teeth he kind of had this snarl when he smiled that made him look like a badass drug dealer in a movie. He got a fluttering feeling when he looked at his friend; he felt excited and ashamed all at once. He knew he could never tell anyone, least of all Daryl, since he knew his friend well enough to know he would beat his ass for sure so all he could do was act more brave, wilder even, than he actually was to fit in. He would do anything on a dare to keep from being called chicken-shit.

"I ain't no coward!"

He shouted this to the boys watching as he jumped from one building rooftop to the next of the ancient buildings downtown or what passed for "downtown" in Satsuma Grove. They called it "the antique district" but really most of them were just old junk stores that had once been thriving businesses: the old theater, drugstore, hardware store, jewelry store, and others. Now they sold all kinds of crap from old chifforobes, used appliances, and clothing so old they called it "vintage" and hocked grandma jewelry. The past was for sale, at a price. He always thought Satsuma Grove was a funny name for a town uglier than shit with all the run down strip malls everywhere. They would never set a movie here unless it was post apocalyptic. The roads were about to fall apart with giant ruts and potholes from the rains that made your vehicle ride rough as hell but people here loved their festival life. They told themselves Louisiana was the greatest place on planet earth. *I couldn't imagine living anyplace else. I mean, the food alone!* This is what natives said. They distracted themselves with all the festivals, parades, Churchgoing, Mardi Gras beads, and LSU football. Varnado kept dreaming about leaving but he couldn't decide where to go. Maybe it was a lack of imagination. It was troubling since he couldn't seem to project himself somewhere else in the world. How would he talk Daryl into going somewhere with him? There had to be something better.

Even now he had to admit that everything he did was for Daryl's approval. The flame tattoo he had on his neck was to impress Daryl with his coolness. Daryl was still a mystery to him. He didn't talk much or *show his hand* as they said on cop shows. It was like Daryl had a secret and Varnado was fascinated by the mystery. He felt Daryl would open up and show him this secret one day but the drugs and thefts had changed them both. Daryl pounded oxycontin. They weren't kids anymore. They had both spent time in juvie. Varnado had been arrested a few times and did time in lockup for DUI. After all these years, he still felt himself watching Daryl and he was terrified that his friend might already know his secret.

The irony of it all was that Varnado was a respected name about town and across the parish. As a family, they owned all kinds of businesses. Some Varnados sat on school boards and the Chamber of Commerce in Denham Springs, Central, Greenwell Springs, Livingston, Watson, Walker, Zachary, and as far north St. Francisville. The Varnados generally contributed to society but the young man with the flame tattoo was an anomaly to the rest of his clan and to himself for that matter. He was a throwback to some ancient French *Fantomas* strain of Varnado or *Vernadeau* as they were known in *la France profund*.

As he turned onto Florida Avenue, he lost control of his truck and plowed into a hydroplaning white van with the name "Lungcare" stenciled on its side. The van had been hauling ass and careened like a pinball from the truck to a light post due to the angle of impact across the aqueous highway. It all happened so suddenly Varnado didn't know what to think. He sat there for a minute and revved the engine. He pulled slowly up to the driver's side.

"Ask that silly son-of-a-bitch what he was doing!" Varnado

directed Daryl. "Ought to get out and kick his ass!"

"Oh shit," Daryl said.

"What shit? What?" Varnado asked, he was jittery and terrified.

"Dude is dead as hell!" Daryl said. "His face is bloody. Probably hit his head. Maybe pull up in Albertsons' parking lot and I'll take a closer look. Maybe he's still alive."

"What? Are you crazy?"

"What?" Daryl asked. "Take a look at him for yourself."

"You think we should wait for the cops? Because we had an accident? We got all this stolen shit and drugs and you want to be a good Samaritan and talk to a cop. Well, fuck that!"

"Oh yeah!" Daryl turned and a dumb smile spread across his face. "Sorry man. I'm a little high."

"Jesus!" Varnado pulled back onto Florida Avenue and nearly avoided side-swiping a little Cooper car as he did so. "I ain't going to jail for you."

That tickled the shit out of Daryl and he started giggling in that high pitch giggle he couldn't control when he really started laughing about something. It was a disturbing sound coming out of a big guy.

"Shut the hell up!" Varnado yelled. "Stop it! You're freaking me out!"

Daryl kept laughing until Varnado could no longer hold onto his anger and joined in with him.

They parked behind a Popeyes where the parking lot was higher than the flooded street and unloaded the boat into the mudmilk water as Daryl semaphored to Varnado as he backed into a parking space. They could practically unload it anywhere, no need for an actual boat ramp, and just buzz up and down the flooded Highway 16 or use Florida Avenue as a thoroughfare. The truck would hopefully be high and dry there. They would get off on the other side of Denham Springs, but not nearly as far as East Baton Rouge parish. Daryl worked the whole time unhitching the boat with a cigarette burning in the corner of his mouth as he squinted his eyes against the stinging smoke, a spare rollie tucked behind his ear.

Daryl got into the truck and sat opposite Varnado in the

passenger seat. Daryl checked his cell phone for the sixth time, but it still didn't work. Old habits didn't die. Varnado checked his phone again too but fared no better. Daryl tossed his cell out into the water, underhanded, like an offering.

He said, "So much for that shit. This life on the wild bayou now."

"Damn! That's hot work. Gotta rest for a minute," Varnado said as he rummaged through the glove compartment and found a stack of Subway napkins. He used two of the napkins to wipe the sheen of sweat from his forehead. He put on a pair of Ray-Ban knockoffs with dark red lenses he found beneath the zipped case holding the owner's manual. His eyes indistinct black dots behind the red veneer. Now the world bore a scarlet cast. Varnado reached back behind the seat where he had a cooler of beer and fished a can out of the lukewarm water for Daryl. "Coors Banquet?"

"Damn straight," Daryl said. "That's hella good shit."

Varnado slammed his phone into the middle console. "This fucken thing is worthless."

Daryl popped open his beer and took a big swig and said *yaaahhhs* and suddenly looked at him sideways, "What?"

Varnado shook his head, "What-what?"

"Why you looking at me like that?" Daryl said.

"I wasn't!" Varnado's faced turned as red as his sunglasses for a second, so he looked out the window. "I mean . . . how was I looking?"

"Like you was going to say something. I dunno."

"Where's my beer, Daryl?"

"Get it yourself, nephew! I look like your bitch?"

"Bro please! Why you always giving me so much static? I was just going to say, we're going to fuck shit up now, son! You wouldn't believe me now if I told you what I see." Varnado bopped Daryl in the chest with the back of his hand. He grabbed a Coors out of the cooler for himself, knocked what remained of the unmelted ice off into the floorboard, the can hissed as he opened it. He chugged half the can. The sky had turned a hazy red behind his shades and clouds streaked around like crimson meteorites in his peripheral vision. He wouldn't be surprised if he saw pink unicorns flying around now. The shrooms were doing their thing. The clouds overhead began to vibrate and the water started to sing a song unlike anything he had ever heard even on Sirius radio.

"Won't be long." Daryl agreed. "We gonna have more shit, money, chicks than we know what to do with."

Varnado smiled revealing his gold tooth, "Poor sons-a-bitches ain't gonna know what hit them."

"All right, let's hit it!" Daryl got back out of the truck. He carried two ten gallon cans of gas, the color of fire, from the bed of the truck and wrangled them back into the built-in fuel compartment.

Over the past day-and-a-half the pair had been on the lookout to steal anything of value they could fence for meth. They weren't just going to do meth; they were going to sell the shit too. The floor of the boat was half-filled with copper piping, construction tools, even several feet of aluminum guardrail from a concrete bridge. They were seeing dollar signs in everything that was easy to grab or was floating on the surface of the water. Whenever they saw someone alone who they thought would be an easy victim they exchanged savage smiles.

Migrant clouds grew like purple mushrooms majesty in the sky. Mother Nature could be a real bitch. Varnado noticed that even the ditchbirds had disappeared. Egrets and herons had more sense than people, he thought. A flock of white herons flew out of a water-pocked field like gawky, adolescent angels as their boat buzzed past.

A woman in her thirties wearing large maroon-framed glasses was walking alone between houses with a black purse held high over her head to keep it out of the foul water. Her dark hair was slicked down on her head from the water like she had fallen head-first as she made her way through the murky streets. As soon as Varnado saw the woman with her purse he grinned at Daryl and scratched at the flame tattoo on his neck. It was a nervous tic he had picked up. His whole body itched. He wondered what the woman had looked like ten years earlier. She had probably been one fine piece of ass back then, he mused. The wet fabric of her blouse caused her hard nipples to poke through her blouse.

"Let's help this poor woman!" Varnado called to Daryl who did as he was bidden. "Hello there, Ma'am! Where you headed?"

"Oh hello," the woman answered uncertainly pushing up her glasses that kept falling down the bridge of her nose. "I'm heading to my sister's house in that neighborhood over behind the antique district. My house took on several feet of water. Power's out. I was hoping I wouldn't have to walk all the way there in this."

"That's an awful long way. We would be glad to ride you over there! It's nice and dry up here beside me." Varnado couldn't help making suggestive facial expressions with his eyebrows. He looked back at Daryl who snickered and put his forehead down so it touched his own forearm so as not to give away their true intentions, but it was too late. Varnado's brain was frying in the heat like scrambled eggs while he watched for the woman's reaction. There was a loud radio static fuzz in his ears that made listening to anything else a challenge.

"Oh, that's okay," the woman said. The shadow of a black cross fell sideways across her face causing Varnado to shove his fingers in his eyes to remove the image but it was still there when he looked again. She was already walking at an angle away from them but the water was suddenly up to her neck as she took this little detour off the street and into the yard of an Acadian style home. She gasped as the water lapped against her face. "I'm okay but thanks for offering." Her face suddenly looked stricken and pale and her eyes grew even larger behind her lenses with visible droplets of water.

"No, really!" Daryl said. "Come on with us. It's no trouble." But there was an ominous tone to his words. "What's your name? Hey, I think I know you! Weren't you a cashier at Canes?"

"Yeah," Varnado snapped his fingers. "I think I know you too. You ever go to Double D Daiquiris? C'mere a minute."

"No no," the woman shook her head. "I'm a Baptist. I go to church. I don't even drink no more." Varnado noticed the woman had two little nubs extending out of her forehead like a junior devil all screwy wormwood.

Varnado's head was on a swivel as he looked about to see if anyone else was about to witness their exchange, "Well now! Ain't you so very proper and special! Too good to take a free ride with us?" He turned his head back to Daryl and murmured something that the woman couldn't hear. This was the first demon he had seen today, and a female one at that!

"I ain't saying that," she said. "I just don't need any help is all. This disaster has taken just about everything from me and everyone else. I just want to get to my sister's place. I'll be fine . . . please." But she didn't continue with what she was saying please about.

Daryl guided the boat right alongside the woman who still held her purse aloft. She couldn't get away from the boat fast enough and they were on top of her now. She grimaced with fear and looked as if she might start screaming. Varnado wondered how he could have ever thought this fat cow had ever been hot. Her fear angered him. The buzzing in his ears grew like a chorus of cicadas. The heat was driving him crazy. His bloody vision grew hazy as he decided what might be done with this she-devil.

"Let me help you with your heavy load here," Daryl said. He reached out with his free left hand and grabbed hold of the strap of her purse. "I'll just take this from you and put it right here in the boat. High and dry. Then, we'll get you in the boat too. All safe and sound."

"No!" She yelled at them but she couldn't keep a good grip on her purse with the water so high. "This is my purse. It's all I've got left." She had sixty-seven dollars in cash, her credit cards, and pictures of her kids in the purse. She pulled back on her purse with all she was worth but Daryl kept yanking on the strap and started laughing like it was a game. She screamed as loud as she could, fearful and defiant, but there was no one around to hear her brave enough to come out and get involved.

"Give it to me, baby," Daryl laughed, "you're a strong one now, ain't you? Calm down and take my hand."

"Telling a woman to calm down," Varnado laughed, "works about as good as baptizing a cat."

"It's all I've got!" She spat water. "Let go, please! I've got kids! Don't hurt me!" She rose up out of the water a little and let out another scream that made the hairs on the back of Varnado's neck stand up. Her mouth was open wide and a fiery red devil's tongue stabbed toward him in midair like a cottonmouth with its big fangs. She had to shut that shit up. He could feel the adrenaline pumping in his veins. A shotgun blast went off deep down in his soul and he was changed in the twinkling of an eye.

While they struggled over the purse, Varnado had picked up

Daren Dean

the oar out of the bottom of the boat. Neither the woman or Daryl were paying much attention to him as he made his way back to Daryl and the woman, keeping himself nice and balanced. He jabbed the oar at the woman and bumped her shoulder with it. She licked at the oar with her forked tongue in a threatening, lascivious manner. The beast gasped with pain but still wouldn't turn loose the prize. Daryl was beginning to lose his composure since he found the situation to be beyond hilarious and it seemed to Varnado that Daryl was weeping like an hysterical angel. The woman had no chance of holding on to her booty although she was fighting like a wildcat. The oar suddenly came down from behind Daryl with a sickening force on top of the woman's head. She cried out, a guttural noise of pain and horror. A crimson mask of blood descended down her forehead and face and licked one of her lenses. She closed her eyes against the blood before she disappeared beneath the surface of the water.

"What the fuck is wrong with you, Varnado?" He slung the purse into the bottom of the boat like some strange breed of fish where it clunked like a brick was in it. "Are you trippin right now, motherfucker?"

"It looked like she was about to drag you into the water with her snake tongue from where I sit," Varnado said. "I probably just—"

"Her what? Ain't you going to try to save—"

The woman suddenly emerged from the water with her hands thrust heavenward in a gesture of supplication. "Help me!" She cried out with what little energy she had left. "I'm drowning! Help me! Please!"

Varnado turned back toward the woman with a mixture of horror and a little fear managed to find its way between the chinks of his drug-induced armor. "Grab onto this oar!" He held the oar out to the struggling woman who appeared to be in slightly deeper water now as the current pushed them along. Just before the woman could grab the oar, he raised it up again in a motion like cutting firewood and whacked her decisively on top of the head again with the edge. She submerged for the second, and last time. Her body did not come back up.

"Oops Varnado," laughed, "my bad."

"Jesus!" Daryl said. "You just murdered that woman! What

the hell did you do that for?"

"Shut up, Daryl!" Varnado said. "Just shut up! Let me think! I got scared when she started bleeding and dying and screaming and everything! I had to kill the beast! The whore of Bablyon!"

"Jesus H. Christ, Varnado!" Daryl looked at Varnado with amazement. "We done lots of things before b—"

"Oh shut up you goddamn crybaby!" Varnado said. "Just get us the hell out of here before somebody sees us!"

"What are you on, man? You need to calm the fuck down. Sit down over there before you fall out of the boat. Ya crazy mother-fucker!"

Varnado stared coldly at him behind his bloody shades.

"Don't look at me like that!" Daryl said. "If you were an Indian, your Indian name would be Crazy Ass!"

Varnado didn't laugh but he did crack a smile, "Well, call me Chief Crazy Ass then!" He pulled out the .38 he had tucked in his waist band at the small of his back and waved it around casually for emphasis.

Daryl revved up the boat and off they went making a little loop and heading out of town. He didn't even know where he was going or why he was going there. A terrible fear gnawed at his gut. He had never known Varnado to be violent—not like this. The image of the oar coming down on the woman's head and cracking her skull open kept replaying in his mind. The water oily with blood and gore. What if someone had seen them? What if they got into trouble and were arrested? He didn't want to go back to jail. They might send him to the Angola for this.

Varnado snatched up the purse to see what the woman had protected so fiercely. He was a little surprised at himself but the woman shouldn't have fought them. She was just a woman. A pow-erful feeling of love for the woman welled up within him. Everything would have been okay if she had just given up her purse. It seemed perfectly reasonable that they could have lived a good life together. When he opened the mouth of the purse, it barked at him like a coyote. There wasn't much in it but a little cash, Burt's Bees, Juicy Fruit, generic tampons, mace on a key chain, some loose change, and other random items. He found a North Carolina drivers license and saw that her name was Crystal. There was a picture of the woman (only she seemed younger, more attractive, than when she was in the water) with a big-beefy red-headed man, probably her husband, with a handle-bar mustache, and two little tow-headed kids. They had likely taken the portrait at Sears in Cortana, or what everyone called *The Ghetto Mall.*

He flicked the family portrait into the water and watched as it curled and floated away. This was what that dumb bitch wanted to die over? Suddenly, he felt she had betrayed their love and he began to weep. He offered to share the cash with Daryl who held up his hand and shook his head no.

"I don't want no part of that!" Daryl shouted. "That's bad juju right there!"

Varnado shoved the cash into the front pocket of his jeans and flung the purse out into the deep water.

## DIXON

My back was killing me after a night sleeping on the ground in the tent outside the church camp. It took me awhile to get up after rolling over onto all fours like a bear. I blinked away the tears as I forced myself to my feet with a groan. It felt like a serial killer was stabbing me in the lower back with an ice pick. I took a couple of Aleve with my coffee. I turned on the Cobra Walkie Talkie and tried Lynette again. Nothing. It probably needed fresh batteries. I knew she would be very worried by now. I promised myself to go back home come afternoon.

There was already a breakfast line leading into the modest little church. I was beginning to think of it as The Island Church in my head. There was a choice between a vat of oatmeal, grits, small hard biscuits with white or tomato gravy, and some modest looking examples of sausage links and cheap eggs but even with extra pepper they didn't have much taste. I ate mine with Louisiana Hot Sauce and toast that gave them a much-needed kick.

After preparing the boat and stocking up on new provisions from Pastor Rob we were finally ready to get back out there. The fire-fighters had supplied us with gas much to my surprise. I was hoping we could help a few more people out before nightfall. The humidity was even higher now if anything.

Noah took a selfie with Genie and murmured something to her. I could tell they were thinking about kissing each other but Jourdan gave him the stern father look and the lovebirds restrained themselves and slowly separated. I told Noah to try calling Lynette on his cell phone to my house landline. There was no response. I even tried her cell phone but she only used it for "emergencies" and that meant she only turned it on when she wanted to make a call. We were on the same plan so it probably didn't work anyway but I felt like I had to try everything.

"Here's an idea. Why don't you ask the fire chief to check on Ms. Lynette?" Noah asked. His mama was able to text him somehow so at least she knew he was okay. I probably shouldn't have kept him overnight this way but he was old enough. He was probably used to hanging out late in the French Quarter most of the night.

"Nah," I told him. "We'll get back by this afternoon."

It was a good question but I didn't want them to waste their time in case it was a false alarm. There were so many people begging for real, legitimate help. I didn't want to be another drain on the work these men were doing so I said nothing. The truth was I hated to ask anyone for anything. I just wasn't built that way.

Under the awning of the church, an elderly woman in a lavender pantsuit said to an unimpressed white-haired lady with a discernible mustache, "I never heard the weatherman say nothing about flooding or that we should evacuate. Why didn't anyone warn us?"

I clambered back onto the Blue Betty II and Jourdan and Noah gave the boat a heave back into the bracken. The boat engine growled back to life. We did a big U-Turn and I gave everyone a wave as we sped back in the direction from where we had come. A lot of kids and older folks cheered like we were putting on a show. A shelf of water flashed into the sky and reflected a stunning rainbow as we cut the water. I looked back as we drove away at the little church on an island. If there is a God, that had to be his work.

We sped through a snaking two lane road just under the I-12 overpass where I saw an elderly man with iron gray hair walking in water up to his waist leading an appaloosa horse by a lead rope. He seemed burdened by a magisterial sadness. The horse pulled a rowboat. A young boy with a crewcut walked on the other side of the horse with a grim-faced adult expression. The water was up to the boy's chest. I wondered why the old man with the craggy face didn't keep the boy out of that nasty water and put him up in the boat and out of harm's way. It was hard telling what was in the water, everything from snakes to chemicals, and raw sewage. Maybe the boy didn't want to ride in the boat, there was that, but it didn't seem responsible on the old man's part.

Behind the boat, what had really grabbed my attention, was what looked like a shiny silver coffin with chrome decorating the lid. The coffin had likely been dredged out of the ground due to the flood and was now tethered by a length of rope to the boat. I'm sure it was a relative and I hoped, for the old man's sake, it wasn't his wife though that seemed most likely. I had the strangest feeling of déjà vu but I didn't know what it signified. I guess it made me think of Lynette and how I couldn't reach her and was afraid to think what it could mean. My eyes teared up on me unexpectedly. I wiped them away so Jourdan and Noah wouldn't see. I hadn't so much as sniffled in years. The old man leading the horse from under a full head of iron gray hair never even glanced our way as we sped on. His flinty, expressionless face said it all.

About that time I saw a billboard on the side of Range for an urgent care clinic that made me laugh despite myself. It was a young woman with a thought bubble over her head and she's thinking, *I think I will get sick now.* I assumed there was some context I was missing but alone like that on the billboard, it really didn't make sense. Looking around at all of this flooding, I couldn't have agreed more.

The address the fireman sent us to was on the other side of town near a KOA campground, the old cemetery, the big city park, a Walmart, a Dollar General, a Voodoo Daddy's, a couple of ancient flooded strip malls, and well-beyond the high school that visitors often remarked upon, saying it looked like a penitentiary a mile outside of town. There were big houses on River Road that were flooded out but those were rich people with tons of insurance and money to burn but it was still sad to see. The further we went, the deeper the water seemed to get or maybe the lack of landmarks to compare things to made it look that way. It was all underwater like the place had been reclaimed by old Poseidon himself.

I felt better with the crew I had working with me now that the girl and her dog were being taken care of by Pastor Rob. Jourdan wasn't saying much but at least I knew he spoke English. For his part, Noah was a little blue now that his lady love was ashore but I couldn't entirely blame him for that. He'd be more focused now, more of a help. He was busy now swatting some free-loading fire ants off the boat with an old t-shirt.

What we were doing was dangerous work but I knew it was the right thing to do at the same time. I tried to put the dangers out of my mind. I had seen just about everything over the years but I just wanted to do what I could and then get back to Lynette by dark.

A sign in front of a two-story house made from a sheet of drywall with red spray paint warned ominously: *LOOTERS WILL BE SHOT ON SITE!* Some people weren't too big on spelling or they were literalists. Much of the land north of us hadn't ever flooded like this in Satsuma Grove but points south of the interstate were much lower and it was more common. As a result, most folks I knew didn't have flood insurance. Why would you pay extra if you weren't in a flood zone but the simple answer I came to later on my own was simply because this is Louisiana. After this disaster was in the history books, the insurance offices would be locked up tighter than Fort Knox out of fear of their own policy holders when they found reasons, technicalities in the fine print, not to make good on their near worthless policies.

I looked at the address again on the little piece of white paper. It was still 13105 Lake Pointe Drive but we'd been going in circles trying to find it. First of all, there wasn't a lake anywhere nearby that I knew about. There was supposed to be an elderly couple stuck in their attic but the water didn't appear deep enough here though that could easily change with the topography of the land. We came to a subdivision on dry land and let Jourdan out. He would try hoofing it a few blocks over to see if he could find the house and we would come back in 15-20 minutes. Not too far from where we let him out a country girl of about fourteen in a cowboy hat, riding a white, Arabian mix over a kind of natural levee. She gave us a curt little nod that said she didn't need any help, thank you very much, she was on a mission. I gave her a little salute and wished her the best of luck on her mission in my head.

We hadn't gone far when we came to a stretch of road near a church where a long line of traffic sat like a car lot with people in their cars or out milling around. We came at the road from the East where there were maybe a dozen or so people out of their vehicles staring at a sight I will not soon forgot. A man lay atop the cab of a half-submerged pickup truck holding on for dear life. It looked like a savage embrace as much as a handhold. He was in a strong current of white water pelted him in the face. It looked like he was being waterboarded. He must have driven too far down the road and misjudged the depth or the current because the road was now dissected by water but dry at both ends.

Noah tapped me on the shoulder and pointed. An alligator, maybe eleven or twelve feet in length in my judgment, was sitting on a hunk of concrete, twisted rebar, and a veritable bonfire of castaway trees. The creature's head was enormous and he appeared to be well aware of the man on the truck. Perhaps he was biding his time or just resting. We had seen a lot of displaced wildlife, but this was the first alligator I had seen though it was not unheard of to see them in the area during hurricanes and floods. We had already seen more snakes than I wanted to think about.

I motored over to the road, as close as I dared to get, to see if we could ascertain what was happening with the man on the truck.

"He lost control of his truck," said a fat man with a Confederate flag t-shirt who waved his fancy cell phone around. "I saw it all. He had a load of cattle with big-ass horns. The whole damn rig went belly up and we never saw them again. Probably got swept away."

"Jesus will help him, uh huh!" A tiny black woman, a good church lady, wearing an obvious wig on her head aired her thoughts on the matter. It was more hat than wig from where I sat. "That what Miss Eunice say! Praise his name!" She held her hands palms up, heavenward.

"Is someone coming to save him?" I hollered toward the crowd.

"Jesus will!" The church lady said. She threw a fist in the air to punctuate her statement. She started dancing in a circle like she was doing a rain dance and raising-the-roof at the same time.

"We ain't in church now!" A white woman's voice answered her call from the opposite side of the road.

Miss Eunice spun around, "Who said that? Don't you blaspheme now! Why, look at ya! You ain't nothing but *boosie* your ownself! The Lord in church, and He out here too!"

"You're ratchet!" The other woman clapped back but I couldn't tell who had said it.

Everyone ignored her comments anyway. She seemed slightly touched. No one knew who she was affiliated with though there was a nursing home not far away she might have escaped from. She knew how to dress though, I'll give her that. She had a kind of purple dress getup with a big purple hat she flopped on top of her ill-fitting wig.

"I called 911, but with all this water nobody could get near enough. There's been a National Guard helicopter circling around in the area. Maybe they're going to try to airlift him. The problem is all the trees in the area. They will really have to thread the needle."

"Think we should risk it?" I asked Noah.

Noah nodded but his face looked a little green.

"If we get swept past him, it looks like we'd end up in those rapids down in the river below," I said more to myself than Noah.

The group of bystanders gasped.

"Oh Lord Jesus!" Miss Eunice hollered.

"What happened?" Noah shouted at me.

"The alligator moved toward him!" A black man in aviators and a military uniform hollered at us. "See if you can get close to him!"

"Oh boy," I said. "We're going to have to do something quick. Even if the gator don't get him, he won't be able to hang on much longer."

Another man's voice on the street carried over the water as he proferred useless advice to his young son, "Now, a gator is just as scared of you as you are of him."

"Help!" The man called weakly out of the side of his mouth like a swimmer as the water gushed over him like he was a bronze figure in a fountain.

It was frustrating to be so close to him but unable to really do anything useful to help him. None of the onlookers were trained to do anything like this.

"Let's give it a try," Noah said. "We got to try, don't we?"

"I'm going to take us over there," I pointed to the water between the truck and the road. If we miss him, with any luck, we'll end up in that standing water over there and out of the current."

"Where?" Noah asked.

"On the other side of the road, parallel to it," I pointed again.

Noah nodded.

"The only problem is when we first pull up were going into the current and we're going to bump the truck. We might dislodge the truck and then we'll have made everything worse. It's awfully dangerous for him. He might end up in the Amite."

"We got to try," Noah repeated. He picked up a rope and I showed him how to make a slip knot right quick before handing it back.

"Try to get this out to him when we get close."

"Don't do it!" A woman screamed.

"They've gotta save that man!" Another woman's voice hollered back like she was having a conversation at the top of her voice.

I tried to maneuver between the road and where the truck was hung up. Just as predicted the current banged us into the truck and it moved. I was afraid the truck might become dislodged. The man hollered and his hands slipped a little but he held on. The gator turned his big head toward us. His mouth opened like he was saying hey! I put Noah on the tiller. I grabbed the rope from Noah. I tried to get the man to grab it when I threw it. He tried blindly reaching his hand out to grab the loop but between the water coming over the top of the truck and his weakened state it was obviously not going to work. If we had come upon him a little earlier it might have worked. And if I were a younger man I might jump from my boat onto the truck but I might have ended up in the water too.

"What's your name?" I yelled.

"Cody!"

I couldn't understand his last name.

"Cody!" I said. "Try to grab onto this rope!"

"Trying!" He said. "Tell my daughter I love her if I don't make it. Can't hold on much longer."

"She knows! We'll get you," I said but just then the motor started sputtering. I looked back and for some reason, just inexperience I reckon, Noah had the rotor out of the water. Or maybe something had slammed into it. I wasn't sure which, but now our boat was moving partially in the current and toward the big gator who looked like he might pounce.

"Get it back down in the water!" I hollered at Noah.

He nodded in response but he was struggling with it.

The alligator bit the air and I could hear his mouth snapping open and shut like he was going to chew one of us up. As the boat spun in the water we had to hold on for dear like we were on a carnival ride and the side of the boat rammed into the refuse pile and I swear I was just a couple of feet from the big boy's chompers.

Now we floated harmlessly along the near side of the road and in the shallows. I was sorry not to make it to the man but relieved we hadn't gone over the edge and down below into the Amite.

"I'm sorry, Mr. Dixon!" Noah said. "Something slammed into the engine or the blade. Killed it. That's why I yanked it up but then I couldn't get it back down."

"It's all right," I said. "Let's try another pass. We'll change places. I'll drive and you can throw the rope to him this time. First, see if you can restart her."

Just as we were reconnoitering the situation the sound of a Black Hawk helicopter came out of nowhere going *swoosh, swoosh, swoosh* overhead. It was beginning to hover above the tree line as it began to descend neatly between trees and power lines. The tree branches were whipped violently by the wind shear from the helicopter's blades. The side door was open and a guardsman was hanging out to survey the situation. The wind speed generated from the rotor as the pilot navigated a path between the canopy was strong enough that some of the onlookers held their hands in the air and turned away their faces. We did the same from where we sat in the boat but I tried to watch through my hands.

The guardsman was lowered slow down to the man on the truck. He was lowered a little and raised back up several times like a yo-yo. The pilot seemed to be having difficulty maintaining his position. Finally, the guardsman's boots barely touched the roof of the pickup before he suddenly ascended fifteen feet up and then he was lowered down again. He was yelling something at the man on the truck but the man didn't seem to hear him. One of the cowboy's boots had come off. He looked up at the guardsman on the rope, raised his upper body on one hand and reached his other hand straight into the sky.

At that moment, the white water tore the cowboy off the truck roof and ripped his body into the current of the Amite. We were all shocked because it looked like he was just about to be saved.

Seconds later, the alligator whipped his impressive body around like a bullwhip being cracked and dove into the water after the man and disappeared from sight beneath the surface of the water. The group on the street gasped in a collective expression of sickening disappointment. The helicopter ascended quickly as if to give chase from the air as the guardsman continued to dangle on the line narrowly missing the power lines. The river eventually wound its way toward Frenchtown Conservation Road and combined with the Comite where it passes under 190. The cowboy's body would end up there in the spruce pine hardwood forest unless the alligator found him first.

According to the map a Livingston Parish Deputy Sheriff showed me it was supposed to be around here somewhere but all I could see were individual houses, an occasional mobile home, and a little convenience store with two ancient gas pumps out front. There was a subdivision of which I couldn't see much, it was too far away to be Lake Pointe. I cut the engine. As I did I heard the whine of another engine. It was a fast approaching speedboat that looked expensive but the characters in it didn't look like the original owners.

"I know those guys." Noah said. "They're tweekers."

"Who are they?" I asked.

"It's Heaven's boyfriends. The driver's name is Varnado. I know that much."

"Heaven huh?" We both fell silent as we waited for the boat to hum right up next to us. We had to find out what they wanted.

"Hey there, boys!" The one called Varnado said. He was grinning like a coon with his eyes at halfmast. He was far from what anyone would call sartorial; wearing sunglasses, faded blue jeans, no shirt, and work boots. Now that Noah had said something, I recognized both of these clowns from hanging out several doors down in the rental house with the drug-dealer gal. Her bug eyes were like wildcats with a bad case of poison ivy fighting each other for control of her brain. The rumor in the neighborhood was that the little girl had poisoned Lazy Jeff. I remembered him from well before he had ever hooked up with the methhead chick. He had never been much with the ladies, so he had been proud as a peacock showing her off when she first moved in with him. Lazy Jeff was all right, but a little slow on the uptake.

It would have been hard to miss Varnado. The flame tattoo on his neck and a bloody red heart with feathery green angel wings wrapped in barbed wire on his bare chest.

"What're y'all doing all the way out here?" He talked a little funny but I was familiar. He was holding his mouth in such a way that suggested he had a big wad of Skoal tucked in his lower lip. His body was still wiry and muscular, despite the drugs. He sneered as he looked down on us from the larger boat leaning forward with his elbow resting on his propped up knee.

A young man, about the same age as his partner, appeared at the tattooed one's side scratching a full beard said, "Ya'll need some help?" He exchanged glances with his buddy and they smirked at each other—I did not like those smiles. They were both acting squirrely. Probably high on something, what I guessed.

"Well!" I shouted back with my hands on my hips as their eyes lingered over Noah. "Just with the Cajun Navy trying to find folks for the fire department. They don't have enough boats for flooding like this. We're due to report back now!"

It was clear they weren't out to help anyone. I noted the scrap metal piled in the boat. These boys were up to no good. Selling scrap for cash to buy more drugs with. I didn't much like the way the tattooed one was eye-fucking us the whole time. Noah wasn't experienced enough to know what he was looking at but we were sure missing Jourdan about now. They might have second thoughts if they got a look at the stocky Cajun.

"Just you and the boy?" The tattooed man spat an amber streak into the water.

"My name is Noah!"

It dawned on me just how young Noah was. He talked like an adult sometimes but he almost looked girlish with his smooth-cheeked skin and he hadn't begun to fill out yet either. These two wouldn't pay him much notice at all. It was the two of them against me. I had to figure out a way to keep the boy and myself safe.

"Now ain't that funny with this flood and all!" The tattooed one guffawed. "Maybe you should ask God for help, Noah."

Noah's wide-eyed expression said it all. He looked away from the men and cast his eyes down toward the water as if there was something of interest down there.

My stomach was now a little queasy from nerves. I could feel the anger building inside. I didn't like being threatened. I took a deep breath and my chest puffed out. These guys were sizing us up. What they saw was a kid and a broken down old man. I kept a couple of knives and machetes on board but I no longer carried firearms. I had thought I'd put violence and all of that behind me after Desert Storm and getting myself clean a few years later. If they had met me back then . . . well, let me put it this way, I had about every firearm known to man in the utility room I'd converted to a gunroom. My wife called it the armory back in the day. These boys were younger than I was when I was overseas fighting Saddam.

"What kind of goodies you got in there?" His greedy eyes indicating everything in our boat.

"Goodies—?" I asked.

"You got any cash?"

"Not for you, I don't." I reached down and pulled out the bigger of the two machetes I kept in the boat for whatever purpose it could serve. I hoped it might prove a deterrent in this situation. I smacked the wide blade against the palm of my hand for emphasis and gave them boys my war face.

"These two look familiar," Varnado said over his shoulder to his partner.

"No," I said. "We don't know you."

"That's because you do know us!" Noah hissed like an accusation. "And we know you! You're Heaven's boys!"

"Heaven's boys?" The big one said. "We don't work for her."

"You believe that shit?" Varnado scoffed. "Me and Daryl here smash that whenever we get the urge. She even pays me for it." He giggled an unnatural sounding hyena laugh as he stole a glance at Daryl.

Daryl shook his head in disbelief, "Heaven's boys! That skank . . . they know us." He looked down at the deck with a grimace, "I'm saying they know who we are! They can identify us. Not like that other one you took care of back there."

The tattooed one had a shocked expression on his face as if he had just been picked out of a police lineup already. He looked guilty and ashamed all in the same moment. If he hadn't been holding a gun, I would have been tempted to laugh. As it was, I wish

Noah had stayed silent. Now that they knew we could identify them, it didn't bode well for us. I stared at Noah so I can tell him to quit talking with my eyes but he continued to stare accusingly at them the way a kid will, self-righteously, when he knows he's absolutely not wrong.

"Oh hey!" Daryl snapped his finger. "I know this old man. He lives down the street from Heaven. He's that trucker lives with that handicapped, old broad! That big blue Kenworth's always parked in the driveway! His wife's always like..." Then he put his hand over his face like he was holding an invisible oxygen mask, breathing hard, clutching at his neck with the other, and acting like he was going to fall down. Then he fell into a fit of laughter. I wanted to choke them both with my own two hands.

Varnado blurted out, "Blue Betty! Oh, hell yeah! That's one nice rig you got!"

"That's a big 10-4!" Daryl punched Varnado's shoulder. "He's that old trucker dude."

No one said anything for about ten seconds. We all just stood there staring at each other. The tattooed one was rubbing his goatee like a pet.

"It might have been better for you if you hadn't knowed us." Varnado shook his head regretfully and sighed heavily. "Because now . . . you're both going to have to disappear."

Now Noah glanced at me for reassurance but it was too late now. Glancing over my shoulder I hoped to see Jourdan coming toward us but just a breeze riffling the surface of the water in our drifting wake. When I turned back around Varnado held a Glock almost casually against his knee.

"What are you looking at back there, bud? Is the Cavalry on its way?"

"No sir," I said.

"Sir!?" Varnado said. His eyes wild with hilarity. "He just sirred me!"

"We don't want to hurt anyone," the bearded one said, he was obviously the more reasonable of the pair. "So you'd better put your shaver away, old man."

I put the blade down but not too far out of reach. "Y'all better just go on then."

"Don't tell us what to do! You ain't in no position to tell us dick, sir!"

"What exactly do you want?" I asked, holding out my hands. There was probably more of value in any of the houses on the street and yet they were going to rob us or murder us. It didn't make sense except that these two were in a drug-haze and hadn't even thought to bust into the abandoned houses full of stuff of those who had escaped the floor or tried to before the flood water made it impossible.

"Why, all of it—of course!" He snickered and I could see his snaggle-toothed grin, missing some teeth though I noticed his one gold tooth. It made him look just like a pirate. A couple of hollow-eyed meth heads who would probably kill us for a pack of cigarettes.

I hated feeling so helpless. I was already rethinking my whole position about getting a gun, maybe I'd get a couple of them, after all of this was over. My hand was tapping against my thigh. I knew I could not allow this, whatever this was, to happen without putting up some kind of fight. Just as the tattooed blond jumped into our boat, Noah walked toward him like he was going to confront him, and then gave Noah a vicious shove so that the boy fell down backwards landing on the floor with his hands outstretched catching hold of one of the passenger chairs with one hand as he landed roughly on the deck. All I could really see of the boy now were his legs, blue and orange tennis shoes, and shock of hair.

"Now let's not get violent," I held up my hands, "I'll give you whatever you want. Just don't hurt the boy."

"You hear that, Daryl?" The blond laughed. "He'll give us whatever we want!" This last bit he said in a mocking tone of voice as though I were terrified of him. "That's fucken hilarious!"

"Listen!" I said putting some military bearing into my voice. "You put that gun down and I'll show you what's funny. Kindly take whatever it is you think you want and then get the hell off my boat."

"Whoa!" The one named Daryl laughed. "Billy Badass here! You better watch out or he'll mean-mouth you to death! Hey! Who's this?" His chin jutting upward.

Just then I saw Jourdan walking up the street toward us. He could tell we had company but he didn't know what was going on. He looked pretty intimidating in his cowboy hat, broad-shoulders and balled up fists but I knew for a fact the only weapon he had on him was the Case knife. Sunlight splintered through the clouds and glinted off the silver cross hanging from a chain on his bare chest.

"Get back!" I turned to shout at Jourdan who began to jog-slog his way through the water toward us. The sound of his movements echoing off the houses on either side of the street. "Get back! They've got guns! Call for help!" I waved at him windmilling my arm in a clockwise circle.

Jourdan stopped and his weight shifted onto his back foot. Just as I turned, Varnado had managed to close the gap between us and pistol-whipped me across the face. I went down hard on my bad knee. I looked up and I could see the heart of Christ on his chest close-up now with a red hot flame blowing out of the heart's upper chamber. Varnado grinned down at me now and it looked like something had died in his mouth. He spat another stream of bug juice but this time on my hand as I attempted to regain my feet.

"Have a seat, big man," he motioned to the Captain's chair.

"Take it easy," I said. "Don't do something you'll regret." I wiped the b[B]eechnut on the thigh of my jeans.

"I never do," he haha-ed. "I don't never regret nothing." He extended his arm and I knew exactly what he was thinking about doing. He charged a round and squeezed off a shot in Jourdan's direction but since I was facing away I couldn't see what was happening though my own training said he needed to get a higher grip on the pistol and more of an isosceles stance. He was not someone who was used to handling firearms. "Ya, you better run off, motherfucker!"

"You going to kill this old man?" Daryl asked from the speed boat. "I bet you ain't got the cahonies to do it."

"Is that right?" His eyes bugged out now. Neither of these boys was in their right mind. They were all juiced up. I could see Varnado was the froggy kind who couldn't resist a dare. He raised the business end of the Glock to my head and the look on his face was pretty grim.

*This is how I die,* I thought. *I never dreamed it would end like this.*

"I've got cash," I said to distract him. "Let me give it to you now." I was too far away to make a grab for the gun without getting it right in the face. He only laughed at me. My eyes were tight on his trigger finger. He held the gun parallel to the ground like a gangbanger in a TV cop show.

"I'm going to blow your brain outs…"

"Quit eye-fucking me, son, and just do it already . . ." I whispered quietly like it was my last secret in this world.

*This is it.*

"Put that gun down." It was Noah's trembling voice. Varnado's face blanched for a moment before dissolving slowly into a sickening grin. "Put it down or I'm going to shoot you."

The bearded one made a motion toward the boy.

Noah's voice cracked, "Stay back, Mister! I'd hate to have to shoot you too—don't think I won't. I'm from the 7th Ward in *New OR-lins*," With that pronouncement, he placed his left hand over the right on the handle of the gun from his side to get a better grip. This seemed to make the bearded man take pause. I felt pride for the boy's bravery well up in my heart as if he were my own flesh and blood.

"Look at the way your hand is shaking," the bearded one said. "I don't think you have it in you, kid. You just ain't that tough."

The tattooed man turned toward Noah. It seemed as if I were looking down a long, dark hallway where sound no longer existed; he led with the Glock moving ever so slowly and relentlessly toward the boy. Once I saw his right ear pointing toward me, an ear close to being devoured by a red and yellow flame, I knew what had to be done. But before I could do anything, I saw Noah point the pistol in the bearded one's general direction and squeeze off a round, which sent the beard diving to the deck for cover.

I pushed myself off the cushioned seat and tackled the tattooed one around the waist. Suddenly, we were both airborne as we seemingly hovered in midair before landing unceremoniously on the deck. The wind was knocked out of me and I found myself struggling to suck the air back into my lungs. The Glock went off near my head almost simultaneously and was accompanied by a loud, disorienting ringing in my ears. A few heartbeats later, I found myself staring into the soulless blue eyes of a dead man. He had landed on his gun and pulled the trigger himself. The flames had died out. The sound of the other speedboat buzzing into the distance let me know the bearded one had left his partner behind.

I rolled over to my hands and knees, "Are you okay?"

Noah still clutched the weapon in his hands with an expression of shock on his face. He simply nodded at me like a child who had just done a bad thing but still hoped to avoid the consequences. If he had said anything I would not have been able to hear it with the painful ringing tone in my head. I snatched the Ruger out of Noah's hands and regarded it for a minute. I then kicked the dead man's weapon away and felt his neck artery for a pulse.

"Did I?" Noah stuttered. "Did I kill him?"

"Shhh, don't worry!" I said. "He shot himself when I landed him on. It wasn't you."

"Oh my God," he whispered. "I thought I . . ."He stumbled toward the body.

"Don't touch him!" I snapped at Noah a little meaner than I meant to. I covered the man's body with the tarp.

I had to sit down. My legs were shaking so bad. It wasn't fear but rage that spiked my adrenalin. The methheads tried to kill us! I was ready to fight but now the other one was long gone. The cops would have to deal with him. I grabbed a flask out of the front panel and took a swig to steady my nerves. When the liquid courage made its way down my throat and into my gut I walked over and patted Noah on the shoulder. He didn't look none too steady. His complexion had gone pale. He handed the Ruger over without me even having to ask. I took it and put in the waist band of my jeans at the small of my back. I hugged his neck, "You done good, boy. You done good today." He half hugged me back and patted my shoulder. His whole body was shaking. I eased him down to sit on one of the bench seats. "I'm proud of you."

"I'm sorry," Noah said. "I didn't mean to."

"You might have saved both our lives," I said. "You distracted him."

## NOAH

It was almost 11pm when we finally got back to Eden Church Road.
It took some time but the police had met us at the island church.
They asked Mr. Dixon and Jourdan a shit-ton of questions. They
took me into the Church, their command center since the police
station had flooded, and asked me what had happened over and over.
They acted like they believed us but they wanted to be thorough and
that meant raking us over the coals.

It was all a blur. I told them the truth so Mr. Dixon didn't
have to lie. They told me I was brave but after they took Angelina's
Ruger and then that I was in big trouble unless I told the truth. They
tried to call her but the phones were still down. The big fat cop didn't
like me calling Angelina by her name. I could tell by his accent he
wasn't from around here. He was basketball player tall for one. Louisiana people around here weren't that tall unless they were foreign-
ers and by that I mean they weren't from here. Normally, they said,
they'd take me into custody but these were not normal times with the
flood and all. The police department, and the fire department across
the street, flooded. They let me go with Dixon back home "for now"
they said. They would have more questions for me once things were
back to normal.

"We know all about that piece of shit Varnado," Officer
Nash opined confidentially. "He didn't win any civic awards. We'll
find his partner. Those boys been in the middle of trouble around
here as long as I can remember."

"That tweeker shot himself with his own gun when I charged

him," I said. "If you blame anyone, blame me."

"We'll suss out the truth in the end, son."

Before I left I saw Genie. She smiled at me and gave me a little wave like she was about to ask a question in school. She was a little freaked out over the whole deal. She let me hug her but it wasn't romantic, like when we were in the boat before. It was like I was a friend from a long time ago that she barely remembered. It was weird but maybe she just seemed that way or maybe she had thought twice about me. Genie stayed with her dad at the church. We didn't even really say goodbye. It was awkward with her daddy staring daggers into my soul.

She was walking toward me with a smile on her face one second but her daddy was saying, "*Viens ici, asteur,* gal!"

I knew I wouldn't ever forget her. I couldn't forget that smile. It started in her eyes. I had her cell number in my heart and decided to worry about it later. I didn't know how I would get to Lafayette to see her anytime soon. I was so tired from the last couple of days. My brain refused to think about it anymore than that. Was this how love was supposed to work?

"Damn," Mr. Dixon sighed, as he drove the boat right up to the front porch of the old Acadian style. The Spanish moss in the live oak of the front yard was hanging so low it seemed to make a little canopy just above the front door or like mermaid hair. The roof was going to need work. I probably could have touched the moss if I had stood up in the boat. There was still Mardi Gras beads stuck in the branches from who knows which festival, or year even. The entire front yard was a bayou now. The water was up a couple of feet on the bricks of the little ranch. It was no need asking what was wrong.

"I need to check on Lynette," Mr. Dixon said. He tied the boat to the satelite TV dish pole next to the house. There was no light, not even a candle burning in the house. The sound of the wake lapping against the house echoed between the houses.

"It doesn't look like anyone's home, Mr. Dixon," I said. "It looks like your house got flooded out."

"I know it, son. I still need to check on things. Hopefully someone came and carried Lynette to a friend's house. Before you go home," he said, "stay here in the boat for a minute."

Even in the darkness I knew something wasn't right. His

voice trembled when he spoke but not like he was afraid. The house seemed empty. Even Mr. Dixon's dog wasn't barking. Our house was just a couple of houses down the street and I was anxious to check on Angelina even if things were not great as they could be between us I still loved her. I could see light from candles or maybe the hurricane lamp on the fireplace mantle from where I sat in the boat. It was very quiet. The generator must have stopped working. I strained to see if I could see Miss Lynette moving around in through the windows. A few people seemed to be back home on our street but because of the hour and the electricity still being out it was hard to tell. According to Pastor Rob, some people had tried to leave but they just got stranded on I-12 heading east toward I-55 between overflowing rivers. The lucky ones had made it temporarily up an exit ramp but a lot of them didn't have any food or water.

I was hoping she was okay. She was always worried about our neighbor, Heaven, as if she were a Satan worshipper or something. She claimed Heaven killed her own husband just before I moved back. I remembered "Lazy Jeff" as everyone on the block used to call him, but only vaguely since I was just a kid then. I remember he let me ride on his riding mower with him once while he mowed his big backyard.

Mr. Dixon pulled himself up onto the front porch and clomped across the wood boards. He called for Slash and whistled. He cocked his head and listened just outside the front door before he went in. I couldn't help thinking again of replaying the whole incident on the boat in my mind. I didn't shoot anybody but I was trying to. It was a relief that I didn't kill Daryl the way it went down with Mr. Dixon and Varnado. It was self-defense like they always said on cop shows. I knew that. The tattoed guy was pointing his gun at us. He was about to shoot the old man and we all knew it. Where was his boss? Where was Heaven? No one was at her house either. Even if someone was there, it was probably in the same shape as Mr. Dixon's house. She must have got out somehow.

A low wailing sound came from within the house. The sound caused the hairs to stand up on the back of my neck. I knew it meant something bad. We hadn't been able to get in touch with Miss Lynette since earlier yesterday. Mr. Dixon had been in there for a good long while. It was clear he had probably found her in the house but I

Daren Dean

didn't want to think about it. It made my stomach sick. Something in me wouldn't allow specifics of whether she was dead or not into my mind, but she was. I knew she was.

I snuck a Swisher Sweet from the old trucker's stash and lit it with a pink Bic he had probably borrowed off Miss Lynette. I knew he wouldn't give a care. Just sitting there smoking was enough to do until he came back out. I didn't even really like smoking but I liked the sweet taste on my lips and tongue. A Monster drink would hit the spot about now too. I wanted to wait for him in case he needed me. I let my mind wander back to Genie, everything about her. Her eyes, her dark hair, the cut of her cheekbones, the way she called me *beb* in the boat real quiet so her daddy wouldn't hear her. Her long arms and lean legs like a new colt. I'd never thought about Cajun girls before. Her taking selfies of us on the sly when we we're on the boat together. I hoped she would send one to me.

I took my cell phone out and texted, *How are you doing, beb? Did you make it back to Lafayette?* I stared at the screen in hopes she would text me right back but nothing happened so I slid my cell phone back in my pocket. She probably couldn't get on the internet. Her daddy was probably too cheap to get a real plan. Mine was one of the few working since I had an off-breed company. I don't know why it worked, but the big companies didn't. They must use different satelites. Tripp paid for my phone plan. I heard people complaining about their phones not working on the radio call in show before I'd gone out with Mr. Dixon. The DJs were trying to get information from anyone across several parishes that had any information. It was mostly people calling to say they were looking for someone or wanted to know some information but there weren't many answers to be had.

When Mr. Dixon finally came out onto the porch he was in no particular hurry. He leaned against one of the wooden columns holding the porch up pinching the bridge of his nose and sighing heavily. He had a green pint bottle of whiskey. I could smell it on him already. I could hear the sound of the whiskey when he tipped it up to drink. He coughed after his second drink like he was trying not to bust out crying. It scared me to see him, a tough old man, about to cry. They were married forever. They were a perfect matched set like the little rooster and hen salt and pepper shaker Angelina had on our kitchen table as long as I could remember.

"She's gone," he said. "It's like the Titanic in there. Everything floating around on the water. I found her on the bed. There's water all up under the bed where she . . . in the house."

"Do you . . . can you tell . . . what happened? I mean . . ."

He didn't say anything for a minute until I thought he wasn't going to answer me. "It's okay, son. She had lots of medical issues. It was probably just too much for her." There was a catch in his throat. "I can't say for sure what it was."

"I'm so sorry."

"The generator quit too," he said like an afterthought. After a few moments he whispered quitely to himself, "I don't know either, baby." He hung his head like I never saw him do before. "It just hit me," he made a sound deep in his throat and his face grimaced like he was holding back the world, "I lost the one I love and who's going to love me now?"

I stared at him. I didn't know what to say. I nodded my head like I understood, but these were uncharted depths.

"Go on home," he said. "Wait a minute." He pulled his wallet out of his back pocket and folded some bills over between his fingers. "I want to thank you for all your help. I really appreciate you. If I had known all this was going to happen. I don't know."

I help up the palm of my hand. "I can't take your money, Mr. Dixon. Not now."

"I want you to have it, Noah." His voice sounded hard, determined. He came off the porch, waded down into the water, and grabbed me by the wrist and put the bills in my hand. "Please." He closed my fingers over the wad. Then, he held out his arms and I leaned down from where I sat in the boat and he hugged me hard. "Thank you. You're a fine young man."

"Thank you, sir," I said. I didn't know what to say. I hugged him back.

He pushed me back and looked at me. His eyes were brimming with tears. He looked at me the way a dad looks at a son once in a blue moon. He nodded his head like he was agreeing with something I had said. I thought I knew what he meant.

"Go on home, buddy," he said. "I know it's hard but when you see Angelina—call her Mama. You only get one, you know. In her condition she might not . . . well, you just never know. Okay?"

"Okay."

"Just take the boat over there so you don't have to get down in the water. I'll get it tomorrow."

"You sure you don't need me to stay with you?" I asked.

"Go on now. Just take the boat. I'll come get it tomorrow. Just tie it up at that metal railing to your porch. You remember the knot I showed you?" I nodded. Mr. Dixon untied the rope from the old satellite pole and tossed the end of it into the boat. He gave the boat a big shove as he walked backward to stand up on the porch.

"I'm sorry about Miss Lynette." I couldn't think of anything else to say that didn't sound dumb or lame as the boat floated toward my house. "I'll check on you tomorrow."

I saw his shadow under the little porch hold up a hand like he was waving and what he said next, suddenly sad and old, echoed like surprising lyrics to a song between the houses, "She speaks back through my heart."

## ANGELINA

I stumbled out on the porch hoping for the smallest breeze in the humid night, smoking with my oxygen tubes pulled down under my chin, when Noah and Dixon pulled up in the boat to Dixon's house. The neighbors had always saying I was going to blow myself up. Whenever someone said that I'd snap right back at them, *Good!* That usually shut them up. The power was out anyway so no chance of going out with a bang.

The frogs and insects were singing their hearts out. My eyes were loosely closed, fluttering open every so often as if someone might be sneaking up on me, and whisper-praying to God for miraculous healing. So far he hadn't outright healed me but there were days at least I felt like I had some energy to get up and wash the dishes, load and run the dishwasher, or maybe vacuum the rug in the living room before I gave up the rest of the day to staring at my cell phone. I tried to be thankful for all the little miracles.

Noah and Dixon were just shapes in the night but their voices echoed across the water and between the houses unmistakably. I could hear every word. Dixon's deep, growling voice was a strong contrast to Noah's higher, croaking adolescent voice. Noah was so big now, I wasn't used to it yet. I still remembered the tiny jumper I dressed him in as a baby, with dark jeans and what looked like red suspenders over a blue shirt that made him look as snuggly as a little stuffed Teddy Bear. They seemed to talk for a long time.

Lynette was dead. When Dixon groaned in the house I somehow knew what he had found. I hadn't seen Lynette or anyone

Daren Dean

because I hadn't been feeling well, so I hadn't been out of bed but a few times. Lynette was the type of woman who preferred the company of men over women. If I'm being honest, I'm the same way too. Some women have female friends but my only female friends were more the kind of girls I partied with years before Tripp left us for his doubtful career as a musician in New Orleans and his new girlfriend. I guess they lived on love. It wasn't fair but I knew I couldn't compete with a healthy girl who was probably not even thirty yet. I wondered what they talked about. I guess they had music in common.

I heard the boat bump against the porch next door. We had been lucky since our house was old and had been trucked in according to Mr. Jule many years earlier. It set up higher than the brick ranch style houses in the area, which were just on concrete pads. There were only two houses on our street like this one.

I suddenly felt terribly nauseated. I flicked my cigarette butt out into the void of water. It sounded like I was floating down the river on a house boat though the flood levels seemed to be subsiding a bit. I went back inside and barely made it to the bed before I collapsed into my blankets. The sheets smelled moldy and like garlic and onions. I would have to wash the bedding once the water was back on.

I wasn't sure how long I slept when I heard his footsteps on the front porch before I heard his voice softly calling. "Mama?" A thrill went through me just hearing my son's voice call me that for the first time in a long time. Tripp had poisoned him against me but could have done worse had we wanted to. I had tried not to talk him down in front of the kids at first, but it was hard not to speak my mind after a while.

"I'm in my bedroom," I sat up in bed and listened though my head spun so it felt like I was drunk but it wasn't from drinking although until now I was beginning to feel better since the flood had caused me to miss my last round of chemo at Baton Rouge General. I didn't want want him to think all I did was lay in bed even at this hour. It was one of those irrational responses like when your phone buzzes, someone has awakened you from a dead sleep but you assure them you were awake the whole time for some reason. I threw back the blankets, put my feet into my house shoes, grabbed my robe off the foot of the bed. I slipped into it as quickly as possible and knotted the belt at my waist. I sat back down on the edge of the bed while I waited for the dizziness to subside.

I heard him kick his shoes off at the door. I heard him groan a little. Had he been hurt out there helping Dixon? If I had been thinking straight when Noah left I would never have let him go out there. It was fine for a grown man to do what he thought was right but another thing for a young, teenaged boy.

"Are you okay?" Noah asked tentatively as he opened the door and found me sitting there. "I was worried about you." His words stabbed me in the heart. Tears immediately sprang to the corners of my eyes and I tried to thumb them away so he wouldn't know but I still wanted to see him.

I pointed toward the window, "Push the curtains aside. Open the blinds. It's so dark in here. The power hasn't . . . well, you know that already. Talk about worried! How was it?"

"It's bad everywhere," he said. He sounded older. He used the footboard to guide himself from the door to the window. When he moved the curtains, it was surprisingly bright outside. The moonlight streamed in bluish-green. His hair was plastered on his head. I could smell the salty odor of sweat on him. There was something different about him. "I joined the Cajun Navy today. We were all over Livingston Parish. We helped a bunch of people. Did you see my note on the fridge?"

"I saw it," I studied his face and I could tell he really had been worried about his mother. "Come sit next to me." I held my arms out to him but he looked away as if he hadn't noticed.

"I'm dirty," he warned. "I probably stink really bad."

"Don't worry about all that," I said, "I'm just glad my son is home safe."

His shoulder-blade leaned into my chest due to the angle he sat on the edge of the bed. He allowed his head to lean on my shoulder. I could feel the exhaustion in his body. He suddenly began to weep silently. I didn't think he would want me to ask so I held him like that for a couple of minutes. The sounds we normally heard at night like the hum of cars on the I-12, the bawling train that normally clattered through town, and even the comings and goings of our neighbors in their vehicles at all hours had been replaced by an eerie silence. The only sound was the lapping of water against the floor joists in the crawlspace under the house. At least, all the trash and cans and accumulated junk beneath the house would be cleaned out by the tide of putrid waters.

"Miss Lynette passed," he said in a quiet voice. "I feel so bad for Mr. Dixon. He's alone now."

"I know. I'm sorry. She had been in bad health for a long time. I think they both knew it was coming."

"So have you," he said, very quietly, "been in bad shape." There was a gentleness to his face I hadn't seen in a very long time. "I wish I . . ."

"Shhh. I know," I touched my lower lip to stop the tremor. "I'm sorry about that too, buddy. I'm sorry you have a mom who can't take care of you like she should but I want you to know I'm still here."

"I'm sorry too," he said. "I'm sorry for everything."

"Don't waste your time apologizing," I said. "You don't need to say your sorry for anything. I'm your mom. I love you no matter what. And I'm still here."

I could feel his breath on my arms. My crying eyes made my vision blurry but it didn't matter since I didn't need to see anyway. I had my son with me. That was all I needed for now. I hugged him hard against me although I could feel him pulling away ever so slightly. He wasn't a little boy anymore.

A sound erupted from him like a sharp object had been ripped out of his body suddenly, "Mama! Mom . . ." He sniffed loudly. He whispered, "I did something bad. I . . ." He buried his face into my shoulder like when he was a little boy. I could feel his own tears dampening my blouse. This wasn't like him. Normally, he was an adolescent volcano of anger. He didn't finish his sentence.

"It's okay," I said. "Try not to think about it tonight. Go into the bathroom. There's a hurricane lamp in there on the counter. It's turned down real low but you can turn it up a little so you can see what you're doing. I want you to go in there and get cleaned up a little. You can take your clothes off and throw them in the laundry. Get a wash cloth out of the closet and use the water from the tub. I filled it up before it was too late just in case. Clean yourself up real good. Use the bar soap. Put on some clean clothes. You will feel one hundred percent better. Okay?"

He leaned back and looked at me. "Okay," he said with a nod. He arose from the bed and the sound of the mattress and box springs complaining as he stood.

I heard the floorboards creak as he walked into the bathroom. I wanted to force myself to get up and follow him in there. My son was home. The weight of him in the house was comforting. It felt like he had been gone for years. I wanted to take the wash cloth from him and wash his back but he was a young man now and I knew I couldn't. I knew it but it didn't stop me from wanting to treat him like when he was a little boy. I couldn't help but remembering his light brown hair, almost blond, those big blue eyes, and his chubby little cheeks. Now his face was all angles. His skin was sunburnt from being out on the water. He had high cheekbones like me it turned out.

"There are two geckos on the wall in here!" Noah said.

"They're okay," I said. "Just eating the bugs for us."

"You almost see right through them," his voice marveled.

I wish I could go back in time and do things differently with Tripp, so Noah and Jessica could have had a normal home life. I wish I could build a time machine back to happiness when my family was still together. I had let the love slip through my fingers like water. Love was like water since there was nothing grab onto but I was thankful for this: I was happy to hear him, my son, in the next room. All the noises were his noises. We were together. Neither of us had to be alone anymore, unless we wanted to be or decided to be.

## PRESLEY

The smell of meat cooking on our gas grill was making my stomach growl. The meat odor mingled with the citronella smell coming from the waterlogged candles Jamie Lynn had managed to light. The flood waters had disappeared and those of us who were still on Eden Church Road couldn't help but feel crazy happy and blinking in the sunlight on our lawn chairs and camping chairs and feeling hopeful that we'd made it. You'd think everyone would be depressed and feeling kind of bad, but it was just the opposite.

"Let's get everything out of the freezer," Jamie Lynn said. "Well cook it up. Go ahead. I'll see if the grill is going to work."

"Make sure the little gas tanks didn't float away," I said.

"We can use charcoal if that's the case," Mr. Allen said. "This here can do both, or either one."

The power was still out and no word as to when it would come back on. They had turned it off so people wouldn't get electrocuted.

"Let's have a block party!" Jamie Lynn was staring into the barely cool freezer with a cigarette dangling unlit between her lips. She was wearing a top with Minnie Mouse on it and a pair of pink short shorts. "Go knock on Angelina's door and see if she has any freezer meat that needs cooking up! Tell her to bring any alcohol she has too! And, I know that one's got alcohol!"

I shook my head, "You mean Crazy Cancer Lady! Don't make me go over there again. She yelled at me."

"Angelina, you mean!" She gave me a stern look, trying to

play the part of an actual mom, and it almost made me laugh. She was already drinking Jose Cuervo Gold margarita in a proper plastic margarita glass without ice even though it was only ten in the morning. Her latest boyfriend, Mr. Allen, had brought over the Jose Cuervo, two six packs of Canebrake beer, and about fifteen pounds of mudbugs. He lived in a trailer court off Acadiana avenue.

"Go on up and down the street! Knock on everyone's door! Tell them to bring anything out of their freezer they want cooked up. Allen has volunteered to be our cook! Isn't that right, Allen?" She slapped him on his butt with her hand and then grabbed one cheek and shook it real good. "Mmm, mmm."

*So gross!*

He saluted using a big silver spatula that he had been calling Excalibur. It felt like we had just started a brand new festival and we were the Krewe of Eden Church Road!

I didn't want to do it, but I slipped on my green Crocs and walked across the squishy grass to Angelina's house. A lot of people on our street weren't even home. I guess all the smart people left, but they would be back one way or another to pick up what was left of their lives or to rebuild.

When I knocked on the door, I was surprised when a cute guy with a chiseled face and angry sunburn answered the door. I thought he looked kind of familiar but the name wouldn't come because I was dreading the bald lady would answer.

"Hi," he said.

"H-hi…there," I said.

"It's me, Noah," he said. "You forgot me?"

"Noah?" I said. "No way."

"Yeah," he laughed. Despite his sunburn, his face looked kind of pale at the same time just beneath the surface. There were dark circles under his eyes like he had been up all night. He was shirtless and I could see all his lean muscles. He slipped his fingers into the pockets of his blue jeans.

I knew I was supposed to say something else but his pale blue eyes were hypnotizing me. I had never felt anything quite like this.

"Did you need something…Presley? Presley!"

"That's me," I said. "Um, Jamie Lynn wanted me to come over and ask your mom if she had any meat in the freezer? Since the power went out probably everyone's meat is going to go bad. We're going to cook everything on the grill. Bring whatever you've got . . . the meat and stuff . . . we'll cook it up . . . yeah?"

"Okay," he said. "Sounds like a good idea. I'll see what we've got in here. When should we come over?"

"You're coming over?" I was so nervous I could hardly speak.

"Sure, why not?" He said.

"You're coming over?" I repeated like an idiot.

"Yes." He kind of narrowed his eyes at me like he was trying to figure me out. Maybe he thought I was a special needs kids. "I'll bring Mom too if she's feeling up to it."

I stared at him but tried to keep my eyes glued to his. "Great!" I said suddenly. I turned and walked quickly back to my house across the squishy lawns again so I wouldn't say or do anything else to embarrass myself. The last time I had seen Noah was—it had been a long time. He had been skinny and short back then. But now, oh my gawd. He looked good, really good.

I turned around and cupped my hands over my mouth, "It's a block party! Tell everyone! Krewe-of-Satsuma Grove!" I pivoted back around and started jogging to my house. I was so excited I didn't know what to do with myself. I knew tomorrow we'd have to start ripping up the carpet and linoleum from the floors and throwing all of our stuff out but that didn't seem to matter as much now. We had lived through it all somehow.

Mickey came running up from the marshy side yard yipping at me. I don't know where he was or how he didn't get floated away but here he was! I swooped him up in my arms and he licked my face. He was muddy but I was so happy to have my puppydog back. He almost didn't even look like a dog anymore with his fur so covered in mud. He looked more like a clay sculpture, but I was a dog-mother again.

I noticed the statue of the Virgin Mary against a white backdrop almost like a book in front of Mr. Jule's and Hope's house. It was kind of wrong to know that she had been through so much. It was like the Virgin herself had undergone the same ordeal as us even though we weren't religious though I had gone to church and Bible camp just so Jamie Lynn could "do her thing" as she had put it. She actually said this to people when we were grocery shopping at Albertsons! She is so embarrassing! I'm not even going to lie.

The Virgin's face was calm but she seemed to be crying black tears. I remembered once asking Hope, "Why do people pray to Mary?"

"We pray for Mary to . . . whatever . . . intercession! Yes, this is the word," Hope said. "Her son can't refuse to give her nothing she asks him for."

I didn't necessarily believe all of that but I guess I believe in God. I believed there was something out there. I might not know much about anything but I could feel a spark of meaning when I saw the tennis shoe and the colored Mardi Gras beads hanging on the telephone lines. Was it a sign of hope or just plain old grief? The weeping Mary might not be real, but even an atheist was going to need grace after a disaster like this.

# Epilogue

*The mudmilk waters had long since receded and seeped back into the banks of the Amite and the Comite rivers like spirits charged to wreak havoc upon the land and now dwelling beneath the earth again until such a day of apocalyptic necessity, when they might once again be called upon by fickle gods. Now, such people as were left in the parishes: East Baton Rouge, Ascension, Livingston, Tangipahoa, and more were driving the byways and streets where black mold clung to drywall, water-logged possessions were stacked and balanced along the curbs and on the front yards like some garish display of tragic, modern art. "Here's what I have sacrificed to the flood gods of Louisiana," those orphaned possessions said. The rotting stench was incredible for the better part of a year. The towering garbage heaps piled in front of houses in every neighborhood spoke for the residents of Satsuma Grove, but the government listened with a deaf ear.*

*A sign in front of a house on River Road proclaimed: DON'T LOOT! LOOTERS WILL BE SHOT! SAVE FOR FEMA!*

*Insurance companies doing the Devil's arithmetic decide what the contents of a life are worth and even whether those lives should be funded again to rebuild the future. "Now you too can qualify for a business loan to rebuild it all on your own dime! Build ye houses anew on artificially elevated earth!" The agents and their secretaries hid behind locked doors to protect a hypothetical pittance against outraged policy holders after a carefully planned contingency loophole is discovered in the contract. The winding tropical storm and flood were unnatural acts of a senseless God.*

*The rancid stacks, leaning towers, of refuse from human lives, lay waiting for an accounting that would never fully materialize. The smell of mildew was in the air. More than one person said, "It was like a bomb went off" in an effort to describe their imploding lives. While also knowing they shared this with their neighbors and relatives, and also knowing just to let it go, and not allow it to eat you up since Louisiana people know this cycle of devastation and renewal. It* had become more than a way of life but a vital signifying part of what was and would be for the next year. Driving through the junkyard of leftover lives.

Some residents were beginning to come back and were adding to the piles as necessity dictated. The lucky ones had seen only a few inches of water encroach the borders of their home, while the majority measured the flood waters in their homes upon the wall by the foot. Most had seen a couple of feet and others had narrowly escaped with their lives by punching a hole in their roof with a sledge hammer or used a chainsaw or whatever tool was handy that allowed access, until they were plucked off the roof by a Black Hawk helicopter. There was a water line of demarcation upon the walls of the houses that told a tale like rings on the inner trunk of a tree.

A lucky few had FEMA trailers parked on their front lawns now as they repaired and rebuilt their homes. Green and orange SERVPRO trucks cruised the streets of Livingston Parish. Still others had to drive back into the disaster zone to scrape the mud and rotting insides of their house like a cancer patient. "If I can just rebuild it, I can sell it and move on," some wept. Others moved to live with family members in Baton Rouge, in New Orleans, while others fled the state for good or to family members who had started new lives in Houston as long ago as Katrina. Those who had the funds leveled their home, brought in enough dirt to rebuild four feet above the existing ground level as dictated by new building codes, and sold their lives to the next person with enough faith to believe this kind of flooding wouldn't happen again in their lifetime.

Stacks of ripped drywall rested on the ground with the lichen of black mold yet creeping along the surface near the curb like a rare fountain made to discharge sofas, couches, recliners, mattresses, boxsprings, headboards, chifforobes, dressers, appliances and kitchen tables. There were piles of mildewed clothing with a rank, sour-rotting stench, testifying to ruined lives in the ebullient light of a Louisiana afternoon. A library of photo albums and books also stacked the yards with a black-blighted purple and white leprosy on the covers and human faces on each page should one care to thumb through the images documenting the fond memories of holidays from Mardi Gras to Christmas. Anyone driving through the area could see the devastation and activity to know that tears had been dried over the inescapable question of why, to which there was no good answer except to look to one's faith or the explanations of the experts who spoke of climate emergency and the unsustainable life. The Mary statues in front of every other house on Eden Church Road wept intercessory tears.

The green, purple, and gold Mardi Gras beads tossed from the joyful hands of men, women, and children from the parish floats during happier times remained tangled and enduring in tree limbs and power lines like the implacable hopes of unbounded and undivulged dreams. An echo of voices, murmuring from months, decades, and into the future and yet trembled and reverberated from the past, "Hey lady! Throw me some beads!"

## ABOUT THE AUTHOR

Daren Dean is the author of seven books: *Far Beyond the Pale, I'll Still Be Here Long After You're Gone: Stories, The Black Harvest: A Novel of The American Civil War, This Vale of Tears, Roads, The New Salvation and Other Stories. The Black Harvest* was nominated for several awards, including the Pen/Faulkner, the W.Y. Boyd Award for military fiction, and the Midlands Author Award. Roads was a featured Indie review in Kirkus Reviews in 2023. Dean is an associate professor of English and Creative writing at Lincoln University of Missouri. He lives in Missouri with his wife and children.

www.ingramcontent.com/pod-product-compliance
Lightning Source LLC
Chambersburg PA
CBHW030521020726
47494CB00004B/1188